THE COAST OF CHICAGO

THE COAST OF CHICAGO
Stuart Dybek

faber and faber

LONDON · BOSTON

First published in Great Britain in 1991
by Faber and Faber Limited
3 Queen Square London WC1N 3AU

Phototypeset by Input Typsetting, Wimbledon
Printed in England by Clays Ltd, St Ives Plc

'The Palatski Man', 'Blood Soup', 'Visions of Budhardin',
'The Wake', 'Horror Movie' and 'The Apprentice'
first published in *Childhood and Other Neighbourhoods*
in the USA in 1986 by The Ecco Press, New York
copyright © by Stuart Dybek 1971, 1973, 1975, 1976,
1978, 1979, 1980

'Chopin in Winter', 'Bottle Caps', 'Lights', 'Blight',
'Bijou', 'Nighthawks', 'Hot Ice' and 'Pet Milk' first
published in *The Coast of Chicago* in the USA in 1990
by Alfred A. Knopf, Inc., New York, and simultaneously
in Canada by Random House of Canada Ltd, Toronto.
Copyright © by Stuart Dybek 1990

A CIP record for this book
is available from the British Library

ISBN 0-571-16219-3

Contents

The Palatski Man

He reappeared in spring, some Sunday morning, perhaps Easter, when the twigs of the catalpa trees budded and lawns smelled of mud and breaking seeds. Or Palm Sunday, returning from Mass with handfuls of blessed, bending palms to be cut into crosses and pinned on your Sunday dress and the year-old palms removed by her brother, John, from behind the pictures of Jesus with his burning heart and the Virgin with her sad eyes, to be placed dusty and crumbling in an old coffee can and burned in the backyard. And once, walking back from church, Leon Sisca said these are what they lashed Jesus with. And she said no they aren't, they used whips. They used these, he insisted. What do you know, she said. And he told her she was a dumb girl and lashed her across her bare legs with his blessed palms. They stung her; she started to cry, that anyone could do such a thing, and he caught her running down Twenty-fifth Street with her skirt flying and got her against a fence, and grabbing her by the hair, he stuck his scratchy palms in her face, and suddenly he was lifted off the ground and flung to the sidewalk, and she saw John standing over him very red in the face; and when Leon Sisca tried to run away, John blocked him, and Leon tried to dodge around him as if they were playing football; and as he cut past, John slapped him across the face; Leon's head snapped back and his nose started to bleed. John didn't chase him and he ran halfway down the block, turned around and yelled through his tears with blood dripping on his white shirt: I hate you goddamn you I hate you! All the dressed-up people coming back from church saw it happen and shook their heads. John said c'mon Mary let's go home.

No, it wasn't that day, but it was in that season on a Sunday that he reappeared, and then every Sunday after that through the summer and into the fall, when school would resume and the green catalpa leaves fall like withered fans

1

into the birdbaths, turning the water brown, the Palatski Man would come.

He was an old man who pushed a white cart through the neighbourhood streets ringing a little golden bell. He would stop at each corner, and the children would come with their money to inspect the taffy apples sprinkled with chopped nuts, or the red candy apples on pointed sticks, or the *palatski* displayed under the glass of the white cart. She had seen taffy apples in the candy stores and even the red apples sold by clowns at circuses, but she had never seen *palatski* sold anywhere else. It was two crisp wafers stuck together with honey. The taste might have reminded you of an ice-cream cone spread with honey, but it reminded Mary of Holy Communion. It felt like the Eucharist in her mouth, the way it tasted walking back from the communion rail after waiting for Father Mike to stand before her wearing his rustling silk vestments with the organ playing and him saying the Latin prayer over and over faster than she could ever hope to pray and making a sign of the cross with the host just before placing it on someone's tongue. She knelt at the communion rail close enough to the altar to see the silk curtains drawn inside the open tabernacle and the beeswax candles flickering and to smell the flowers. Father Mike was moving down the line of communicants, holding the chalice, with the altar boy, an eighth-grader, sometimes even John, standing beside him in a lace surplice, holding the paten under each chin; and she would close her eyes and open her mouth, sticking her tongue out, and hear the prayer and feel the host placed gently on her tongue. Sometimes Father's hand brushed her bottom lip, and she would feel a spark from his finger, which Sister said was static electricity, not the Holy Spirit.

Then she would walk down the aisle between the lines of communicants, searching through half-shut eyes for her pew, her mind praying Jesus help me find it. And when she found her pew, she would kneel down and shut her eyes and bury her face in her hands praying over and over thank you Jesus for coming to me, feeling the host stuck to the roof of her mouth, melting against her tongue like a warm, wheaty snowflake; and she would turn the tip of her tongue inward and lick the host off the ridges of her mouth till it was loosened by saliva and swallowed into her soul.

Who was the Palatski Man? No one knew or even seemed to care. He was an old man with an unremembered face, perhaps a never-seen face, a head hidden by a cloth-visored cap, and eyes concealed behind dark glasses with green, smoked lenses. His smile revealed only a gold crown and a missing tooth. His only voice was the ringing bell, and his hands were rough and red as if scrubbed with sandpaper and their skin very hard when you opened your hand for your change and his fingers brushed yours. His clothes were always the same – white – not starched and dazzling, but the soft white of many washings and wringings.

No one cared and he was left alone. The boys didn't torment him as they did the pedlars during the week. There was constant war between the boys and the pedlars, the umbrella menders, the knife sharpeners, anyone whose business carried him down the side streets or through the alleys. The pedlars came every day, spring, summer, and autumn, through the alleys behind the backyard fences crying, 'Rags ol irn, rags ol irn!' Riding their ancient, rickety wagons with huge wooden-spoked wheels, heaped high with scraps of metal, frames of furniture, coal-black cobwebbed lumber, bundles of rags and filthy newspapers. The boys called them the Ragmen. They were all old, hunched men, bearded and bald, who bargained in a stammered foreign English and dressed in clothes extracted from the bundles of rags in their weather-beaten wagons.

Their horses seemed even more ancient than their masters, and Mary was always sorry for them as she watched their slow, arthritic gait up and down the alleys. Most of them were white horses, a dirty white as if their original colours had turned white with age, like the hair on an old man's head. They had enormous hooves with iron shoes that clacked down the alleys over the broken glass, which squealed against the concrete when the rusty, metal-rimmed wheels of the wagon ground over it. Their muzzles were pink without hair, and their tongues lolled out grey; their teeth were huge and yellow. Over their eyes were black blinders, around their shoulders a heavy black harness that looked always ready to slip off, leather straps hung all about their bodies. They ate from black, worn leather sacks tied over their faces, and as they ate, the flies flew up from their droppings and climbed all over their thick bodies and the horses swished at them with stringy tails.

The Ragmen drove down the crooked, interconnecting alleys crying, 'Rags ol irn, rags ol irn', and the boys waited for a wagon to pass, hiding behind fences or garbage cans; and as soon as it passed they would follow, running half bent over so that they couldn't be seen if the Ragman turned around over the piles heaped on his wagon. They would run to the tailgate and grab on to it, swinging up, the taller ones, like John, stretching their legs on to the rear axle, the shorter ones just hanging as the wagon rolled along. Sometimes one of the bolder boys would try to climb up on the wagon itself and throw off some of the junk. The Ragman would see him and pull the reins, stopping the wagon. He would begin gesturing and yelling at the boys, who jumped from the wagon and stood back laughing and hollering, 'Rags ol irn, rags ol irn!' Sometimes he'd grab a makeshift whip, a piece of clothesline tied to a stick, and stagger after them as they scattered laughing before him, disappearing over fences and down gangways only to reappear again around the corner of some other alley; or, lying flattened on a garage roof, they'd suddenly jump up and shower the wagon with garbage as it passed beneath.

Mary could never fully understand why her brother participated. He wasn't a bully like Leon Sisca and certainly not cruel like Denny Zmiga, who tortured cats. She sensed the boys vaguely condemned the Ragmen for the sad condition of their horses. But that was only a small part of it, for often the horses as well as their masters were harassed. She thought it was a venial sin and wondered if John confessed it the Thursday before each First Friday, when they would go together to confession in the afternoon: Bless me Father for I have sinned, I threw garbage on a Ragman five times this month. For your penance say five Our Fathers and five Hail Marys, go in peace. She never mentioned this to him, feeling that whatever made him do it was a part of what made him generally unafraid, a part of what the boys felt when they elected him captain of the St Roman Grammar School baseball team. She couldn't bear it if he thought she was a dumb girl. She never snitched on him. If she approached him when he was surrounded by his friends, he would loudly announce, 'All right, nobody swear while Mary's here.'

At home he often took her into his confidence. This was what she liked the most, when, after supper, while her parents watched TV in the parlour, he would come into her room, where she was doing her homework, and lie down on her bed and start talking, telling her who among his friends was a good first sacker, or which one of the girls in his class tried to get him to dance with her at the school party, just talking and sometimes even asking her opinion on something like if she thought he should let his hair grow long like that idiot Peter Noskin, who couldn't even make the team as a right fielder. What did she think of guys like that? She tried to tell him things back. How Sister Mary Valentine had caught Leon Sisca in the girls' washroom yesterday. And then one night he told her about Raymond Cruz, which she knew was a secret because their father had warned John not to hang around with him even if he was the best pitcher on the team. He told her how after school he and Raymond Cruz had followed a Ragman to Hobotown, which was far away, past Western Avenue, on the other side of the river, down by the river and the railroad tracks, and that they had a regular town there without any streets. They lived among huge heaps of junk, rubbled lots tangled with smashed, rusting cars and bathtubs, rotting mounds of rags and paper, woodpiles infested with river rats. Their wagons were all lined up and the horses kept in a deserted factory with broken windows. They lived in shacks that were falling apart, some of them made out of old boxcars, and there was a blacksmith with a burning forge working in a ruined shed made of bricks and timbers with a roof of canvas.

He told her how they had snuck around down the riverbank in the high weeds and watched the Ragmen come in from all parts of the city, pulled by their tired horses, hundreds of Ragmen arriving in silence, and how they assembled in front of a great fire burning in the middle of all the shacks, where something was cooking in a huge, charred pot.

Their scroungy dogs scratched and circled around the fire while the Ragmen stood about and seemed to be trading among one another: bales of worn clothing for baskets of tomatoes, bushels of fruit for twisted metals, cases of dust-filled bottles for scorched couches and lamps with frazzled wires. They knelt, peering out of the weeds and watching them, and then Ray whispered let's sneak around to the building where the horses are kept and look at them.

So they crouched through the weeds and ran from shack to shack until they came to the back of the old factory. They could smell the horses and hay inside and hear the horses sneezing. They snuck in through a busted window. The factory was dark and full of spiderwebs, and they felt their way through a passage that entered into a high-ceilinged hall where the horses were stabled. It was dim; rays of sun sifted down through the dust from the broken roof. The horses didn't look the same in the dimness without their harnesses. They looked huge and beautiful, and when you reached to pat them, their muscles quivered so that you flinched with fright.

'Wait'll the guys hear about this,' John said.

And Ray whispered, 'Let's steal one! We can take him to the river and ride him.'

John didn't know what to say. Ray was fourteen. His parents were divorced. He had failed a year in school and often hung around with high-school guys. Everybody knew that he had been caught in a stolen car but that the police let him go because he was so much younger than the other guys. He was part Mexican and knew a lot about horses. John didn't like the idea of stealing.

'We couldn't get one out of here,' he said.

'Sure we could,' Ray said. 'We could get on one and gallop out with him before they knew what was going on.'

'Suppose we get caught,' John said.

'Who'd believe the Ragmen anyway?' Ray asked him. 'They can't even speak English. You chicken?'

So they picked out a huge white horse to ride, who stood still and uninterested when John boosted Ray up on his back and then Ray reached down and pulled him up. Ray held his mane and John held on to Ray's waist. Ray nudged his heels into the horse's flanks and he began to move, slowly swaying towards the light of the doorway.

'As soon as we get outside,' Ray whispered, 'hold on. I'm gonna goose him.'

John's palms were sweating by this time because being on this horse felt like straddling a blimp as it rose over the roofs. When they got to the door, Ray hollered, 'Heya!' and kicked his heels hard, and the horse bolted out, and before he knew what had happened, John felt himself sliding, dropping a long way, and then felt the sudden hard smack of the hay-strewn floor. He looked up and realized he had never made it out of the barn, and then he heard the shouting and barking of the dogs and, looking out, saw Ray half riding, half hanging from the horse, which reared again and again, surrounded by the shouting Ragmen, and he saw the look on Ray's face as he was bucked from the horse into their arms. There was a paralysed second when they all glanced toward him standing in the doorway of the barn, and then he whirled around and stumbled past the now-pitching bulks of horses whinnying all about him and found the passage, struggling through it, bumping into walls, spiderwebs sticking to his face, with the shouts and barks gaining on him, and then he was out the window and running up a hill of weeds, crushed coal slipping under his feet, skidding up and down two more hills, down railroad tracks, not turning around, just running until he could no longer breathe, and above him he saw a bridge and clawed up the grassy embankment till he reached it.

It was rush hour and the bridge was crowded with people going home, factory workers carrying lunch pails and businessmen with attaché cases. The street was packed with traffic, and he didn't know where he was or what he should do about Ray. He decided to go home and see what would happen. He'd call Ray that night, and if he wasn't home, then he'd tell them about the Ragmen. But he couldn't find his way back. Finally he had to ask a cop where he was, and the cop put him on a trolley car that got him home.

He called Ray about eight o'clock, and his mother

answered the phone and told him Ray had just got in and went right to bed, and John asked her if he could speak to him, and she said she'd go see, and he heard her set down the receiver and her footsteps walk away. He realized his own heartbeat was no longer deafening and felt the knots in his stomach loosen. Then he heard Ray's mother say that she was sorry but that Ray didn't want to talk to him.

The next day, at school, he saw Ray and asked him what happened, if he was angry that he had run out on him, and Ray said, no, nothing happened, to forget it. He kept asking Ray how he got away, but Ray wouldn't say anything until John mentioned telling the other guys about it. Ray said if he told anybody he'd deny it ever happened, that there was such a place. John thought he was just kidding, but when he told the guys, Ray told them John made the whole thing up, and they almost got into a fight, pushing each other back and forth, nobody taking the first swing, until the guys stepped between them and broke it up. John lost his temper and said he'd take any of the guys who wanted to go next Saturday to see for themselves. They could go on their bikes and hide them in the weeds by the river and sneak up on the Ragmen. Ray said go on.

So on Saturday John and six guys met at his place and peddled toward the river and railroad tracks, down the busy trucking streets, where the semis passed you so fast your bike seemed about to be sucked away by the draft. They got to Western Avenue and the river, and it looked the same and didn't look the same. They left the street and pumped their bikes down a dirt road left through the weeds by bull-dozers, passing rusty barges moored to the banks, seemingly abandoned in the oily river. They passed a shack or two, but they were empty. John kept looking for the three mounds of black cinders as a landmark but couldn't find them. They rode their bikes down the railroad tracks, and it wasn't like being in the centre of the city at all, with the smell of milk-weeds and the noise of birds and crickets all about them and the spring sun glinting down the railroad tracks. No one was around. It was like being far out in the country. They rode until they could see the skyline of downtown, skyscrapers rising up through the smoke of chimneys like a horizon of jagged mountains in the mist. By now everyone was kidding him about the Ragmen, and finally he had to admit he couldn't find them, and they gave up. They all peddled back, kidding him, and he bought everybody Cokes, and they admitted they had had a pretty good time anyway, even though he sure as hell was some storyteller.

And he figured something must have happened to Ray. It hit him Sunday night, lying in bed trying to sleep, and he knew he'd have to talk to him about it Monday when he saw him at school, but on Monday Ray was absent and was absent on Tuesday, and on Wednesday they found out that Ray had run away from home and no one could find him.

No one ever found him, and he wasn't there in June when John and his classmates filed down the aisle, their maroon robes flowing and white tassels swinging almost in time to the organ, to receive their diplomas and shake hands with Father Mike. And the next week it was summer, and she was permitted to go to the beach with her girlfriends. Her girlfriends came over and giggled whenever John came into the room.

On Sundays they went to late Mass. She wore her flowered-print dress and a white mantilla in church when she sat beside John among the adults. After Mass they'd stop at the corner of Twenty-fifth Street on their way home and buy *palatski* and walk home eating it with its crispness melting and the sweet honey crust becoming chewy. She remembered how she used to pretend it was manna they'd been rewarded with for keeping the Sabbath. It tasted extra good because she had skipped breakfast. She fasted before receiving Communion.

Then it began to darken earlier, and the kids played tag and rolivio in the dusk and hid from each other behind trees and in doorways, and the girls laughed and blushed when the boys chased and tagged them. She had her own secret hiding place down the block, in a garden under a lilac bush, where no one could find her; and she would lie there listening to her name called in the darkness, Mary Mary free free free, by so many voices.

She shopped downtown with her mother at night for new

school clothes, skirts, not dresses, green ribbons for her dark hair, and shoes without buckles, like slippers a ballerina wears. And that night she tried them on for John, dancing in her nightgown, and he said you're growing up. And later her mother came into her room – only the little bed lamp was burning – and explained to her what growing up was like. And after her mother left, she picked up a little rag doll that was kept as an ornament on her dresser and tried to imagine having a child, really having a child, it coming out of her body, and she looked at herself in the mirror and stood close to it and looked at the colours of her eyes: brown around the edges and then turning a milky grey that seemed to be smoking behind crystal and toward the centre the grey turning green, getting greener till it was almost violet near her pupils. And in the black mirror of her pupils she saw herself looking at herself.

The next day, school started again and she was a sixth-grader. John was in high school, and Leon Sisca, who had grown much bigger over the summer and smoked, sneered at her and said, 'Who'll protect you now?' She made a visit to the church at lunchtime and dropped a dime in the metal box by the ruby vigil lights and lit a candle high up on the rack with a long wax wick and said a prayer to the Blessed Virgin.

And it was late in October, and leaves wafted from the catalpa trees on their way to church on Sunday and fell like withered fans into the birdbaths, turning the water brown. They were walking back from Mass, and she was thinking how little she saw John any more, how he no longer came to her room to talk, and she said, 'Let's do something together.'

'What?' he asked.

'Let's follow the Palatski Man.'

'Why would you want to do that?'

'I don't know,' she said. 'We could find out where he lives, where he makes his stuff. He won't come around pretty soon. Maybe we could go to his house in the winter and buy things from him.'

John looked at her. Her hair, like his, was blowing about in the wind. 'All right,' he said.

So they waited at a corner where a man was raking leaves

into a pile to burn, but each time he built the pile and turned to scrape a few more leaves from his small lawn, the wind blew and the leaves whirled off from the pile and sprayed out as if alive over their heads, and then the wind suddenly died, and they floated back about the raking man into the grass softly, looking like wrinkled snow. And in a rush of leaves they closed their eyes against, the Palatski Man pushed by.

They let him go down the block. He wasn't hard to follow, he went so slow, stopping at corners for customers. They didn't have to sneak behind him because he never turned around. They followed him down the streets, and one street became another until they were out of their neighbourhood, and the clothes the people wore became poorer and brighter. They went through the next parish, and there was less stopping because it was a poorer parish where more Mexicans lived, and the children yelled in Spanish, and they felt odd in their new Sunday clothes.

'Let's go back,' John said.

But Mary thought there was something in his voice that wasn't sure, and she took his arm and mock-pleaded, 'No-o-o-o, this is fun, let's see where he goes.'

The Palatski Man went up the streets, past the trucking lots full of semis without cabs, where the wind blew more grit and dirty papers than leaves, where he stopped hardly at all. Then past blocks of mesh-windowed factories shut down for Sunday and the streets empty and the pavements powdered with broken glass from broken beer bottles. They walked hand in hand a block behind the white, bent figure of the Palatski Man pushing his cart over the fissured sidewalk. When he crossed streets and looked from side to side for traffic, they jumped into doorways, afraid he might turn around.

He crossed Western Avenue, which was a big street and so looked emptier than any of the others without traffic on it. They followed him down Western Avenue and over the rivet-studded, aluminium-girded bridge that spanned the river, watching the pigeons flitting through the cables. Just past the bridge he turned into a pitted asphalt road that trucks used for hauling their cargoes to freight trains. It wound into the acres of endless lots and railroad yards behind the factories along the river.

John stopped. 'We can't go any further,' he said.

'Why?' she asked. 'It's getting interesting.'

'I've been here before,' he said.

'When?'

'I don't remember, but I feel like I've been here before.'

'C'mon, silly,' she said, and tugged his arm with all her might and opened her eyes very wide, and John let himself be tugged along, and they both started laughing. But by now the Palatski Man had disappeared around a curve in the road, and they had to run to catch up. When they turned the bend, they just caught sight of him going over a hill, and the asphalt road they had to run up had turned to cinder. At the top of the hill Mary cried, 'Look!' and pointed off to the left, along the river. They saw a wheatfield in the centre of the city, with the wheat blowing and waving, and the Palatski Man, half man and half willowy grain, was pushing his cart through the field past a scarecrow with straw arms outstretched and huge black crows perched on them.

'It looks like he's hanging on a cross,' Mary said.

'Let's go,' John said, and she thought he meant turn back home and was ready to agree because his voice sounded so determined, but he moved forward instead to follow the Palatski Man.

'Where can he be going?' Mary said.

But John just looked at her and put his finger to his lips. They followed single file down a trail trod smooth and twisting through the wheatfield. When they passed the scarecrow, the crows flapped off in great iridescent flutters, cawing at them while the scarecrow hung as if guarding a field of wings. Then, at the edge of the field, the cinder path resumed sloping downhill toward the river.

John pointed and said, 'The mounds of coal.'

And she saw three black mounds rising up in the distance and sparkling in the sun.

'C'mon,' John said, 'we have to get off the path.'

He led her down the slope and into the weeds that blended with the river grasses, rushes, and cattails. They sneaked through the weeds, which pulled at her dress and scratched her legs. John led the way; he seemed to know where he was going. He got down on his hands and knees and motioned for her to do the same, and they crawled forward without making a sound. Then John lay flat on his stomach, and she crawled beside him and flattened out. He parted the weeds, and she looked out and saw a group of men standing around a kettle on a fire and dressed in a strange assortment of ill-fitting suits, either too small or too large and baggy. None of the suit pieces matched, trousers blue and the suit-coat brown, striped pants and checked coats, countless combinations of colours. They wore crushed hats of all varieties: bowlers, straws, stetsons, derbies, Homburgs. Their ties were the strangest of all, misshapen and dangling to their knees in wild designs of flowers, swirls, and polka dots.

'Who are they?' she whispered.

'The Ragmen. They must be dressed for Sunday,' John hissed.

And then she noticed the shacks behind the men, with the empty wagons parked in front and the stacks of junk from uprooted basements and strewn attics, even the gutted factory just the way John had described it. She saw the dogs suddenly jump up barking and whining, and all the men by the fire turn around as the Palatski Man wheeled his cart into their midst.

He gestured to them, and they all parted as he walked to the fire, where he stood staring into the huge black pot. He turned and said something to one of them, and the man began to stir whatever was in the pot, and then the Palatski Man dipped a small ladle into it and raised it up, letting its contents pour back into the pot, and Mary felt herself get dizzy and gasp as she saw the bright red fluid in the sun and heard John exclaim, 'Blood!' And she didn't want to see any more, how the men came to the pot and dipped their fingers in it and licked them off, nodding and smiling. She saw the horses filing out of their barn, looking ponderous and naked without the harnesses. She hid her face in her arms and wouldn't look, and then she heard the slow, sorrowful chanting and off-key wheezing behind it. And she looked up and realized all the Ragmen, like a choir of bums, had removed their crushed hats and stood bareheaded in the wind, singing. Among them someone worked a dilapidated accordion, squeezing out a mournful, foreign melody. In the centre stood the Palatski Man, leading them with his arms like a conductor and sometimes intoning a word that all would echo in a chant. Their songs rose and fell but always rose again, sometimes nasal, then shifting into rich baritone, building always louder and louder, more sorrowful, until the Palatski Man rang his bell and suddenly everything was silent. Not men or dogs or accordion or birds or crickets or wind made a sound. Only her breathing and a far-off throb that she seemed to feel more than hear, as if all the church bells in the city were tolling an hour. The sun was in the centre of the sky. Directly below it stood the Palatski Man raising a *palatski*.

The Ragmen had all knelt. They rose and started a procession leading to where she and John hid in the grass. Then John was up and yelling, 'Run!' and she scrambled to her feet, John dragging her by the arm. She tried to run but her legs wouldn't obey her. They felt so rubbery pumping through the weeds and John pulling her faster than she could go with the weeds tripping her and the vines clutching like fingers around her ankles.

Ragmen rose up in front of them and they stopped and ran the other way but Ragmen were there too. Ragmen were everywhere in an embracing circle, so they stopped and stood still, holding hands.

'Don't be afraid,' John told her.

And she wasn't. Her legs wouldn't move and she didn't care. She just didn't want to run any more, choking at the acrid smell of the polluted river. Through her numbness she heard John's small voice lost over and over in the open daylight repeating, 'We weren't doin' anything.'

The Ragmen took them back to where the Palatski Man stood before the fire and the bubbling pot. John started to say something but stopped when the Palatski Man raised his finger to his lips. One of the Ragmen brought a bushel of shiny apples and another a handful of pointed little sticks. The Palatski Man took an apple and inserted the stick and dipped it into the pot and took it out coated with red. The red crystallized and turned hard, and suddenly she realized it was a red candy apple that he was handing her. She took it from his hand and held it dumbly while he made another for John and a third for himself. He bit into his and motioned for them to do the same. She looked up at John standing beside her, flushed and sweaty, and she bit into her apple. It was sweeter than anything she'd ever tasted, with the red candy crunching in her mouth, melting, mingling with apple juice.

And then from his cart he took a giant *palatski*, ten times bigger than any she had ever seen, and broke it again and again, handing the tiny bits to the circle of Ragmen, where they were passed from mouth to mouth. When there was only a small piece left, he broke it three ways and offered one to John. She saw it disappear into John's hand and watched him raise his hand to his mouth and at the same time felt him squeeze her hand very hard. The Palatski Man handed her a part. Honey stretched into threads from its torn edges. She put it in her mouth, expecting the crisp wafer and honey taste, but it was so bitter it brought tears to her eyes. She fought them back and swallowed, trying not to screw up her face, not knowing whether he had tricked her or given her a gift she didn't understand. He spoke quietly to one of the Ragmen in a language she couldn't follow and pointed to an enormous pile of rags beside a nearby shack. The man trudged to the pile and began sorting through it and returned with a white ribbon of immaculate, shining silk. The Palatski Man gave it to her, then turned and walked away, disappearing into the shack. As soon as he was gone, the circle of Ragmen broke and they trudged away, leaving the children standing dazed before the fire.

'Let's get out of here,' John said. They turned and began walking slowly, afraid the Ragmen would regroup at any second, but no one paid any attention to them. They walked away. Back through the wheat field, past silently perched crows, over the hill, down the cinder path that curved and became the pitted asphalt road. They walked over the Western Avenue bridge, which shook as a green trolley, empty with Sunday, clattered across it. They stopped in the middle of the bridge, and John opened his hand, and she saw the piece of *palatski* crushed into a little sour ball, dirty and pasty with sweat.

'Did you eat yours?' he asked.

'Yes,' she said.

'I tried to stop you,' he said. 'Didn't you feel me squeezing your hand? It might have been poisoned.'

'No,' she lied, so he wouldn't worry, 'it tasted fine.'

'Nobody believed me,' John said.

'I believed you.'

'They'll see now.'

And then he gently took the ribbon that she still unconsciously held in her hand – she had an impulse to clench her fist but didn't – and before she could say anything, he threw it over the railing into the river. They watched it, caught in the drafts of wind under the bridge, dipping and gliding among the wheeling pigeons, finally touching the green water and floating away.

'You don't want the folks to see that,' John said. 'They'd get all excited and nothing happened. I mean nothing really happened, we're both all right.'

'Yes,' she said. They looked at each other. Sunlight flashing through latticed girders made them squint; it reflected from the slits of eyes and off the river when their gaze dropped. Wind swooped over the railing and tangled their hair.

'You're the best girl I ever knew,' John told her.

They both began to laugh, so hard they almost cried, and John stammered out, 'We're late for dinner – I bet we're gonna really get it,' and they hurried home.

They were sent to bed early that night without being permitted to watch TV. She undressed and put on her nightgown and climbed under her covers, feeling the sad, hollow Sunday-night feeling when the next morning will be Monday and the weekend is dying. The feeling always reminded her of all the past Sunday nights she'd had it, and she thought of all the future Sunday nights when it would come again. She wished John could come into her room so they could talk. She lay in bed tossing and seeking the cool places under her pillow with her arms and in the nooks of her blanket with her toes. She listened to the whole house go to sleep: the TV shut off after the late news, the voices of her parents discussing whether the doors had been locked for the night. She felt herself drifting to sleep and tried to think her nightly prayer, the Hail Mary before she slept, but it turned into a half dream that she woke out of with a faint recollection of Gabriel's wings, and she lay staring at the familiar shapes of furniture in her dark room. She heard the wind outside like a low whinny answered by cats. At last she climbed out of her bed and looked out the lace-curtained window. Across her backyard, over the catalpa tree, the moon hung low in the cold sky. It looked like a giant *palatski* snagged in the twigs. And then she heard the faint tinkle of the bell.

He stood below, staring up, the moon, like silver eyeballs, shining in the centres of his dark glasses. His horse, a windy white stallion, stamped and snorted behind him, and a gust of leaves funnelled along the ground and swirled through the streetlight, and some of them stuck in the horse's tangled mane while its hooves kicked sparks in the dark alley. He offered her a *palatski*.

She ran from the window to the mirror and looked at herself in the dark, feeling her teeth growing and her hair pushing through her skin in the tender parts of her body that had been bare and her breasts swelling like apples from her flat chest and her blood burning, and then in a lapse of wind, when the leaves fell back to earth, she heard his gold bell jangle again as if silver and knew that it was time to go.

Blood Soup

Busha was calling him.

He ran into her room. She lay in the dark clutching the crucifix, her toothless gums chewing with prayer.

'Oh, Busha,' he said, 'nobody's home.'

She closed her eyes and her crouplike breath came easier.

'*Usiadź*,' she whispered, patting the bed for him to sit.

He sat beside her for the first time since they'd brought her back half conscious from the hospital. It was only a matter of time, they'd been told. But she'd hung on for two weeks.

'You take care of me now, Stefush.' She smiled. 'Remember how I take care of you?' Her arm rose to smooth his hair back, skin transparent as a lampshade, bones like yellow candles beneath the network of veins.

'How are you feeling, Busha? Can I get you something?'

'Dying, Stefush.'

'No, you're not, Busha. You're going to get well.'

'Too old. No strength.' She held his wrist and closed her eyes again. He was suddenly afraid that she would die with only him there. The room seemed oppressive, reeking of camphor and Vick's, shades drawn against the sunlight, the tops of the nightstands and bureaux cluttered with medicine bottles and photographs of all her children and grandchildren. Even now Busha made him feel that secret he'd always felt between them, that in her seemingly unlimited power to love them all she loved him specially. It was the kind of love he thought must have come from the Old Country – instinctive, unquestioning – like her strength, something foreign that he couldn't find in himself, that hadn't even been transmitted to his mother or any of Busha's other children.

The holy pictures of Jesus and Mary gazed down from over Busha's bed with sorrowful eyes, hair flowing, their flaming hearts crowned with thorns, pierced by swords, and dripping blood. When he was little, Busha would give him a dime if he kissed them and he could still remember the taste of dusty glass on his lips. He wished he believed in them strongly enough now to pray for her. She was sweating.

'Can I get you water?'

She opened her eyes. '*Zupa*' – she swallowed – 'soup.'

'What kind, Busha? Chicken noodle? Tomato? I'll make some.'

She rolled her head *no* on the pillow, making a sour face, smacking her grey tongue. '*Czarnina*.'

'What?'

'*Czarnina*. Blood soup. *Rozumiesz*?' she asked.

'Yes,' he answered, he understood. He remembered her making it years ago, a strong-smelling mixture of carrots, apples, prunes, flour, sour cream, parsley, thyme, and duck's blood. She'd kept two full pickle jars of the blood in the refrigerator and he would open it late at night to stare at them, liverish red beside the sweating-glass gallon of milk, waxed paper rubber-banded over their tops, and featherless duck heads on the lower shelf floating in a pot of clear water. It was Easter, rainy, they were all at Busha's, arriving with coloured hard-boiled eggs, ham, kraut, *kielbasa*, freshly grated horseradish. When his uncles saw the soup simmering on the stove they began laughing and joking.

'Hey, Ma must have been feeling run-down again.'

'Time for the family's oral transfusion.'

They sat at the ping-pong table on the back porch as she ladled it steaming into bowls.

'Try, Stefush. Make you strong. Grandpa loved it.'

But he wouldn't.

'It's fruit soup, Stefush. Just take a taste.'

He sipped off the tip of a spoon. Heavy and sweetish, the taste coating his tongue like velvet, but beneath the sweetness something dark and overly rich, like marrow. No, he insisted, he didn't want any more. He was ready to cry.

'Take jar from dresser and go to Józef's,' Busha said, pulling herself up from the pillow, squeezing his wrist. 'He give you.'

'That's your holy water in there, Busha.' He didn't try to

explain that his uncle Józef had sold the meat market he'd owned the last twenty years.

'Bring me.'

He brought her the Miracle Whip jar. The evaporating holy water looked like urine with a cloud of residue at the bottom. She dipped her fingers and made the sign of the cross, then spilled the rest on to the wilting lily someone had propped beside the bedpan.

'You get for me, Stefush.' Again it was like a secret between them, a magic to keep her alive.

'OK,' he promised. His legs were weak, his back sweaty. All he wanted was to get out of that room. His parents would be back soon anyway.

'Take quarter for yourself,' she said, pointing to the little change purse on the dresser.

'No, Busha, you don't have to give me money. I'm too old.'

'Stevie, take quarter. I know you smoke.'

He unsnapped the purse and took a quarter. 'Thanks,' he said.

He washed the jar out with hot water and put it in a bag, then took two dollars from the teapot where his mother kept loose change. His brother, Dove, was in the backyard throwing a rubber ball off the brick wall of the apartment building next door. In the sunlight, with traffic passing, it hardly seemed real to Steve that he'd just been in a dark room with a dying woman.

'Wanta come with?' Steve asked.

'Where to?'

'Uncle Joe's old meat market.'

'Taking the Alley Heartaches?'

'Yeah.'

Dove had nicknamed them Alley Heartaches earlier that summer when they walked the alleys instead of streets to the dentist. The alleys made them almost forget where they were going. Trees arched over wooden backyard fences like a green arcade, the fences were lined with garbage cans to pick through, smells blasted from black ventilators behind stores and factories. Steve had made up a double called the

Butchie, who lived in the Alley Heartaches, distinguishable from Steve only because of the clothespin he wore in his hair. The Butchie would ambush them whenever Steve ran ahead and turned into a gangway. Dove would find Steve unconscious, a victim of the Butchie, or the Butchie himself would appear, grinning like a maniac beneath his clothespin to bombard Dove with garbage. But Steve didn't feel like the Butchie now. They walked along in silence. He hadn't even bothered bringing a clothespin.

'I thought you were supposed to watch Busha,' Dove said.

'Busha *told* me to go.'

'For what?'

'*Zupa.*'

'*Zupa?*'

'Soup, jerk. We're going to get Busha soup.'

'Why does she want soup?'

Steve ignored him. Instead he started humming, then singing:

> 'Gimme dat *zupa zupa zupa.*
> Gimme dat oompha oompha oompha.'

He sang it over and over in different voices, making a sound like a tuba at the end.

'They're gonna be mad when they get home if you're not there,' Dove said.

'Shut up and sing, dimp. And march!'

> 'Gimme dat *zupa zupa zupa.*
> Gimme dat oompha oompha oompha.'

The sign on the window still read JOE'S MEATS. Plucked chickens dangled scaly yellow claws above the faded plastic parsley and spattered sheets of butcher paper. Steve looked for the skinned rabbits his uncle usually hung among the chickens but there weren't any.

Inside, shoppers crowded before the glass meat counters while the butchers called out numbers. A lot of the talk was in Spanish. Little Mexican kids played in the sawdust on the floor, sweeping it into mounds as if they were at the beach, the way Steve remembered doing when he was smaller. He and Dove stood at the end of the counter watching the butchers in their red-smeared aprons lugging sides of meat and trays heaped with innards from the clunking, safelike freezer door.

Big Antek was still there, behind his wooden chopping block, surrounded by huge knives, hacksaws, and cleavers, his boozer's nose like a clown's, whacking the cleaver through gristle with the same abandon that had cost him three of his fingers on his left hand. He saw them and grinned. When he came over he had a cold hotdog for each.

'What you guys want?'

Steve slipped the empty Miracle Whip jar out of the bag. 'My grandma needs duck's blood to make soup.'

'We don't sell fresh blood no more,' Antek said. 'It's against health regulations.'

'You mean nobody can get it any more?'

'I can get Busha some,' Antek whispered, 'but not till Saturday. We only get ducks for the weekend now. How's she doing?'

'Bad. Everyone's waiting for her to die.'

'I know a guy you can get some from right away, maybe,' Antek said. 'At least he used to have it. Ain't seen him since around Christmas. We used to drink together when I worked at the Yards. He's a little crazy. Raises pigeons. Sometimes sleeps on the roof with them. In fact, that's what they call him – Pan Gowumpe – "Mr Pigeon" in English.' Antek had scribbled the name and an address on a torn corner of butcher paper. 'Be careful in that neighbourhood,' he cautioned, dropping his voice, 'the coloureds are moving in.'

They left the meat market, Dove puffing at his hotdog and flicking it as if it were a big cigar. On the next corner, by Goldblatt's, the blind man played accordion. He played with his back to Twenty-sixth Street and the music had always seemed like an invisible boundary to Steve.

'Here, give him this quarter and watch his dog,' he told Dove.

The dog raised its wolfish head off his paws and opened its

eyes when the coin clunked into the cup. The eyes gleamed silverish blue-green, like mother-of-pearl.

'See? The dog's blind too.'

They crossed the boundary of wheezing music. A block down, a loudspeaker over the door of a used-furniture store crackled old Temptations hits. The sidewalk was jammed with secondhand furniture and refrigerators. Instead of supermarkets and department stores the street was lined with Goodwill clothing shops, noisy bars, and abandoned storefronts.

'Let's go in here and look around,' Dove said before an Army-surplus store.

'We don't have time to fool around. Busha's waiting. And don't stare at people,' Steve said as a bearded black man went by, testifying to the traffic.

Steve kept checking addresses against the paper Antek had given them. Finally, they stopped before a maroon-brick apartment building surrounded by a broken pipe fence. Doorbells dangled from frayed, disconnected wires in the entrance hall. The cracked plaster beneath the mailboxes was crayoned with names from years of tenants.

'This place doesn't even have an address,' Dove said.

'Well, this is where it *should* be. Here's Gowumpe – fourth floor.'

The bulbs were burned out on the stairway. They climbed towards the foggy gleam of the skylight. At the far end of the hallway on four, the fire-escape exit stood ajar, emitting a streak of blue summer sky, though hardly enough light to see the doors.

'Now what?' Dove asked.

'It didn't give an apartment number.'

They could hear radios playing behind some of the doors.

'Pan Gowumpe! *Pan Gowumpe!*' Dove hollered down the corridor.

'Shut up! Jesus Christ! You want the crazy people to come out?'

They ducked through the exit and crouched on the fire-escape landing, but none of the doors opened.

'Let's try the roof,' Steve said. He only half meant it. A

narrow metal ladder ran up the side of the building and over the roof.

'I'm not climbing that,' Dove said.

'OK, chickenshit, then wait here and hold the bottle.'

'I'm not waiting here alone.'

'Then climb the goddamn ladder.'

The rungs were rusty and when Steve got on behind Dove the bolts moved in the crumbling mortar and for a moment it seemed as if the entire four-storey fire escape were swaying loose against the side of the building.

'Yaaahhh,' Dove screamed.

'Keep moving or you'll get paralysed,' Steve said.

Dove kept climbing slowly, hand over hand. Once over the edge, he sat down hard on the roof, digging his finger-nails into the tar as if the building might suddenly tilt and slide him off.

A wind that hadn't been blowing on the street fanned across the blazing tar. It was tacky beneath their gym shoes. A twisted TV antenna lay embedded on its side, tangled in wire. A wooden shed the size of a newspaper stand leaned by the chimney. Beyond it, against the peaked skylight, a row of coops stood on a raised wooden platform. Hard corn scattered below them like gravel. The panes of the skylight were crusted with pigeon droppings and splashes of white-wash.

They walked over to the coops. Two pigeons fluttered off. They watched them sail away over the roofs and trees, and circle the copper green steeple of St Kasimir's.

'I wonder where all the other pigeons are,' Steve said.

A cooing howl, half pigeon, half ghost, came from behind them. They froze.

'Go away 'fore you get pushed off,' a voice rasped from the wooden shed.

'We're looking for Mr Gowumpe. Antek from Joe's meat market gave us this address,' Steve said quickly.

'I know you made the massacre! I can identify you!'

The wooden door opened a crack. A weasel-shaped face peered out with whitish eyes.

'All we came for was to buy some duck's blood for soup

for my sick grandma. See?' Steve held up the Miracle Whip jar.

'How much you pay?'

'Are you Pan Gowumpe?'

The door opened out wider. A small, stooped black man wearing a mailman's hat squatted on a buckled mattress crammed between the walls of the shed. Around him, stacked cardboard boxes, overflowing ragged clothes, and newspaper threatened to topple.

'The Pan's *gone*,' the man said.

'He's dead?'

'Dead? Sheeit! That old bastard ain't never gonna die. Too mean, too crazy. Still getting it up. Health inspectors tried running him out for keeping ducks, roosters, whatnot downstairs. Then somebody come up here and massacre all his pigeons he been raising twenty years. He's *gone*, that's all.'

They looked at the coops again, this time noticing clots of feathers, brownish stains, flecks of skin spattered on the wood and panes. Steve put the bottle back in the bag.

'Do you live in *there*?' Dove asked.

'Come on in, my man. Have a look around.' The man grinned, showing bad teeth, gesturing like a doorman.

'We gotta go,' Steve said. 'Sorry to bother you.'

'Hey, what about your grandma? You really want duck's blood?'

'She makes soup with it.'

'Maybe I can get you some.'

'You know where Pan Gowumpe moved to?'

'Maybe I do.' He took his mailman's hat off and rubbed his hand over woolly grey hair. His scalp showed through like varnished wood. 'Cost you a buck.'

'OK,' Steve agreed, 'But you get us there first.'

The small man turned back and groped in the shed for a leather mail sack. He slung it over his shoulder and clamped a padlock on the shed door. 'We go this way,' he said, raising a trapdoor from the roof.

They followed him down the alleys, waiting while he stopped to examine garbage cans, stuffing empty pop bottles in his mail pouch.

'Were you a mailman?' Dove asked.

'I *am* the Mailman. That's what folks around here call me. Nobody messes with the US Mail.'

He stopped at a dumpster behind a supermarket. Flies swarmed from crates as he picked through spoiled peaches, stuffing wilted lettuce and carrots into his sack. 'You gotta live off the city same way country people live off the land. Like the rat does. You ever eat garbage?'

'Only when he makes me,' Dove said, pointing to Steve.

'You make your little brother eat garbage?'

'It's just a threat,' Steve said.

'Wait'll you guys are old. Won't be no threat. Don't matter if you're white or red or black – you'll eat what you can eat. Garbage, dog food, even drink duck's blood.' He started to laugh. 'How sick your grandma anyway?'

'She thinks she's dying.'

'And this duck soup gonna cure that? Man, I gotta get me some.'

'Gimme dat *zupa zupa zupa*,' Dove started singing.

'That's good,' the Mailman said, and started singing along with him.

They sang until they reached the end of the alley. Cars whished by. Across the street, Douglass Park stretched for blocks. It had been in the news the summer before when a riot followed a fight between a white softball team and a black one.

'You sure this is the way to Gowumpe's?' Steve asked.

'Shortcut,' the Mailman said.

A group of black guys, playing softball behind a rickety backstop, ignored them as they entered the park. The Mailman led them into the trees, down a path that twisted through a dense jungle of bushes. When they could see the lagoon sparkling through a gap in the bushes he motioned them down. Together they crawled to the edge of the lagoon and crouched where it got soggy, behind a screen of reeds and cattails. Out toward the middle, beyond the lily pads, a family of white ducks glided.

'*Zupa*,' the Mailman whispered, grinning.

'Christsake,' Steve said, under his breath, 'you're crazy. You said you were taking us to Pan Gowumpe's.'

'Not exactly. I said I could get you duck's blood. Look, I know the Pan. He treats them birds like family. He ain't gonna give you shit, nohow. Whole time I knowed him he ain't give me nothin' but an egg now and then – him healthy and me starvin'.' He fished into his mail pouch and came up with a handful of dried bread crusts. 'People throw these out for the birds – there's folks throw away their entire lives. You gotta start learning to see what's around you for the taking.'

He snapped off a corner of bread and skimmed it out so that when it touched, a circle spread on the water as if a fish had been feeding.

'They're turning,' Dove said.

'Course they are. Ducks know what a free meal is. Now, don't make no noise.'

He continued flipping bread out. They crouched, watching the ducks racing one another to gobble it down. Each throw brought them a little closer to shore.

The Mailman carefully emptied the sack out between his legs and handed it to Steve, who was trying to see what had been in it.

'When I get the ducks outa the pond you get between them and the water and pounce this over one. You gotta be quick 'cause they already gun-shy from kids throwing rocks at 'em.'

He was tossing bread near the shore now and began to creep backward, laying a trail of crusts. Two of the more aggressive ducks were already paddling at the mossy edge of the lagoon.

Steve held himself rigid among the reeds. Up that close their white feathers dazzled as if the sun were beating harder. He could see the scales on their vibrant orange webbing as they waddled, squishing, over mud. He was sweating, dizzy with the scorched smell of cattails, his eyes seeming to magnify the tiny pond world so that he could see the wake that water spiders left in the scum, translucent minnows darting through his reflection, turquoise bands on damsel flies. Something had gone wrong with the day. He felt disconnected, as he did sometimes walking to the dentist with Dove when he'd realize it would be so simple to turn around and not go. But he wouldn't turn and it would be like someone else still walking in his body. Then he thought of Busha – a vision of her struggling for breath in that shade-drawn room cluttered with photographs and holy pictures like frozen scenes from her life. Why did she want to go on living? But when he thought that his stomach knotted. He wanted her to live. The world would be too unnatural without her.

'Now, boy!' the Mailman whispered.

Steve sprang up and the ducks erupted in a flurry of feathers. The big drake he lunged for flapped past his shins, almost knocking him down. Two ducklings were trapped a moment between him and Dove and the Mailman, who were shooing with their arms, and when one of them tried squirting past him for the water he pounced with the sack.

The Mailman let out a whoop. 'Told you I'd get us a duck, boy!'

They crouched, breathing hard, around the sack. The duck quacked worriedly inside. Steve's legs felt drained of strength.

'It's the littlest one,' Dove said.

'We ain't gonna roast him,' the Mailman said.

'What are we gonna do?'

'Carry a knife?'

'No,' Steve said.

'Got the jar but no knife, eh?' The Mailman looked at him scornfully.

'We better let him go,' Dove said. His voice quavered; his face was flushed. Steve could see he didn't like what was going on.

'What about your grandma's soup? Gonna let her die?'

Dove looked down, as if he were studying the weeds. The Mailman went over to the pile of junk he'd dumped out of his sack and picked up a Seven-Up bottle. He rapped it against a rock half submerged in the reeds. It didn't break. He smacked it again. It still didn't.

'We're not gonna kill it?' Dove whispered to Steve.

The Mailman was still rapping the bottle. Suddenly, it shattered, leaving him holding the jagged neck.

'Sheeit! A man could cut his finger off.' He came over and handed it to Steve. 'Hold this a second.'

Steve set it down in the grass. The Mailman was slowly lifting up an end of the sack, squinting in. A stream of liquid green jetted out.

'Yah!' he yelped, flinching and falling backward into a sitting position. 'I'm blinded!'

The duck had its tail end out, trying to wriggle free, spurting a steady stream of green. Dove and Steve were trying to stuff the bird back under the sack.

'Man, what you doin' with that duck?' a voice drawled.

Four black teenagers stood on the path. They all had baseball gloves and the guy speaking was holding a bat.

'Who told you honkies you could come to our pond and steal a duck?' he asked. 'This here's a black park. Ain't you got no respect? I'm asking you a question, honkie.'

'I got respect,' Steve said. It sounded phony as soon as he said it.

'You got sheeit, that's what you got.' He walked over to the pile of bottles and rotten vegetables the Mailman had emptied, and scattered them about with the bat. 'Been stealing our garbage, I see. You dudes are litterbugs too.'

The other three guys laughed.

'Say now, son,' the Mailman said. He was still dabbing his eyes with the tail of his shirt.

'Ain't *your* son, you crazy old nigger. What you doin' bringin' this white cheese here? I heard about you when I was little. They used to say you come at night for kids to stuff 'em in your mail sack. Goddamn, I oughta bust yo' head.' He cocked the bat, then whirled on Steve. 'Empty out your pockets, man.'

Steve turned them inside out. One of the guys picked up the money and dropped it into his baseball mitt. The guy with the bat flicked two fingers into Steve's shirt pocket and lifted out his pack of Kools.

'You too young to smoke,' he said. 'Goddamn! Picking on defenceless animals. Man, I oughta kick your white asses from here to the Anticruelty Society. In fact, that's exactly what we are gonna do unless you get your ass outa here *now*. And I mean run, motherfuckers!'

They ran, stumbling through the bushes when they lost the path, then out across the shaggy outfield grass.

'Hold up,' the Mailman yelled, nearly collapsing when they reached the infield. He was panting hard and holding his heart. They waited for him to catch up, then helped him over to a park bench under the shade of a tree, across from a bus stop.

'One of them dollars was mine, goddamn!' He leaned his head back. One of his nostrils was leaking blood and there was green duckshit on his collar. 'I'm a sick man. I needed that *zupa*. I need a cure.'

'They didn't get the jar,' Dove said. He handed it to Steve, the paper bag twisted and sweaty from his fist.

A bus pulled up and a few of the people stared.

'We gotta get out of here,' Steve whispered. 'It's getting late.'

'OK,' the Mailman said, 'I'll take you to Gowumpe's. It ain't that far.'

They cut between the shells of condemned buildings, their broken windows clouded with plaster dust, and inside, the remains of rooms – overturned tables, flattened couches – amid the wreckage of fallen ceilings, as if the people who'd lived there had left in a hurry. Steve kept looking for something familiar to help them find their way back. He wasn't exactly lost, but disoriented about what streets to take. He didn't want Dove or the Mailman to know.

The Mailman led them to a backyard crowded with junked cars, weeds sprouting through hoodless engines.

'He lives up there,' the Mailman said, pointing to the third floor of a building that almost touched the El tracks. All its windows were smashed out.

'Nobody lives in there,' Steve said. 'It's ready to fall down.'

'Told you he's *gone*, boy. I watched him move in there. He tried to shake me, but I followed him. Look at that.'

'What?'

'Pigeons.'

Pigeons lined the tracks. Once he noticed them, Steve realized he'd been hearing them coo. They fluttered back and forth between the tracks and the windowsills on the third floor.

'See how they goes inside? Pigeons don't ordinarily go inside. Go on up.'

'Ain't you coming with us?'

'We wouldn't get nothin' if I did. See, we had a little disagreement over whose pigeons they were at the other place, me living on the roof and all. The Pan think I called the health inspectors on him. Like I told you, he's *gone*. You go. I'm gonna be waiting right out here for you. Don't forget what you owe me neither.'

'You saw they got my money.'

'I'll settle for some of that *zupa*. I'll go home with you guys and when your grandma makes it you sneak some out for me.'

'That's wasn't our deal.'

'Then I'll go back with you to get my dollar.'

They shoved the unhinged door aside and Steve and Dove started up the stairs. As soon as they got beyond the sunlight from the doorway it was hard to see. The stairs were covered with rubble.

'Careful,' Steve said, 'there's no banister.'

The Mailman was hissing something after them, but they couldn't quite hear him and didn't stop.

'I think he said he'd curse us if we tried to screw him,' Dove whispered.

They reached the second floor just as the stairs began to rumble. The walls shook and plaster rained down. There was a roar. They could actually feel as well as hear the El go by.

'The tracks must almost be touching this wall,' Steve said.

The train's echoes clattered behind as they walked down the second-floor hallway, past old rooms with sooty wall-papered walls. The doors had been removed. Light filtered in through broken-out windows facing west, sun nearly at eye level and blinding as if the suspended particles of dust were tiny mirrors. They entered one of the rooms and stared out the window, directly even with the El tracks. Pigeons were resettling in the wake of the train. They were pecking at something scattered among the ties.

'It's close enough to climb out and jump to the tracks. Hey, we can jump from here, then run down the tracks before the next train comes and make it to the next station, climb up

on the platform and take the train home without paying.'
Steve boosted his leg over the windowsill as if he were climbing out.

'Don't do it,' Dove pleaded.

'You must think I'm crazy.'

'Listen,' Dove said. 'Hear that? It sounds like a snake charmer.'

'It's a clarinet.'

They followed the sound up to the third floor.

'It's wedding music,' Dove whispered.

Steve had recognised it too. He didn't know the name of the song, but the words went 'Oh, how we danced on the night we were wed'. The melody was Gypsylike and whenever it was played at weddings the old people danced with dreamy looks on their faces and sometimes wept if they were drunk. He knocked softly at the door it was coming from. The playing stopped. He knocked again, a little harder. No answer.

'Mr Gowumpe, Antek from Joe's butcher shop said you could sell us some duck's blood for soup.'

He knocked again. He explained, talking at the keyhole, about his grandmother. It was totally silent on the other side of the door except for the cooing of the pigeons.

'Pretend you're walking away, down the stairs,' Steve whispered to Dove. 'Make a lot of noise.'

'Sorry to bother you,' he said loudly to the door. 'Goodbye.'

Dove stomped off. Steve flattened himself against the wall by the door. He could hear creaking movement on the other side, then the doorknob clicking quietly open. An enormous bushy head of white cowlicks peeked out, looking down the stairs.

'Mr Gowumpe,' Steve said.

The man jumped and slumped back against the doorjamb, sliding down, clutching the top button of the long underwear he wore. Dove came running back upstairs just as the man was crawling back inside. He rolled over heavily and lay on the floor beside his metal clarinet.

'You gave him a heart attack,' Dove said.

The man lay there staring blankly at the ceiling. The floor

was spread with newspapers splotched by bird droppings and weighed down with bricks. A torn bedspread hung over one window, tinting the late-afternoon light rose. The old man crossed his arms over his chest and closed his eyes.

'Mr Gowumpe, Mr Gowumpe,' Steve said, 'Are you all right? Should we go for a doctor?'

A huge white goose waddled out of another room and nuzzled the old man with his beak.

The man opened his eyes. Beneath his shaggy white eyebrows they were the blue of a gas flame. He grimaced, showing his teeth, and at that moment the goose said in a voice very much like a parrot's, 'Doctor? Doctor? What does doctor know?'

The goose continued opening and closing its beak, but no more words came out.

The man had sat up. 'He right,' he said, nudging the goose. 'Even if sick I don't need a doctor. I look sick to you?'

'Why are you lying on the floor?' Dove asked.

'Nice floor. Besides, you give me little scare, I give you little scare.'

Fowl were strutting across the room now – iridescent roosters, speckled hens, white ducks. Pigeons landed on the sill and perched, cooing and swivelling metallic throats.

'Can you make the goose talk again?' Dove asked.

Gowumpe grimaced again, teeth looking powerful as a horse's, and the parrot voice came out of the goose. As soon as the goose heard it, it began to open and close its beak. 'Why your *busha* sick? Just old?'

'It started when she fell down the stairs and broke her hip.'

Gowumpe began to laugh. '*Czarnina* no fix that,' he sputtered. 'It's thick stuff, but you can't make cast from it. Can't make miracle either. When time to die, then time to die.' With each burst of laughter the birds circled faster. 'Maybe if you make soup out of Christ's blood. Ever see old ladies kissing relics? Blessing throats with candles, blessing eyes, ears. Hey, nobody blesses asshole. Why not? Has its troubles too.' He'd changed back to the goose's voice. 'How you find me?'

'The Mailman showed us,' Steve said.

'Mailman! Hey, he dirty, thiefing sumnabitch!'

'He's sick too,' Dove said. 'He needs some soup too.'

'Ain't goddamn sick. He been cursed. Crazy old lady in the old building put evil eye on him for snooping in her garbage. She think the Mailman Russian spy!' He exploded into laughter and the roosters began to circle the room again. 'He think blood soup gonna help him get it up again, understand? Push-push. Soup gonna make him push-push.' He was flushing red under his white mane, stamping the floor in time to his laughter. Every time he said 'push-push' he worked the middle finger of his left hand in and out of the fist of his right. They could feel the walls quaking the hilarity back, then the floor shaking, plaster sifting from the ceiling. A flight of pigeons beat in through the window. Dove clapped his hands over his ears as the El roared by as loud as if the tracks had split the room. The air swam with plaster dust and feathers.

'Seventy-five! Seventy-five! That's how old Gowumpe!' He was cawing in the voice of the goose. 'And still push-push!'

The train was racketing away. 'How old you?' he asked, pointing at Dove.

'Nine.'

'Nine, no push-push. Though possible! I'm still in Old Country when nine. Didn't know a damn thing. Nobody knows at nine. What you know?'

'Nothing,' Dove said.

'See, what I tell you? How old you, *dupa*?' he asked Steve.

'Thirteen.'

'Understand *dupa*?'

'It means "behind",' Steve said, ' "butt", something like "asshole".'

'That's right. See, thirteen years and you know "asshole". Seventy-five years and what I know?'

'What?'

'More *dupa*.'

He stomped across the room, gesturing for them to follow, chickens squawking out from under his feet. 'Hey, pick up your feet over newspaper,' he yelled at Steve and Dove.

'Glass doorknob.' He pointed. '*Dupa* throne always behind

the door with the glass doorknob.' He flung the door open and grabbed Dove by the collar. 'Look down, don't fall.'

On the other side the floorboards jutted out a foot, then dropped three stories into darkness. Plumbing dangled from bare lathing. Gowumpe grinned, all the while grunting, lip-farting, pantomiming tremendous explosions.

'One day health inspector will be poking nose down there and killed by Gowumpe shit bomb!'

'You mean you really *go* hanging over the edge?' Dove asked, astonished.

'Show you something else.' Gowumpe got down on his hands and knees, opening and closing his mouth repeatedly without making a sound. The goose waddled over immediately, its beak opening and closing in the same way, and with a short beat of its wings hopped to his back. Gowumpe crawled across the room to his silver clarinet, then slowly rose, the goose taking short steps up his spine, until he was standing straight with the goose perched on his head. He theatrically tilted his clarinet towards the ceiling and blew, and at the same time the goose extended its neck, honking in perfect pitch, spreading its wide, white wings.

Together, holding the note, wild white hair, white throat, white wings, they seemed to fill the room.

Dove and Steve applauded.

'Ten years together,' Gowumpe said, raising his eyebrows toward the goose. 'Goose older than you.'

He stooped and the goose hopped back to the newspapers.

'What you got in the bag, little boy?' the goose asked.

Dove took the Miracle Whip jar out of the bag and showed it to the goose.

'Oh, yes, you're the little boy who wants some blood. Most little boys just want feathers.'

'Boys, I tell you something,' Gowumpe broke in. 'I used to work in the Yards. You know? Armour, Wilson, Swift, all of them. Twenty years ago it was big ting. On Thursdays you could smell all over the city. People say, "They're making soap. Making glue." All these DPs working there – it's all right to say it, I'm DP too – Polacks, Lugans, Bohunks. People who knew how to be hungry. Surrounded by all that meat! Sometimes DP on the line would drink some blood. Fresh, right on the job. I see it. Think it would make them strong, cure hangover, good for push-push. Take jars home for women to keep them young. A lot of bullshit.'

'She thinks it will help her,' Steve said.

'No. You don't know yet. There are two kinds of people. Living people and dying people. Living people, they don't hardly know about dying people. They think there are just people. But dying people know there are two kinds. They know no other difference is important – man and woman, black and white, old and young – doesn't matter. Some feel angry, some ashamed, some try to pretend they living.' He looked at both of them. 'Ahccckk.' he shook his head in disgust. 'Hey,' he said to Dove, 'show you something more.'

He led them into the next room, where the goose had come from. The floor was scattered with hard corn. Two old, four-legged, disconnected bathtubs stood in two corners, half full of water and bobbing ducklings. Ducks waddled across wet newspaper quacking. A huge, homemade birdcage, fashioned from chicken wire and screening and full of branches, was set against the wall. Canaries, parakeets, and finches flitted inside.

'People give me birds when they can't keep self,' Gowumpe said. 'Gotta find another place before it gets cold. Look here.'

He carefully opened a door to a small bedroom. Boards had been hammered across its single window like horizontal bars so that the light streaked in leaving most of the room dim. The closet in the corner was doorless. Perched on a bare coatrack, a large, startlingly blue bird blinked. A scarlet crescent of feathers opened like a slash beneath its throat. Two tail streamers arced almost to the floor, their amethyst tips sweeping above the dropping-spattered pie plates of water and cut-up fruits buzzing with flies. It partially stretched its wings, revealing bald, raw skin among the brilliant plumage.

'Been pulling out his own feathers,' Gowumpe whispered.

Suddenly the bird screamed so violently that Steve and Dove pulled the door shut.

'You gonna miss it,' Gowumpe said, opening it and pushing them in to look.

36

Inside, the bird had ruffled itself to double its original size, blue plumes sheening bronze and green, radiating colours as it hung upside down, swinging wildly from the coatrack, its streamer tails whipping the air like antennae from some other world.

Gowumpe pushed them out and shut the door.

'What is it?'

'Don't know. Old lady, dentist's widow, give me.'

They turned back to the main room with its newspaper and corn on the floor, but it looked different to Steve now. He couldn't shake off the image of the bird; its colours were superimposed on the gutted walls. Dove was dabbling his hand in the tub with the ducklings.

'You still want?' Gowumpe asked, pointing to the jar as if Steve might have changed his mind.

'Yes,' Steve said.

'How much money you got?'

'We got jumped in the park on the way here. But whatever it is I'll get it and come back.'

'Robbed. I live here forty years – DPs, Mexicans, coloureds – and don't get robbed.'

'What about your pigeons?'

'That was crazy person who did that.' He took a shoe box off the windowsill. Silverware jangled. He lifted out a butcher knife.

'You come here again or tell someone where Gowumpe living and *shlshsh*,' he said to Steve, running the knife past his own throat.

'We won't tell,' Steve swore.

'You're not going to kill one,' Dove said.

'No, they got little faucets.'

They waited. Another El screamed past, filling the room with pigeons. Dove held his ears and turned his face to the wall till it passed. Finally, Gowumpe came out holding the bag in the palm of a big hand.

'Hold by bottom, too heavy. Feel how warm.'

Dove wouldn't touch it. Gowumpe handed it to Steve.

'Thank you.'

'Sure, *dziekuje*, like you care about old people. If Busha can't drink it get doctor to pump it in – stick tubes in her

37

nose, tubes in arms, make her prisoner in old people's home. Nice guy. OK, get outa here. I gotta take nap. Stay up half the night keeping rats away from birds.'

'Goodbye,' they said.

'Goodbye, Dupa Yash and Nothing Head,' the goose cackled as the door closed.

They peered out across a narrow cinder alley into the dark underpinnings of the El tracks. Instead of going back down the way they'd come, they used the exit at the other end of the hall.

'The Mailman must still be waiting at the other door,' Steve whispered. 'As soon as a train goes over we'll run across under the tracks. As long as we follow them it'll get us home.'

'We promised him some,' Dove said.

'He can get his own. Jesus Christ! You want him following us?'

'What if he sees us?'

'Just keep running.'

'If he catches me are you gonna stop?'

'He's not gonna catch you, asshole, if you keep running. He's too old. Get ready.'

They could hear the train, still blocks away, rumbling towards them, then it was streaming overhead and they clambered over a downed cyclone fence and sprinted across the alley.

It was like entering a forest of girders. Light came in slats through the tracks above, throwing the bleached shadow of tracks before them. The girders crisscrossed at intervals, forcing them to flip the V centre of beams. Steve cradled the jar against him like a football. His shirt was sweaty and stuck to the paper bag. They kept looking back. If the Mailman was following them along the girders they couldn't see him. But the shadows moved. They kept jogging.

Rush-hour trains hurtled in both directions, coming at shorter intervals, soot and sparks showering down. The air smelled scorched with the friction of screeching steel and the hiss of pneumatic brakes.

'Here it comes.' Dove kept yelling as each train pursued

them; yelling as if they were actually running on the tracks instead of the shadows of tracks, and were being overtaken and crushed in the deafening roar when the slats of light above were blotted out to mere laser flashes between cars. Steve glanced back. Dove was running with his hands over his ears, his mouth gaping. Steve couldn't hear if his brother was screaming.

The tracks followed the alley, running above its blackened walls, broken backyard fences, and wash hanging from dirty lines. The cross streets were crowded with people coming home from work, coming alive for night – neon blinking on in stores, music blasting from bars. So long as Steve and Dove stayed under the tracks it was as if they were invisible.

By the time they hit Twenty-second, Steve knew they were safe. He was a block ahead of Dove, so he sat on a girder to wait for him to catch up. He knew he should have felt more winded, but he didn't. He felt he could continue running for miles. He was thinking of coming home with the blood, of making the soup, of the house filling with his aunts and uncles, everyone drinking and joking, the washtub brimming with ice and cans of beer and pop floating in the freezing water.

'I can't run any more,' Dove said, slumping down on the girder. 'Which side is the appendix on?'

'The other one.'

Another train went over. Dove clapped his hands over his ears and closed his eyes.

'Recognize where we are?' Steve asked. 'There's the dentist's office.' It was a four-storey tan-brick building. In the dusky light the bricks looked pink. 'Wanta stop by for a filling or two? Come on, we can take the Alley Heartaches from here.'

They walked down Twenty-second, past the dentist's, and cut down a gangway into the alley. The sky was lilac over the backyard trees.

'I banged my ankle on a girder,' Dove said, stopping to pull down his sock.

'You'll live. Stop faking.'

'I'm not,' Dove mumbled, limping.

'We got it!' Steve yelled at him. He started strutting and singing:

> 'Gimme dat *zupa zupa zupa*.
> Kick in the *dupa dupa dupa*.'

He was hopping along behind Dove, kicking him in the pants in time to the words. Dove trudged, head down, ignoring him. He wasn't sharing any of the elation Steve was feeling.

'Sing!' Steve said.

'Quit it!'

'A real sorehead. What's your problem?'

'We promised the Mailman. He was sick too. And what if he finds out where we live?'

'The Mailman!' Steve suddenly whirled around. 'Holy shit! I just saw him duck behind us. Run!'

He took off full speed down the alley. Dove tried to keep up but quickly fell behind. Steve kept going. He wanted to run till he was out of breath, to burn up whatever was making his blood jump like electricity. Running always made him feel there were possibilities. He wasn't anxious to go home, for the day to end, though he wished the explanations were over. The closer they got, the less real the celebration he'd imagined with his aunts and uncles became. There was a dread beneath his excitement he didn't want to face – a rising feeling of smallness and helplessness at the heart of his elation. He could visualize the Miracle Whip jar sitting for weeks in the refrigerator, the blood coagulating in the cold. By the time he reached the empty lot behind Baynor's Drugs he was breathing hard. He sat down in the high weeds behind the billboard that screened the lot from the street. He took the bottle out of the bag. It was plum-coloured, not brownish, the way he remembered it. He wondered if the twilight was doing that. He unscrewed the cap slowly, took a deep breath of weed-scented air, then carefully sniffed the jar, ready to fight down nausea. It smelled like vinegar. There was a sweet, earthy smell beneath the sourness that was familiar. He took a drop on the end of his finger. It was too watery. Beets.

He tasted it.

Gowumpe had given him beet juice.

He sank back in the weeds and lay looking up at the wafer of moon solidifying over the garage roofs. He closed his eyes, trying to think of what he'd say when he got home, trying to think of Busha. But his mind kept drifting back to the strange bird burning with its own colours, living in a closet. He could hear Dove panting up the alley. He dipped his finger into the jar and drew a streak across his forehead, then screwed the cap on and put the jar into the torn bag. He lay back in the weeds, groaning, eyes half shut.

'The Butchie got me . . . the Butchie got me.'

Dove was crying, holding his side.

'Go to hell! You bastard!'

'I'm hurt bad,' Steve said, raising his head out of the weeds.

'Hey! You're bleeding! What should I do?'

'Get a priest. I'm dying.'

'I'll get Baynor.'

Steve jumped up, laughing.

Dove stood watching him wipe his head with leaves.

'You didn't fool me. There's no Butchie. The Mailman wasn't following us either.'

'Quit faking. Admit it. You were crying. You thought they got me.'

'You're the one always faking,' Dove said.

Steve took the jar out of the bag. 'Dare me to drop it?'

'Go ahead. It's Busha's.'

'Think I won't?'

'Yeah.'

'*You* save Busha.'

He flipped the jar up over the garage roofs. It turned end over end against the fading sky and seemed to hang like a kicked football, then plunged down. Dove lunged forward to catch it, only to flinch as it touched his hands, jerking his elbows back into his stomach desperately as the jar hit the pavement with the muffled explosion of glass, splattering the cuffs of their jeans, the white laces of their gym shoes.

Visions of Budhardin

The elephant was there, waiting in the overgrown lot where once long ago there had been a Victory garden, and after that a billboard, but now nothing but the rusting hulks of abandoned cars. The children grew silent as they gathered to inspect it: the crude overlapping parts, the bulky sides and lopsided rump, the thick squat legs that looked like five-gallon ice-cream drums, huge cardboard ears, everything painted a different shade of grey, and the trunk the accordion-ribbed hose from a vacuum cleaner. They stared back at Budhardin's eyes looking at them through the black sockets above the trunk. The holes were set too close together for a real elephant and made it look cross-eyed and slightly evil.

They couldn't see inside where Budhardin sat on a stool looking out at the world, his feet on pedals, hands manipulating levers, body connected to a network of lines and pulleys, a collar gripping his forehead for swinging the limp trunk, a clothesline tied around his waist running out the tail hole.

The children walked around, examining it from every angle.

'What in the fuck!' Billy Crystal said. He took his knife out and carved the date into the plaster rump and after it his initials, B.C.

Most of the kids chuckled even though they were familiar with the initials joke. A few threw stones, watching them bounce off, leaving dents in the paint job. Others had run across the lot to the alley, rummaged through the garbage cans, and began their bombardment of rotten tomatoes, banana peels, apple cores. Pedro 'Chinga' Sanchez raced in balancing a glob of dogshit on a popsicle stick, arching it as if it were a hand grenade. It splattered high off the humped back and was followed by a rain of beer cans and Petri wine bottles. Buddy Holly Shwartz sneaked up behind, grabbed the tail, and gave it a yank.

'Hey, it's just a goddamn clothesline!' he announced. They tried to light it up but nobody had any lighter fluid on him, so all they were able to do was get it smoking like a slow wick.

The elephant had closed its eyelids and stopped swinging its trunk from side to side. It stood perfectly still while they discussed pulling its trunk out by the roots or coming back with some gasoline to roast it.

'Ah, fuck it,' Billy Crystal finally said, and they wandered off in little groups.

After they'd gone Mr Ghazili, who owned the little combination grocery–candy store on the corner, shuffled over. As always, even in winter, he wore his house slippers, still speckled with pink paint from some job long ago. He stood looking up at the elephant, chewing his cigar. Little by little the elephant raised its lids.

'That's you in there, isn't it, Budhardin?' Ghazili said.

The elephant nodded its trunk.

'You might look a little different, but I'd recognize those eyes anywhere . . . same as used to stare up at me through the candy counter. Yeah, you liked them liquorice whips. I remember the time you bought out my whole supply and went outside giving 'em away to all the kids telling 'em you were Jesus Christ. So they tied you to a phone pole and started beatin' you with them liquorice whips. I had to run out there and untie you.'

Two tears rolled down the elephant's face.

'Yeah, I remember . . . always alone . . . except for that friend – what was his name? – kid who got runned over . . . And now, a big tycoon! Yeah, I been readin' about you in the papers. Used to try and show people, but nobody around here's too interested in that kinda stuff, you know. Wouldn't of believed it was the same little fat kid anyway.'

Budhardin didn't answer. He had failed to provide the elephant with a mouth.

'Your tail's smoking pretty bad back there,' Mr Ghazili said. He went around and rubbed the sparks out of the fibres. They stood looking at each other. Fistfuls of silver dollars, wristwatches, rings, suddenly issued from the trunk, spilling at Ghazili's feet.

'No, no,' he said, 'I don't want nothing. Just came by to say hello.' He shuffled closer, his slippers crunching over the pile of coins, and patted the bump right above the elephant's trunk, then shuffled away.

Budhardin stood alone watching the day get older inside the sweltering body, wishing he could have told Ghazili the story. It was a story about two peasant boys on their own – their families dead, perhaps from plague. They find a huge plaster elephant standing in a field, left behind by a circus, and take to living in it. But the elephant is in poor repair and at night swarms of rats try to get in through the holes. During the day they wander about the deserted countryside scrounging for food. Once, they come upon a village, completely lifeless, with everything locked, and stare in through the bakery window at a fabulous display of cookies and frosted pastries.

He couldn't remember how it ended. It had been two years since the story had begun recurring in a series of haunting flashes and he still was unable to get beyond the two boys standing before the bakery window, their faces pressing against the glass. Sometimes people would say it sounded vaguely familiar but, like him, they found it impossible to recall the ending.

He let his mind drift and found himself counting cars that passed. It was rush hour. He remembered how he and Eugene used to stand on the corner making endless surveys of cars. Long lists of dates and check marks under columns headed CHEVYS, MERCS, HUDSONS. What made it exciting was when something unusual came by, like a Packard, Eugene's favourite, a model called the Clipper. It had a silver captain's-wheel emblem on the hood. Eugene was always planning how someday he'd pry one off and mount it in his room. Instead he was killed by a maroon '52 Studebaker. The kind in which the front and rear look almost identical, both shaped like a chrome artillery shell – a model Eugene hated passionately.

They'd planned their Dreammobile together – the car they'd drive across-country to the Pan American Highway down to the Amazon – fins like an El Dorado's, long low hood like a Kaiser's, curves like a Jaguar's. They disagreed on whether it would have chrome spoked wheels or spinners with small blue lights.

They'd plan and wrestle on the 'Boulevard', a four-foot median strip of grass separating double-lane traffic. Flat on their backs, rolling over each other between the roar of engines, the rush of tyres only inches away on each side from where they struggled, gulping exhaust fumes. Of course Eugene was no match for Budhardin's greater bulk, but Budhardin would usually let him win. Eugene would wind up, flushed and panting, kneeling on Budhardin's shoulders to keep him pinned, and Budhardin would relax under the light body, turning his head in the crushed grass to watch the hubcaps spin endlessly by.

Once, when they were lying like that in the middle of five-o'clock traffic, a motorcycle jumped the median strip. The biker flew over the handlebars and before he hit they both distinctly heard him yelling, 'You motherfucker!' at whoever had forced him out of his lane. Somehow he got back up, but when he took off his helmet blood was trickling out of his ears, and when he tried to talk all that came out was a reddish-pink froth. He sat down hard and slumped over, choking, and the next thing Budhardin knew, Eugene had run over and was cradling the biker's head in his lap so he could breathe. Later, walking home, Eugene started to cry because he had blood all over his jeans and he figured his old man was going to beat the shit out of him for ruining a pair of trousers.

After Eugene died somebody had drawn a circle with pink-coloured chalk on the street and an arrow pointing to it with the words EUGENE'S BRAINS. Even after a season of fall rain and traffic, on his way to school he'd still been able to see the faded chalk letters on the asphalt before they finally vanished under snow.

It was getting dark now. He began to pedal. The elephant lumbered across the lot, crunching over tin cans, crashing through blowing newspaper. He turned up the alley, his shadow blotting out the shadows of the power lines against the backyard fences. He kept moving till the moon slid unbearably across his eyes in silver spots and blood rushed in waves through his head, making him too dizzy to take another step. He'd known that he was going to pass by the spot, but he hadn't expected his reaction to be this strong. It was the smell – the same smell after all these years – of rain-rotted wood, decaying leaves, catpiss fungi, of some wonderful weed the name of which he still didn't know, and behind it all the hint of damp flower beds. He stuck his trunk into the narrow Secret Gangway and inhaled.

He butted his head against the dark opening between two garages, but it was impossible for him to get any closer to the backyard on the other side. Even back then, as a child, he'd been barely able to squeeze through.

Eugene had discovered the place. He had been going there with Jennifer R., who was a grade ahead of them. Through the passage there was a yard with grass sprouting up like a wheat field around their knees. A broken birdbath stood in the middle, lopsided and dripping moss. Off to one corner, under a huge oak, was an old arbour so completely entwined with vines that the light inside was green. An old invalid lady owned the house, but her back-porch shades were always drawn and once inside the arbour, no one could see in.

They used to take turns going under Jennifer's dress. The elephant began to shudder, standing there with his trunk still in the gangway, remembering it. First the green sunlight inside the arbour and then kneeling down and entering the world of Jennifer, her legs and the way the light came through the flowered dress she wore, palms sweating, taking down her panties and *looking*.

He'd kneel there for a while and then it would be Eugene's turn and then his turn again. Once, on the way there, Eugene said, 'I'm going to kiss it today.' And so when it was Budhardin's turn he kissed it too. And Jennifer said, 'Oh! He kissed me there!' to Eugene and Budhardin pulled his head up, feeling himself blushing, and said to Eugene, 'Didn't you?' And Eugene was rolling around laughing.

Another time Eugene brought a little rubber hammer from a play-tool kit and they took turns tapping Jennifer. She seemed to like it.

The time after that Eugene asked her if she wanted to see them. At first she didn't want to but finally she did.

'We'll both show her,' Eugene said. 'One, two, three, pull it out!' Budhardin tried but he couldn't. He stood there frozen with guilt and embarrassment, his fly open, on the brink of damnation.

'C'mon,' Eugene said, and then he reached into Budhardin's unzipped trousers and pulled out his penis. They both had boners. Jennifer started giggling. Eugene was playing with himself. He tried to get Jennifer to but she wouldn't. She was afraid of germs.

'Look, no germs,' Eugene said, grabbing Budhardin's and jerking it gently.

The elephant was moaning and ramming his huge grey head into the telephone pole that stood in front of the gangway, concealing the entrance from view of the alley. Now that the dizziness had passed he was all twisted up inside and realized he couldn't just stand there any more, he had to keep moving.

He could move off, but he couldn't stop thinking. He remembered the time they went to Ghazili's and bought balloons, then walked down the alley towards the gangway.

'What are these for?' Budhardin asked.

'You put them on your prick,' Eugene said.

They practised with a few. Budhardin struggled with a red one, stretching it over the head of his penis.

'It looks like Santa Claus,' Eugene said, laughing. He had worked a yellow one partially on. 'You know what I'd like to try? Sticking one of these up Jennifer and then blowing it up inside her. I wonder if she'd like that.'

They were jerking each other off while talking.

'How could they have made this a mortal sin?' Budhardin said.

'A mortal sin!' Eugene looked at him, shocked. 'Whataya mean a mortal sin?'

'It's against the Sixth Commandment,' he said. He'd thought Eugene had realized that, that they had been sharing in a pact of mutual damnation. The closeness of damning themselves together had actually been more important than the physical pleasure.

'I wouldn't have done it if I'd known it was a mortal sin.' Eugene was looking at him as if he were weird. 'You mean you knew it and still did it?'

'It's OK,' Budhardin said quietly. 'If you didn't know it was a mortal sin then it wasn't one.'

'You sonofabitch,' Eugene said – he was almost crying – 'I coulda kept doing it then if you hadn't of told me!'

After Eugene went to confession he told Budhardin he'd never go to the arbour again. The priest had made him tell the whole story and for penance told him to wait until no one was looking, then to put his finger in the flame of one of the vigil candles and hold it there a moment, only a moment. And then to meditate on how eternity was a never-ending series of such moments except the fires of hell were not one tiny flame but an inferno roaring like the bowels of a furnace.

Without Eugene, Jennifer wouldn't return either. Budhardin felt more alone than he ever had before. He could still remember in third grade, before he'd made Holy Communion, asking the priest, 'If God is good how could he create something as terrible as hell?' The priest had explained that maybe hell really wasn't full of fire, that the real torture was the terrible loneliness of God withholding his love. Now he knew what that meant. Before he met Eugene he'd accepted himself as damned. From as far back as he could remember he was secretly aware of possessing a genius for understanding catechism, and it became clear to him early that he could never accept what was necessary for him to be saved. Like Lucifer, he was too proud to bow and scrape for God's love. But he hadn't grasped the extent of the pain – not until he was cut off from Eugene, could see the look of repugnance that came into his face, realized he had been cast aside as an 'evil companion'. He couldn't endure it, and so he decided that to win back Eugene's friendship he'd have to win his soul.

He went to Frenchie – an older, crazy guy in his twenties, who'd been in the navy, knew every dirty joke in the world, had naked women tattooed on his ass, wore sandals, a little moustache, and a knot of beard growing out from under his lip instead of his chin. Everybody knew Frenchie was weird and avoided him. He'd come up to kids on the street, grinning as if he were their best friend, and mutter through yellow teeth, 'How 'bout a little, my man?'

Frenchie traded him a pack of dirty playing cards. On one side were regular suits and numbers and on the other were photographs of people doing things together he'd never even imagined. He showed Eugene the deuce of hearts, on the one side of which was a woman smoking a cigarette with her snatch. They went together to the arbour to look at the rest.

'Look at the size of their pricks!' Eugene said. 'I can hardly wait till I get older.'

'Let's see if you got any bigger,' Budhardin said.

That set the pattern. Without Jennifer it became more intense between the two of them. And afterward Eugene going to confession and promising Christ he wouldn't do it any more. Father Wally warned him he was turning into a homo and urged him to pray for strength to withstand these terrible temptations. Sometimes after they did it Eugene would get sullen. Once he started to cry. But there were other times when he said he didn't care any more, would suggest that they try something new off the cards, and Budhardin would feel a flush of joy, knowing that he had gained in his contest with Christ.

One of the times that touched him most came when Eugene was serving Mass. It was the feast of St Lawrence, a martyr who had been grilled alive rather than deny his faith, and Eugene was wearing a white-lace surplice over a cassock, scarlet for blood. The bell rang for Communion. Father Wally turned, holding the chalice full of hosts, and stopped, as always, to give Communion to the altar boys first. They knelt before him on the plush carpeted steps leading to the altar, their eyes closed and mouths gaping in readiness (the way Eugene had knelt before Budhardin the day before). He could see Eugene's face blushing in the candlelight and the look twisting the priest's features when Eugene bowed his head, refusing to receive the host, Father Wally suddenly realizing that someone with mortal sin on his soul was helping to serve Mass.

They never openly kicked Eugene out of the altar boys. He was just never asked to serve Mass again. Eugene never complained, but Budhardin could see something changing within him – as if he were living in a trance, the way he slept through class with his head buried in his arms or how he walked into streets without checking traffic. That's when Budhardin conceived his plan of collecting the souls of the other boys, till there would be no one left in innocence to swing the censer or carry the heavy missal from the right side of the altar to the left during the Offertory or to mumble the Latin responses. He'd show them the cards; he'd tell them the names of the others who'd already seen them. Frenchie let him use his basement to show stag films. Budhardin took them them there one by one, running the film in the dark, the light passing through cobwebs, focused on the cinder-block walls, and just at the right moment he'd stop the machine and ask them, 'Would you trade your soul to see what comes next?' He already had the deeds made out, ready to sign. They always laughed when they scrawled their names in the light of a flickering candle.

The elephant gazed up. He had been traipsing down the alleys for blocks, crossing the empty streets in between, and continuing on. Now he could see the spire of the church rising over the two- and three-storey roofs against a moon as pale as a pane of smoked glass. He remembered walking down the same alley in a cold drizzle and seeing the spire shrouded in fog the day of Eugene's Requiem Mass.

Inside the church everyone was weeping and he was never more struck by the brutality of the service, with its incredibly gruesome *Dies Irae*:

> O day of wrath! O dreadful day!
> When heaven and earth in ashes lay.
> As David and the Sibyl say.

He knew that inside the catafalque Eugene's soul was black as the black-silk vestments of the priest, black as the woollen habits of the murmuring nuns.

> What terror shall invade the mind
> When the Judge's searching eyes shall find
> And sift the deeds of all mankind!

Eugene had died in mortal sin and now while they were chanting he was burning in the fires of eternity. He wouldn't have been surprised to see the flames begin to eat through the coffin from the inside out.

> Before Thee, humbled, Lord, I lie,
> My heart like ashes, crushed and dry,
> Do Thou assist me when I die.

And finally he knew none of it was true, not hell nor heaven, nor good, nor evil, nor God, nor any trace of Eugene called a soul. Only eternity was real. And him standing in the alley in the rain. He had turned then and walked to the arbour. Jennifer was there, dressed in black and crying. He was crying too. Rain was running in rivulets through the lattice and he got down on his knees in the mud and buried his face against her, trying to burrow up her skirt. She struggled away from him, slapping his face, slipping backwards. He fell on top of her and tried to open his trousers.

'It's true what they say about you,' she hissed. 'I hope they get you like they said.'

'What?' he said. She'd stopped struggling.

'After the funeral, they're going to get you . . . all the boys. For stealing Eugene's soul.'

And that evening he was awakened by a soft howling outside his window. In the yard he seemed to see figures moving. He got back in bed. He heard stones tapping against the pane. He looked out the window. In the yard he saw the figures beckoning to him, chanting, 'Give us our souls.'

Sometimes he'd wake and there would be a garbage-can fire just beyond the backyard fence and it would seem to him someone was in it softly screaming. No one spoke to him at school – students or nuns – it was as if he were invisible and he stopped going. One night he heard the pebbles again. He looked out the window. The yard was covered with snow. There were children below, digging a hole, a grave in his backyard, and lowering a dirt-smeared coffin into it. 'Here he is,' a voice said, 'close to you. Give us our souls in return.' The next morning he burned the deeds in an empty coffee can, scattered the ashes along dawn-empty streets, and left for what he thought would be forever.

The elephant stood before the massive church doors curling his trunk around their wrought-iron handles, but the doors were locked. He looked at the sky. It was growing lighter – not the sky itself but the expanding haloes of the streetlights.

There was a side door he had used when it had been his job to ring the bells. They had given him the job because he wasn't able to be an altar boy – they couldn't find a cassock to fit him in third grade, when they picked the torchbearers, and without first being a torchbearer one could never be an altar boy. The bells were operated electrically. It was simply a matter of inserting a key at precisely the right second and switching on the bells for the correct number of rings. He'd listen to the bongs spreading out across the neighbourhood and picture himself swinging from the rope, scattering pigeons, up in the steeple.

As always, the door was open. Inside, it was dim; none of the electric ceiling lights were on. Only the glow from the racks of multicoloured vigil lamps and the red sanctuary light suspended above the altar. The statues stood in the niches, coloured reflections flickering off their martyrs' wounds, their stigmata, their muscles knotted in spiritual exertions, their eyes stony with visions.

He dipped his trunk in the holy-water font and sucked, then quickly swooshed the water out. It was salty and stale from a thousand fingertips, with some kind of fungus floating at the bottom as in a dirty fishbowl. The tottering font crashed to the floor, shattering marble.

He shambled up the aisle toward the altar. The communion rail was closed and he tried to climb over it. The rail swayed beneath his massive weight, then collapsed in a succession of snaps like a chain of firecrackers.

The altar was carefully set: vases of lilies, candles in their golden candelabra, the enormous red missal Eugene used to struggle to carry. Budhardin swept them off with one flick of his trunk, trampling them all into the carpet, then, rearing, seized hold of the base of the enormous wooden crucifix that hung over the altar, dominating the front of the church. His trunk coiled around Christ's nailed plaster feet, the blood streaming down like nail polish from hundreds of wounds above. He could feel something give and thrashed harder. High above, Christ's head shook loose, bouncing down off Budhardin's back and rolling down the altar stairs before finally coming to rest, blue eyes staring out at him from thorn-studded brows. He turned back, letting the cross take the entire weight of his body, wrenching his torso wildly back and forth till it all suddenly gave, toppling slowly like a tree, dragging the entire wall above the altar down with it.

When he came to, he was halfway down the stairs, luckily still resting on his stomach. A cloud of plaster dust hung thick like incense in the red light of the sanctuary lamp. He was surrounded by rubble, and parts of plaster and marble bodies lay strewn about him, hands still folded in prayer, broken wings, pieces of haloes. Where the ornate reredos had risen above the altar was now a gaping hole, BX cables dangling through shredded lathes. The tabernacle still remained, cast iron and indestructible as a safe.

He slowly forced himself up, the broken timbers sliding off his back, and remounted the stairs to finish the job. Before the tabernacle stood the monstrance, like a gold Inca sun flaring out dagger rays, and at its centre a huge empty eye, where an enormous white consecrated host – Christ's body and blood – would be inserted during Benediction. He slid the monstrance aside and parted the silken curtains that concealed the tabernacle doors.

'Dear God! What are you doing?' a voice screamed from the back of the church. An old nun came doddering up the aisle from out of the dark shadows, holding a tray of coloured votive candles, probably here early to arrange the church for another day.

'What are you doing?' she shrieked.

In the gleam of candles he recognized her – Sister Eulalia, more bent and wrinkled than ever. He stood staring as if he expected her to realize who he was and start to scold. Instead the candles were clattering to the floor from her tray.

'Dear God,' she kept repeating, 'oh, my Christ!' Her eyeballs looked swollen behind rimless spectacles; he could see her toothless mouth gasping for breath as she began to choke, leaning against a pew and clutching at her heart. He didn't want to see her fall.

He turned back to the tabernacle, ripped the curtains away, and swung open the golden doors. The light inside seemed blinding, like radium cased in lead. He heard a cry slice through the hollows of the church, more like a war whoop than a scream, and felt a sudden weight on his back. Sister Eulalia was atop him, kicking chunks out of his hide with her sturdy nun's shoes. He tried to reach back for her with his trunk, but she gave it a twist that almost tore it off, then started lashing him across the eyeholes with the floor-length walnut-bead rosary she wore coiled around her midsection. Half blinded, he trumpeted in pain, staggering down the stairs, stumbling over the altar rail, while she lashed on, drumming with her heels and shouting curses.

He swung his body around and around in circles, trying to pitch her off, reared and bucked, but she hung with him. His body careened off the front pews and into the rack of vigil lights in front of the grotto of Our Lady. Her body was sandwiched between him and the rack. He heard her gasp and slammed her against the rack again and again until she crumpled to the floor.

He looked at her lying there among the shattered over-turned candles spreading out their puddles of tallow, her black veil covering her face like a Muslim woman's, her shredded habit up around her hips, exposing her black underwear. The church was reeling. He fingered her with his trunk, pulling away what was left of the habit. She opened her eyes and looked up at him in terror.

'No, no,' she screamed. 'I'm a bride of Christ! I'm God's wife!'

What am I doing, he thought, has it come to this? He plodded away, wanting only escape, down the centre aisle to the front doors, but they were still locked. His head was clearing, but his ears had started to ring. To ring wildly! Then he realized it was the bells.

He hurried down the side aisle toward the doorway he'd come in. Just as he feared, Sister Eulalia had dragged her battered body to the bells and was sounding the alarm.

Before he could make it to the door the rest of the nuns had swarmed into the church.

He turned from them and lumbered back down the aisle, his rump skidding as he tried to cut the corner, knocking over another rack of vigil lights. The nuns rushed after him, some of them clumping through the pews to cut him off. He galloped past the main aisle, remembering there was one more door he still might escape through – the sacristy entrance. He hurdled the broken communion rail, two nuns hanging on to his tail.

The altar boys, led by Billy Crystal, came storming out of the sacristy holding their long-pole candle extinguishers like lances. He braked and wheeled, scattering nuns, and reversed field. The church was a screaming echo chamber. The rear was in flames where he'd smashed into the virgil lights. He tried to fishtail a corner but his momentum was too much and he crashed headfirst through a confessional. His body was wedged so tight he couldn't move.

They hauled him out through the sacristy exit, still stuck in the confessional box, and set him on his side, where he lay futilely kicking his legs. He was in a little garden the nuns tended back of the church, a rock grotto with a goldfish pond, a garden hose trickling water over the rocks. In front he could hear the sirens of fire trucks and smell the billowing smoke. All around him people were pacing and whispering, and someone was winding chains around his legs.

'The firemen want to come around back this way,' a voice warned.

'No, not till we get rid of *him*.'

He could hear the forklift's metal wheels grinding towards him down the flagstone path. The forks lowered and the chains were slipped over them, then the forks hoisted Budhardin, and they all began their silent procession out of the grotto and down the alley. It was just past dawn – grey light streamed through his sockets.

They marched slowly behind the jerky pace of the forklift: altar boys in one column, still holding their extinguishers, and nuns in the other, telling their beads in unison.

The alley wound behind the water-filtration plant and they

left it for a huge storm drain, the forklift travelling so smoothly down the concave passageway that the procession had to jog to keep up. When they finally re-emerged, the sunlight was blinding.

They stood where the drain ended in a broad lip that angled into a steep concrete runoff above the drainage canal. He could smell the acrid industrial stench of the sludge-thick water below mixed with the gentle scent of the milkweeds that sprouted in long shoots like a curtain along the bank. They were murmuring the Sign of the Cross over him and when they got to 'and of the Holy Spirit' he felt them all shove together. He began to roll slowly at first, picking up velocity till he was travelling trunk over rump, the wooden confessional splintering around him and grey chunks of his body flying off, faster and faster till he bounced through the high weeds, somersaulting over the bank and landing with a resounding *bonk* in the metal bottom of a garbage scow.

He lay there stunned, as much from the fact he wasn't drowning in the quicksandlike water of the canal as from the concussion. He heard the bees he'd disturbed buzzing above him angrily in the crushed milkweed. He heard shouts and realized they had seen what had happened and were coming to finish him off. A huge hole had broken open in the elephant's side and the sky he looked out at was so blue he wanted to live just to see it. Why did they have to shout so? Lukewarm rust-stained rainwater that had gathered in the bottom of the scow was soaking through the cracks in his hide. He could see bits of mosquito larvae, suspended flecks of rust, swirls of grease. He licked it off his dry, cracked lips. The water sloshed back and forth across the bottom of the boat. A shadow passed overhead, blotting out the sun. Suddenly it struck him he was moving! He looked up into the girders and saw wheeling pigeons beneath the underside of a bridge. He could see the traffic passing overhead. The scow floated out from under, back into the sunlight. It was in the middle of the river. On each side huge glittering walls of skyscrapers loomed like canyons of glass.

He shifted so he could peer out of the eyeholes. The drop gate was partially lowered and he could see out of the front. The scow was entering the mouth of the river, passing the light tower on the delta. The water was dark brown but beyond that he could see the green horizon of the sea.

'Hey' – someone was knocking on his head – 'hey, Elephant.' He turned back toward the gaping hole and found himself staring into the angelic face of Billy Crystal. 'Hey,' Billy said, 'I told them I was gonna see if you was dead, but instead I untied us and pushed off. You shoulda heard the assholes yelling. Fuck them!'

Budhardin smiled.

'Where you think we're heading,' Billy Crystal said, 'Europe?'

'Maybe,' Budhardin said, 'or maybe the Yucatán. Depends on the current.'

'Well, we got rainwater to drink and garbage for bait and your tail for a line, and I can use this as a fishing pole,' Billy said, shaking his extinguisher. 'The only trouble is there's rats sittin' up on the bow.'

'Don't worry,' Budhardin said, 'there's room enough for both of us in the elephant.'

'South of the border!' Billy Crystal said, his choirboy mouth breaking into a grin. 'Fucking A!'

Bottle Caps

Each day I'd collect caps from beer bottles. I'd go early in the morning through the alleys with a shopping bag, the way I'd seen old women and bums, picking through trash in a cloud of flies. Collectors of all kinds thrived in the alleys: scrap collectors, deposit-bottle collectors, other people's hubcap collectors. I made my rounds, stopping behind taverns where bottle caps spilled from splitting, soggy bags – clinking, shiny heaps, still sudded with beer, clotted with cigarette ashes from the night before.

I'd hose them down and store them in coffee cans. At the end of the week, I'd line up my bottle caps for contests between the brands. It was basically a three-way race between Pabst, with its blue-ribboned cap, Bud, and Miller. Blatz and Schlitz weren't far behind.

That got boring fast. It was the rare and exotic bottle caps that kept me collecting – Edelweiss; Yusay pilsner; Carling's Black Label, with its matching black cap; Monarch, from the brewery down the street, its gold caps like pieces of eight; and Meister Brau Bock, my favourite, each cap a ram's-head medallion.

By July, I had too many to count. The coffee cans stashed in the basement began to smell – a metallic, fermenting malt. I worried my mother would find out. It would look to her as if I were brewing polio. Still, the longer I collected, the more I hoarded my bottle caps. They had come to seem almost beautiful. It fascinated me how some were lined with plastic, some with foil. I noticed how only the foreign caps were lined with cork. I tapped the dents from those badly mangled by openers. When friends asked for bottle caps to decorate the spokes on their bikes, I refused.

One afternoon I caught my younger brother in the basement, stuffing my bottle caps into his pocket.

'What do you think you're doing?' I demanded.

At first he wouldn't talk, but I had him by the T-shirt,

which I worked up around his throat, slowly twisting it to a knot at his windpipe.

He led me into the backyard, to a sunless patch behind the oil shed, and pointed. Everywhere I looked I could see my bottle caps half buried, their jagged edges sticking up among clothespin crosses and pieces of coloured glass.

'I've been using them as tombstones,' he said, 'in my insect graveyard.'

The Wake

Evangeline's mother had died and Jill was going to the wake. She put on her black-leather car coat even though it was a warm evening, and knotted a black-nylon scarf bandanna-style over her hair.

'Be careful what you say,' her mother warned as she left the house. 'You know how over-sensitive Vangie is.'

Jill walked down Twenty-second toward Baynor's Drugs, where she was supposed to meet Rita. They had planned to go to the wake together. The streetlights were on already though it was still light. The same old men and women she always saw on Twenty-second stood hosing their tiny squares of grass. The sidewalks smelled like rusty pipe. Jill was going to have a cherry Coke and smoke a cigarette. She'd left a little early and that's how she'd look when Rita showed up – nonchalantly sipping a drink, smoking, self-possessed, and ready for the wake. Rita was the only friend she had who could appreciate something like that. But when Jill got to Baynor's it was closed. A metal grate was padlocked over the door.

Jill waited on the step under the Rexall sign. She'd realized all along that Rita would be late as usual, but now that she had to stand on the corner it irritated her. She wanted the cigarette she'd planned on, but decided to wait till Rita got there. Even though Twenty-second was one of the big streets in the neighbourhood, traffic was light. She watched it go by, listened to an aeroplane, thought of the people in it going somewhere.

A Pontiac pulled over, muffler rumbling low. There was a liquid promise of power in the sound, even as the car idled at the curb. Jill knew the car was hopped up and looked away so as not to seem interested. She'd vaguely noticed it circling the block – a creamy-white colour with a white convertible top, glittering with chrome, the kind of car guys in the neighbourhood called a Pancho. She'd caught a glimpse of the driver, a guy in a black T-shirt with greased-back blond hair, wearing silver-lensed sunglasses that shone back like mirrors. She knew he wasn't from the neighbourhood. She didn't recognize the car and, besides, none of the local guys would try to pick her up like that any more. They'd nicknamed her Frozen Custard, Miss Tastee-Freez, joked to her face about her being a vanilla sundae with a cherry on top. That's how she liked it. She wasn't going to hang around the neighbourhood forever, get herself knocked up, tied down with a bunch of kids, married to a truck driver. A few of them understood that. Nobody hassled her.

'Hey,' the guy inside the car was calling, 'need a ride?'

Jill shook her head. She could hear the radio throbbing from inside the car, the bass turned up like a rock concert.

'Hey, stuck-up.' He laughed. 'C'mon. You'll like me.'

'I'm waiting for a friend,' she said.

'She's not coming.'

'How do you know it's a she?'

'Just know. And she's not coming.'

Jill could see him flashing a smile like a model's in a suntan-lotion ad. Even his hair flashed. Suddenly she was dizzy; the car looked too white – an egg about to break. The chrome gleamed like the blade of a knife. She felt afraid. Just talking to him had been poor strategy.

She started up Twenty-second. He drove along the curb, the engine rumbling behind her, matching some vibration within her that weakened the back of her legs. When she reached the bowling alley in the middle of the block she went in.

It was air-conditioned. So cold she shivered. The lighting was mint blue. Balls thumped and gained momentum into thunder. Pins exploded at the ends of varnished lanes. She stood beside the popcorn machine. It seemed the bare light bulb the popcorn was piled under gave off heat. She dialled the pay phone next to the machine.

'Hello. Is Rita there?'

'Rita went to a wake,' her mother said.

'Well, this is Jill. I was supposed to meet her at Baynor's.'

'Who's this?'

'Jill. You know, Rita's friend Jill.'

'Well, I don't know nothing about no Baynor's. She don't tell me nothing. You girls just do what you do and don't tell no one. So I don't know. Maybe she forgot. She's very forgetful.'

'Yeah, OK, thanks.' Jill hung up.

She stood in the lobby looking out the window through the blinking neon sign, picturing Rita's fat, frowsy mother. Rita had been her best friend ever since that day in fifth grade she'd shown up wearing those little hooped gold earrings. She'd had a high-school girl pierce her ears. No wonder Rita was screwed up, with a mother like that. Jill could almost smell the booze on her breath over the phone.

'They don't want you calling them alleys – they're lanes now.' A woman with a beehive hairstyle giggled, pushing by Jill. The woman was talking to a guy with long sideburns, punching him in his tattooed bicep. He was grinning down at her, all the while unconsciously tugging at his crotch. It was a reflex Jill had noticed ever since high school. Like spitting. Men seemed to do it when they were unsure of themselves. She'd even seen it on TV ball games – the batter touching himself just before stepping up to the plate. The way some made the sign of the cross, Jill thought. If Rita had been there they'd both be laughing at it; without her Jill couldn't take any more of the bowling alley. Twenty-second looked empty. She stepped out.

She decided not to go back to Baynor's, that Rita had got confused and gone on to the wake. She walked towards Damen so she could stay on the main, well-lighted streets until she had to turn down Eighteenth to the funeral home. It was still light enough so that she wasn't worried. It would be dark coming home, but she'd meet Rita or someone there to walk back with.

She was passing the truck docks, the sidewalk strewn with gravel, air acrid with the smell of rubber and diesel fuel. The traffic here was usually deafening with semis, but today was Sunday. The iron bells from St Kasimir's tolled behind her, answered by the almost musical chiming from St Anne's, the parish she was heading for. They didn't quite agree on striking the hour. A whistle shrilled, cutting through the diffused ringing, then the pavement shook. She stood looking up as a black passenger train roared over the viaduct, windows brassy with the setting sun.

The viaduct served as a natural boundary between her neighbourhood and St Anne's. St Anne's was an old Slavic neighbourhood that had become Spanish. Jill had visited it often when she was younger, before her mother's family had all moved out to the suburbs or died. She'd played there with Evangeline as a child. Evangeline and her mother hadn't moved out. But even some of the older people who had moved insisted on being buried out of St Anne's. Their baptismal certificates were registered there. Father Wojek, the pastor, could say the service in five languages – Latin, Polish, Ukrainian, English, and Spanish. The altar boys now were Mexican kids, their poor-looking gym shoes sticking out from black cassocks. After the service they all would get into their cars and the hearse would lead them up the old streets, past the house where the deceased had lived. Then the cortège would circle the block, passing the house one last time before setting off for the cemetery. It was the saddest part for Jill. She wondered how Evangeline, who sometimes acted half crazy already, would stand the grief the ceremony seemed designed to wring from her.

Parts of the ceremony made her skin crawl. She and Rita had once talked about the kinds of funerals they wanted. Neither of them wanted a big, old-fashioned requiem. Rita said she wanted to die young, when she was most beautiful, and have her naked body frozen in a block of crystal ice and displayed once a year on the anniversary of her death. Jill had an image of a elegant hotel, people in black tuxedos talking quietly, sipping martinis, everyone slightly regretful she had to miss the party. There was even an orchestra with violins and muted trumpets and people dancing, holding a little closer than usual. She wondered how the very rich were really buried.

As she turned down Eighteenth Street she had another image: of Evangeline leaping out of the hearse when it passed her mother's house, weeping, hair wild, those long finger-nails she'd affected since childhood raking the dirt where she kneeled. Poor Vangie, Jill thought.

The houses along Eighteenth no longer looked the same.

A bit shabbier. In places they'd been painted bright colours, the cheap paint already peeling off the mouldy bricks. The graffiti on the fences were in Spanish. She passed the small, sunken front yards, mud-bottomed or overgrown with weeds, in either case littered with cans and bottles. At the end of the block she could see the violet neon sign of Zeijek's Funeral Home.

Zeijek's looked the same, the faded purple canopy over the entrance, the grey three-storey building domed with its fake Russian onions. A few stars were out. She could hear the voices from the tavern across the street, where the men always went to drink during wakes – foreign-sounding as always.

Inside, it was dark, the lobby lit only by a desk lamp that seemed to glow green, reflecting off the blotter. She opened the book beneath it to sign her name and see if Rita's was down yet, but the pages were blank. She walked into the first parlour, past a crumbling wreath that looked set aside to be thrown away. The room was dimly lit and empty, streetlights shining in through stained-glass windows. Folding chairs had been set up, but no one was there yet.

She'd expected to find the family gathered. Friends who hadn't been seen in years. Sometimes it was just such a friend who consummated grief. She remembered when the father of a distant cousin had died, a cousin she'd once spent part of a summer with at a lake, whom she hadn't seen since. Yet, when she stood in line and walked past the casket, it was she who had moved the widow to tears. Her cousin was there too, and had merely said, 'Hi.' But the widow, her aunt, refused to let go of her hands, stared into her eyes, face twisting with emotion, repeating in a whisper, 'Remember?'

Jill was only twelve years old at the time, but she understood what her aunt was trying to express: remember the lake, the sun, we were happy, summer as if it would never end, why must things change?

Walking away from the widow, Jill promised herself she wouldn't be trapped. She had suddenly become aware of time as something active and tangible – real as light – yet everyone around her seemed blind to it. She could actually feel its force like magnetic waves drawing her breath in and out, and realized if she could just maintain this awareness rather than fall back into the stupor of the people around her she could learn to direct her life.

But no one was here. She moved quickly through the parlour into the next room, another parlour, empty as well, and through a third, all empty, looking for Mr Zeijek's office.

She opened a dark-varnished door into a room lit with neon, which stung her eyes after the dimness of the parlours. It looked more like a kitchen than an office, dominated by a porcelain table. The table was ribbed with grooves running down its sides. The way it slanted towards the sink made the room feel tilted. The walls were lined with glass cabinets stacked with bottles of coloured fluids and neatly arranged utensils: wire, coiled tubing, an array of suction cups, needles, forceps, stainless-steel knives, an instrument that resembled a staple gun. One cabinet contained shelves of cosmetics. She opened it and smeared a fingertip of rouge on the back of her hand. This would blow Rita's mind, she thought, thinking of Rita's make-up collection, her endless sketching of mascaraed eyes. She picked up one of the smooth, shining scalpels and slipped it into her purse. She was becoming more conscious of the smell, a combination of chlorine and talcum, and suddenly started to gag. She went to the sink and turned on the taps, the smell of embalming fluid rising from the drain. She vomited and stood gasping over the sink. She felt as if she had defiled the room and she turned the water off and ran out.

The air in the viewing rooms seemed heavier with flowers. She returned to the first parlour. A new wreath stood in the doorway as if it had just been delivered. There were voices, candles had been lit, folding chairs arranged. Mourners congregated in small groups, away from the casket, heads bowed together, chatting inaudibly. Jill scanned the room for Rita. Many of the women were wearing veils. She didn't want to stare, but no one looked familiar.

A tall, balding man, smelling of aftershave, with a gold cross in his lapel, took her elbow, gently steering her toward the coffin.

'She looks beautiful. They did a wonderful job on her,' he whispered.

She knelt before the bier. The casket was lined with crushed silk, its scarlet sheen hot on the heavily rouged cheeks, the carmine lips, the dyed orange hair plastic-looking as a doll's. It didn't look like a real body. They never did. Perhaps they aren't real, Jill thought, just models like store dummies, manufactured like tombstones and coffins. Rita would have liked that idea; she would have found the whole situation hilarious. Jill would have to remember to tell her, to explain that maybe no one really died at all – it was just another hoax perpetrated on children, one she was expected to accept tacitly now that she was old enough to see through it.

But, if so, they'd make a mistake on the model. She'd heard Evangeline's mother had died of cancer, wasted away to sixty pounds. This woman was voluptuous in a tawdry way, her black nightgown lacy at the bosom, plunging to reveal the swell of ample breasts.

'It's nice,' the bald-headed usher whispered. He'd squeezed in on the kneeler next to Jill. 'She never had them that big in life, so she asked they do something about it when they laid her out. It was her last wish.' His finger stroked the curve of breasts and Jill smelled talcum again.

She quickly crossed herself and stood up, making way for the people lined behind her waiting to pay their respects. She was in the line with those waiting to offer condolences, shaking, fighting the urge to gag triggered by the smell of talcum, realizing it was more than just the smell. Her body was rebelling against her impulses – stealing the scalpel from Zeijek, standing here where she didn't belong. She knew she should leave now, go home, but she'd expected something to happen. It was a feeling that had been building ever since she'd heard Evangeline's mother had died, that some ceremony, some gesture, would jolt her life again, open her eyes to the future, revealing a direction the way her uncle's wake five years earlier had. She had disciplined her life, held herself aloof all through high school, but she was coming to feel trapped, in need of a new vision of herself.

A young man with curly blond hair and a reddish mustache looked into her face. He stood between two large wreaths, dressed in a dark-blue suit, a black armband knotted on his sleeve. He vaguely resembled the woman in the casket. There was the same voluptuous curl to his lips. His eyes were bloodshot, as if he'd been crying.

'Thank you so much for coming.' His voice was automatic and flat.

'I'm very sorry,' Jill said, extending her hand.

Instead of accepting it he reached for her shoulders and drew her to him, bending to kiss her cheek. 'Wait for me in the lobby,' he murmured as his lips brushed her ear.

She turned and walked hurriedly down the aisle. Veiled women reached out with old arms as she passed, touching her lightly, whispering, 'Good to see you, dear.'

The lobby was still dark. She leaned against the wall, trying to steady herself, and lit the cigarette she'd been saving since early evening when Rita hadn't shown. It seemed so much longer than an hour ago, standing before Baynor's in the twilight, watching traffic. She'd seen something in his blue eyes more important than grief. She wanted him to show her what that was. Better not to think about it till he's here, she told herself. But when she closed her eyes she could feel his hands on her shoulders again, slipping down her arms, drawing her against him. Hurry, she thought, grinding the cigarette out on the tiled floor.

'What are you doing here?' a woman's voice demanded, echoing from the alcove where the coats were hung.

There was a pitch of hysteria to it and for a moment Jill thought it was Evangeline.

The woman stepped out. Even in the shadows Jill could see how heavily made-up she was, like the corpse's twin, her eyes orchids of eye shadow. 'I saw you butting in on my poor sister's boy.'

'I'm very sorry about your sister,' Jill said.

'Sorry about my sister? How could you be sorry?' She stepped closer, eyes wild-looking, mascara streaked down her cheeks. She was speaking too loud. Jill glanced toward the parlour. People were looking out. The woman pointed at Jill. 'Who invited her?'

'I thought she was someone else,' Jill whispered.

'Someone else? She's *dead!* Oh, God! You bitch! Get her out of here,' she began to scream. 'Get her out!'

The mourners from the next room crowded about the doorway, staring out, shocked, muttering among themselves. Jill could hear the bald-headed man repeating, 'I thought you knew her,' to the women raising their veils for a better look. She could see the blond young man left alone by the casket, kneeling, his face buried in his hands, weeping bitterly.

'It should be you in the casket,' Jill said to the woman, and rushed out the door.

The street was dark. Zeijek's violet neon sign was out. She leaned dizzily against the brick wall, hoping she wouldn't be sick again. *Salsa*, sensual and rhythmic, filtered out of the little bar across the street, light from its sign red on the sidewalk. For a moment she had an impulse to enter the bar and dance, to abandon herself to the music as if it were natural for her to do so, as if she'd lived in this neighbourhood all her life and everyone knew her. But to the men in the bar she would be the ultimate stranger; even as she thought about it she knew she wouldn't go in.

Instead she started back up Eighteenth Street. Windows were open, airing smells of cornmeal and frying oil, radios tuned to Latin stations, voices that stopped suddenly as she passed. She could feel eyes following her from doorways and walked as quickly as possible without breaking into a run along the outer edge of the sidewalk.

A gang of kids sitting on the steps across the street crossed over. She could hear them laughing, voices high and excited like eighth-graders', leather heels clumping behind her in the clumsy gait of adolescence. This was the poorest block, the mud in the sunken front yards smelling of urine and wine.

'Buy a flower?' a delicate child asked, stepping out of a gangway with a cardboard box full of crude paper roses.

Jill kept walking, the little girl with flowers keeping pace beside her.

'Here,' Jill said, fishing out a quarter and accepting a flower.

'Flower is a dollar,' the girl said, still smiling.

'Sorry, I don't have it.' Jill tried to give the rose back, but the girl wouldn't take it. Instead she dropped back a few steps, repeating, 'Flower is a dollar. A dollar.'

'Hey,' one of the guys from the gang behind yelled, 'pay the kid!'

She could hear them clumping faster to catch up, swearing and joking, and kept walking. There was a lighted cart down at the next corner she recognized as the Hot-Tamale Man's. He came to her neighbourhood too, had been coming since she could remember, making summer nights special with his little cart twinkling with Christmas-tree bulbs, steaming with hot tamales and red-hots. She kept herself from breaking into a run. They wouldn't try anything with him standing there. She could see the Hot-Tamale Man under his striped umbrella with its fringe of winking lights, his face expressionless as he watched her approach. A hand grabbed her jacket from behind and she pulled away.

'Would you help me?' she said, ten feet away, trying to sound calm, realizing she'd never said anything to him before except what she wanted on her hotdog, never heard him speak.

He stared down at the slice of onion he was chopping with a paring knife as if he hadn't heard her.

'Could I just stand here with you?' she asked.

Maybe he couldn't hear.

'Nobody's hurting you,' one of the gang said.

'Please,' she whispered.

The Tamale Man opened both compartments of his cart and clouds of steam vapoured about them. She stepped into the steam as if it could hide her, pressing against the cart in its ring of coloured lights. The Tamale Man was poking buns into the compartments with his forceps, snapping them like a claw, then he slammed the covers down and the steam began to vanish. She could see the gang surrounding them. He began to push the cart past her, moving in the direction she'd just come from, the cart hissing, his forceps still clacking. The gang opened to let the cart through, then closed. She watched it roll away, trailing a smell like childhood – wisps of steamed hotdogs and onions.

'Flower is a dollar,' the little girl said.

One of the guys lunged, catching her purse by the strap, but the strap was half worn through already and it snapped off in his hand, leaving Jill still clutching the bag. The rest of them broke up laughing, but the kid left holding the strap whipped it twice across the back of her legs. She could see the high, hard heels on their boots and remembered guys in her neighbourhood warning one another never to go down if they got jumped because getting stomped with those heels cut you to shreds.

'What you doin' around here?'

'I was at the wake. Please,' Jill pleaded, 'my mother died.'

'That's bullshit, man! I can see it in your eyes. You hear this bitch lying about her own mother?'

The Pancho screeched, swinging a U in the middle of Eighteenth, swerved next to her, revving along the curb, the same car she'd seen earlier at Baynor's. The gang stood staring at it.

'Don't just stand there, babe, get in!' the driver called over the roaring pipes.

They were cruising down the boulevard, past the lighted contagious-disease hospital on Thirty-first, up the ramp on to the expressway, under reflecting green signs on overpasses that read INDIANA. The Pancho weaved through traffic, passing with a *whump*, radio blaring. Jill sat back breathing hard, opening her eyes at intervals to see where they were, not sure if she was trying to cry or trying not to.

'Here.' Rita smiled, taking a joint from between the driver's lips, holding it for Jill as she inhaled.

'Relax, babe, enjoy the ride. You're with a class driver,' the blond guy said.

Rita laughed. She was sitting in the middle, between Jill and the driver. Except for a 'hi', she'd hardly said anything, acting almost as if Jill had intruded. She took the joint back, sucked in deeply herself, then leaned across the steering wheel to blow smoke from her mouth into his. They'd been making out on and off like that ever since Jill had jumped in. She watched Rita's lilac-painted fingernails raking through his greasy blond hair while her other hand, joint still fuming between her dime-store rings, teased toward his groin along the inside of his thigh. The car drifted across two lanes, scraping the guardrail before he whipped the wheel back.

'Let *me* drive,' Rita said.

'Drive my car?'

'Yeah,' Rita said, 'that way you can sit next to both of us.'

Jill stared at both of them in the light of the dashboard. She suddenly had the dizzying thought that Rita, her best friend, was setting her up. But Rita's face was cool as usual under a mask of make-up, giving nothing away. The driver was still wearing his silver-lensed aviator shades. His black T-shirt stretched tight over his muscles and part of a skull tattoo was showing high on his bicep where a pack of Kools was rolled in the sleeve. He caught her staring, grinned, then rolled the window down and spat. Wind and engine roared through the car, garbling music, swirling their hair. Jill's scarf blew into her face and she retied it around her throat.

He seemed oblivious of the rushing air, lounged against the open window, one hand nonchalantly playing the top of the wheel, drumming in time to what sounded like pure static. She wondered if he was on some heavier drug.

'Come on,' Rita said.

'OK, but you go where I tell you.' He boosted up in the seat, stomping the accelerator. Jill watched the speedometer jitter over 120 as Rita slid under him, taking the wheel.

'Nice flower,' he said, settling beside Jill. She hadn't realized she was still holding it.

'This might sound weird,' Jill said, 'but I went to the wrong wake.'

'What's weird about that? They're all the wrong one. Hey, honey,' he said to Rita, 'turn at the next exit. I know a great drive-in movie way out in the sticks.' He'd thrown his arms around their shoulders, hugging them all close together.

Jill watched the exit sign looming towards them on the right, but Rita didn't turn.

'Have a ball tonight,' the driver was singing, along with the crackling radio, in a fake hillbilly twang.

'I used to only drive motorcycles,' he whispered to Jill as if confiding a secret, 'but cycles ain't got music. Don't music make everything all right?' He darted his tongue in her ear.

She turned her head to kiss him but caught a glimpse of herself, tiny and distorted, in the lenses of his sunglasses just before closing her eyes. She could see the young man she'd waited for at the wake so clearly in her mind, standing elegant and sad between those wreaths with something in his blue eyes more important than grief. The driver was trying to pry his tongue between her lips so desperately that she could feel its spongy pores. She pushed back in a hard kiss but wouldn't open her mouth.

'You know, the biggest sin is not living when you got the chance,' he said.

'The biggest sin is taking away someone's chance,' Rita answered.

'You missed the turnoff,' he told her. 'You girls don't like the movies, then I'm gonna take you to the ugliest place in the world. After that everything will look beautiful – even your crummy neighbourhood.'

He grabbed the steering wheel and the car squealed, fish-tailing up an exit marked GARY in iridescent letters. The momentum shoved them all closer together and he yanked their jackets back off their shoulders, each of his hands then cupping a breast.

'Both got leather jackets. It's like I got two leather wings.'

Jill could see the windows flashing like acetylene as they sped past foundries and refineries, the sky lit up with the coke aura of blast furnaces, towering smokestacks rimmed with red beacons erupting flame, and the air choking with carbon and smouldering rubber the way it smelled at stock-car races.

He'd worked Rita's sweater up and when the buttons wouldn't come undone on Jill's blouse he jerked them open.

'Yours are bigger,' he said to Rita, 'but she's got pear-shaped.'

'You motherfucker,' Jill said, 'you dirty bastard, you prick, you cocksucker, fucking sonafabitch.' The words were rip-ping out of her mouth, cutting through radio static before being blurred away by wind, every obscenity she could remember hearing on the street, reading on walls, whispered in jokes. She reached in her purse for a Kleenex and smeared her tears. When she stuffed the Kleenex back she felt for the scalpel. Her fingers had gone numb. She was holding something in her fist but couldn't tell if it was the scalpel or a ball pen.

'Can't have beauty without ugliness,' he was saying.

'Who needs this?' Rita asked her, then suddenly spun the wheel and hit the brake. They skidded off the road along the soft shoulder, gravel *ping*ing up over the hood. Jill's neck whipped as the car swerved, the driver's glasses making an eggshell crunch as his head smacked the windshield. As soon as they rocked to a stop Jill was out her door, running through the smoke surrounding the car, afraid it would explode. She scrambled up the incline and back on to the highway, then turned to look for Rita.

Smoke was settling on the red brake lights, the Pancho dug into the edge of a ditch, one headlight beaming up through the weeds. Rita was still inside, but the driver was stumbling out, the heel of his hand pressed to his nostrils.

She ran farther down the highway, then turned again. He was standing on the road. In the dark he didn't look as rangy as she'd thought. His legs were short; his jeans hung lopsided on his hips. There was something vulnerable about him outside the car, like a creature that had lost its shell, his deadly energy drained. They stood staring at each other, listening to Rita gunning the engine and the wheels spinning in the ditch, as if whatever would happen depended on that. When the Pancho dug out in reverse, jolted gears, and bumped forward on to the highway, he shrugged at Jill as if saying goodbye and turned back to the car. It was coasting away slowly and he had to jog to catch up.

'Hold it,' he called, but the car kept rolling. He tried to grab the door but couldn't hang on. He was running alongside, pounding the fender with his fist, cursing and pleading, sounding breathless as the car picked up speed and he ran harder.

Jill watched the taillights shrink, leaving the highway darker and darker. She crossed the grassy median strip and started walking along the gravel shoulder in the opposite direction, towards the dull-red glow in the sky she knew must be Gary. She imagined she could still hear him shouting each time the wind blew, voice pitched high with anger and pain. He was just another kid, she thought, and for some reason the thought startled her. She had a vision of the boy at the wake, kneeling alone, weeping into his hands, and

73

then of all the boys in their leather jackets on the corners, in doorways, hiding their faces and weeping as if they'd lost something very dear to them they could never get back.

Lightning throbbed in a night sky that was more maroon than black and she wasn't sure if it was lightning or a discharge from the steel mills. A single headlight was gaining on her down the highway. She kept walking till the Pancho, one headlight broken, pulled alongside.

'All ours.' Rita smiled as Jill got in. 'Nice, huh?'

'Nice,' Jill said.

'We can go anywhere.'

'Well, where to?'

By the time they got back to the neighbourhood it was raining. The windows were rolled up and steam gathered inside like fog. Drops flattened and rolled across the windshield, absorbing passing headlights. Rita flicked the wipers on and drove slower. Traffic followed in a long, careful line. They cruised down Twenty-second.

'Look,' Rita said, 'Sultana's Beauty Salon!'

Its indigo neon sign glowed behind a padlocked accordion gate.

'There's Leader's Department Store,' Jill said. 'I used to be afraid of its revolving door.'

'Dressel's Bakery, Swanson's Dresses'

'Baynor's!'

Rita turned, driving down side streets, up alleys. Nobody was standing in the doorways. Rain slashed through streetlights on empty corners.

'I wonder if they're all tuned to the same station we are,' Rita said, glancing at the column of headlights in the rearview mirror.

They turned down Jill's block, slowing to a crawl as they passed her darkened apartment building.

'Let's go by yours too,' Jill said.

'You know, he was right about music,' Rita said. 'With the radio playing everything seems all right. I wish I could hear it every minute of my life like they do in movies. I wonder if they could wire a person's brain for that. That's how I'd like to die – listening to music high, driving around at night.'

Jill didn't answer. She felt if she could see the people in

the line of cars behind them they'd be everyone she'd ever known. She'd gone to the wake, and now she could see what Rita was really talking about – it was only your own death that showed how life should be lived. She listened to the music, the electric guitar reaching for the upper, aching registers, a song about an angel, as her house went by again and again.

Horror Movie

He hadn't really been frightened until he went into the bathroom and saw the blood all over the toilet seat, streaks of it running down the bowl, filling in the cracks between the floorboards. He wanted to believe the old Puerto Rican lady from upstairs who'd told him not to worry, that it was just trouble some women have when they're pregnant. The old woman had been waiting for him when he got home late from school after exploring the new neighbourhood. She told him the ambulance had just left with his mother. She said his mother had been worried about him, but the ambulance wouldn't let her stay. He was supposed to go inside and wait for Earl, but he could stay with her if he wanted. She kept lapsing into Spanish, and Calvin went inside to wait, trying not to worry.

But the blood was everywhere, dark clots of it, darker and stickier than blood should look, on the towels wadded in the sink, turning the water in the toilet bowl pink and clouded with what looked either like pieces of tissue of shreds of toilet paper. His first thought was that the old lady had lied, that his mother was dead, that Earl had killed her. Their constant arguing broke like a scab in his mind: how the whole reason they'd had to move was because the caseworker had caught Earl living with them and stopped their cheque. After that his mother had told Earl to work or get out and when she started flinging his stuff out the door he'd grabbed her by the throat, knocking Calvin aside like a fly when he tried to defend her. She had told Calvin, once they moved, no more Earl, but a few days later he was back living with them.

He went into his room and tried playing the basketball game he'd transplanted from their old apartment – shooting a rolled-up sock through a looped clothes hanger – hooking and dribbling, the crowd cheering, the sock flying around the walls, the Big C working the ball downcourt, taking a pass from James in the corner, driving, jumping, pumping.

But he couldn't get the hanger to stick right in the moulding. Every time he took a shot it fell, ending the game, leaving him thinking about his mother and the blood in the bathroom. Finally, he lay down on his bed and squashed the pillow down on his head, praying, 'Jesus, help us,' over and over till the feathers inside roared around his burning ears and he sprang up, suffocating. He thought he'd heard Earl come in and got up to check, but there was nobody there, so he walked out to the back porch.

Down in the alley the big guys were playing basketball. He watched them till the sun sank past the garage roofs, making the broken bottles gleam like copper, thinking of guys he'd known in school who'd been taken out of their homes and sent to orphanages and foster homes. The streetlights came on. Beyond the block of roofs and junkyards a moon the size of a basketball hung over the high-rise housing project. When the game broke up he went back inside.

He opened the refrigerator, its frosty light bulb throwing a pale slab of light. He left the door open till he'd lit the gas burners on the stove. The people who'd moved had taken the fluorescent tubes from the overhead fixture. The blue light flickering off the walls like a police flasher made noises seem too loud – the jelly jar striking the table, the tangled utensils rattling as he felt through the drawer for a table knife, careful of the butcher-knife blade, which always made him nervous. He ate his sandwich quickly, standing by the sink, washing it down with a Nestlé's Quik, letting the water jet from the tap, churning the top to froth like a chocolate malt. He locked the back door, not latching the chain so just in case Earl came he wouldn't think Calvin was trying to lock him out. Then he put out the lights and walked down the long hallway with the bathroom at one end and his room off the middle, into the living room to watch TV. In the dark it looked as if someone were sitting on the couch. He flicked on the lamp. A pair of Earl's trousers were flung over the cushions.

The late news was on, with a special report on Vietnam War victims. Every so often the picture would jump into blinking black-and-grey diagonals, and he'd have to get up to adjust the knobs and move the antennae around. He knew once the set got too warm he'd lose the picture for good, but he hoped it would play long enough for him to see part of his favourite show, *Monsters Till Midnight*. It came on every Friday, old horror movies, most of which were pretty funny, but Earl wouldn't let him watch it any more ever since his nightmares started and he'd wet the bed. Once, after that, when Earl came in drunk and his mother wasn't home, Earl had started messing around, coming at him with his arms stretched out stiff, rolling his eyes, and working his hands as if he were going to strangle him. Calvin had run into his room and Earl had stood on the other side of the door yelling, 'See what that Frankenstein shit done to your head! What you doin' in there? Pissing in your pants?'

He knew he shouldn't watch it now, but that seemed better than just sitting up doing nothing but waiting. The commercials were running and he was feeling jittery, like sitting in a roller coaster before the ride really started but it was already too late to get off. He turned the sound down and sat near the set so he could flick it off if Earl suddenly came in.

Lightning flashed over an old castle and an organ played weird, shaky music. A team of wild-looking black horses clattered over wet cobblestones, dragging an empty black stagecoach behind them. Their enormous eyes rolled and they tossed at their bits, racing under dark trees, galloping through a graveyard, the coach careening off tombstones behind them. HaHaHaHaHaHa mad laughter streamed through the night. Calvin heard something at the door and jumped up, punching the OFF button.

He stood there, the silver dot in the middle of the screen seeming to take forever to fade, waiting for Earl to come in, but he didn't. Calvin went to the door and stood there listening. It was quiet, but every time he decided he'd been mistaken he heard a creak like someone shifting his weight on the other side of the door as if he were listening to Calvin too. He sank slowly to his haunches and tried to peer through the keyhole, but it was stuffed with fuzz. He put his ear to it, listening hard for breathing, but he couldn't be sure he heard any. Finally he crawled away from the door, trying not to make a sound. He was sweating and knew he didn't want to watch the show any more, but he turned the set back on. It flashed into a rolling series of lines; he turned up the sound. Then he forced himself to walk loudly, whistling past the front door, stop, and ask in his toughest voice, 'Who's there?'

No one answered.

'Ain't nobody at the door, Daddy,' he yelled back into the living room.

He turned the set off, removed his shoes, and sneaked past the front door into his bedroom. He undressed in the dark and covered himself up although he was warm. Beneath the covers he brought his knees up and reached under his pillow for his wooden cross. He'd kept it there ever since the night last spring that he and his best friend, James, had gone to the Adelphi and seen a vampire movie. What had frightened him most were the rats swarming across the screen through the sewers, their countless eyes a piercing red, squealing and scrambling over one another's bodies like a current of slimy fur and leathery tails, rushing from the pipes out into the streets, swarming through the windows, twitching snouts and yellow buckteeth filling the screen, almost bursting through the screen itself like circus animals through a paper hoop. They were the vampire's rats overrunning the village and only a cross had turned them back. He and James agreed it was the best movie they'd ever seen, but later that night he'd sensed the rats crawling about his room, waiting for their forces to gather before pouncing on his bed. And he knew they were real, having seen them often enough before, remembered the stench of death that had driven them out of their apartment the summer one died in the wall, and his mother screaming in the middle of the night when one came out of the bathroom and the next day putting out little bottle caps of poison all over the house and telling him he'd die if he touched them. And the time the baby of the lady downstairs had his lower lip chewed away, and later there had been a march through the streets with everyone angry and singing at the same time and the leaders had carried huge rats nailed to sticks above their heads like flags.

All that was in the old neighbourhood before he'd had the

cross. Getting the cross had been James's idea. They'd copped it from a religious-goods store downtown. He lay there thinking about James and himself walking the streets after school, sneaking under the turnstiles and riding the El downtown to see a movie or if they didn't have the money just running through the crowded stores.

Then he was dreaming and in his dreams he and James were racing up the down escalators, going higher and higher, past chandeliers, overlooking each floor, merchandise spread out as far as the eye could see. The people riding down were all giving them dirty looks. He knew they'd tell the store detective. Then they were so high there weren't any more things to buy, just offices with frosted doors and the sound of typewriters, and up even higher, with the escalator changing from smooth gliding steel to one with old rubber steps and black beltlike handrails that jerked along. James had managed to stay in front no matter how hard Calvin tried to catch up, and every so often James would turn back and grin.

He reached the top, where the escalator folded into a bare wooden floor. He stood in a huge dim room, dusty light gleaming through dirty windows, and barely visible through the windows were the smoky tips of skyscrapers. It was some kind of storeroom, full of crates and rolls of material.

'Hey, James, where are you, bro?' he called. But James didn't answer. He walked down an aisle of boxes, half blinded by the sun against the window at the end.

'Hey, James!' he called again. He heard something move down the next aisle and suddenly remembered the store detective and here he was giving himself away by shouting. At the same instant his heart started pounding so hard he was paralysed, like a man having a heart attack. He heard a hiss and looked up. James was standing on top of a stack of boxes that towered among the cobwebbed rafters.

'Hey, Cal,' he started to say, and then the detective rose up behind him, holding an axe with both hands over his head and bringing it down with a cracking noise through James's skull, pitching him headlong off the boxes, James tumbling down and striking the floor all bouncing arms and legs beating up dust.

Calvin ran over to him, crying, 'James! James!' James lay

twisted on his face. One of his legs had come off and there was a jagged hole in the back of his head showing the hollowness inside. And then Calvin realized he was looking at a mannequin – one of those chocolate-looking ones that are supposed to be Negro. Besides, it couldn't be James, it was wearing a dress. He twisted its head around and its wooden eyelids clunked open like a doll's, the doll looking up at him with his mother's eyes from his mother's face. He heard a laughing scream and saw the detective, framed against the blurry blazing window, running up the aisle towards him, axe poised above his head, and felt his heart pound loose in his chest as he tried to rise.

He woke drenched with sweat, someone shaking his bed, until he realized it was his heart pounding so hard it felt as if it were shaking the room. He lay forcing his face into the mattress, clenching his teeth until his jaw ached, trying to regain control. He needed to breathe, to suck in lungfuls of air, but was afraid of moving in the dark. He knew he had to pretend to sleep. If someone was in the room with him, standing over his bed, then his only chance was stillness. If he didn't move, didn't acknowledge the presence by showing his fear, he might be overlooked.

He pretended to sleep a long time, listening to the silence, analysing the steady stream of creaks and rustlings. His body seemed glued to the mattress by his sweat and he began to itch all over.

His left arm had gone totally numb. He slid his right arm under the pillow, feeling for the cross. It was gone. He started to panic, sure someone had taken it away, then he touched it, stuck between mattress and wall. Holding it to his throat, he tried inching off the sweaty area, the sheets unpasting from his back. He reached down and snapped the sweaty elastic band on his shorts, which had been eating into his waist. The air in the room suddenly felt cool and a chill swept over him. He became conscious of having to urinate. His crotch felt so wet that he wasn't sure whether he'd pissed in his bed already or not.

He remembered the times he'd waited like this before, praying for the light, not daring to step out of bed for fear of rats. He'd always made it through to the morning, but his mother had always been in the next room too. He thought of sneaking upstairs and begging the old Puerto Rican lady to take him in, but he knew these were fantasies less real than his fears, that as soon as he moved through the doorway the detective would be waiting at the end of the hall, stalking from the bloodstained bathroom. His muscles clenched till they cramped, the tip of his penis aching, the ache spreading inside his body until the pain began to rival the fear, a part of the fear itself. He heard the back door rattle, then creak as if someone were in the kitchen, the sound so clear he wondered if it wasn't Earl in late, feeling his way drunk. But the thought of Earl sneaking around the house didn't ease the fear. Maybe it had been Earl behind the door all the time. Maybe this was Earl's way of getting rid of him. He could feel his hate and anger trying to well up through the fear, smothered by it each time, cursing the motherfucker oh motherfucker dirty mother you mother mama oh mama.

When he woke again it was Saturday noon. He slipped on his clothes and stripped off the bed sheet, stuffing it under the bed. The new urine stain darkened the yellowed edges of previous stains on the mattress.

He was so hungry he had a stomach ache and he paced the flat, opening drawers and looking through cabinets. He picked through Earl's crushed trousers and found a couple of crumpled dollar bills. He put his sunglasses on and went out the back door, leaving it unlocked behind him, the fall sun glinting off the worn back porches.

Calvin ran down the alley and up Division, change jingling in his pockets, trying to get as far away as he could. His breath came so easily that it felt as if he'd never tire, moving at a place slightly faster than the crowd's, the reflection of his body running wavery beside him in store windows. He couldn't slow down, afraid he'd lose the feeling of excitement he felt out on the streets. He tried to figure out how to use the feeling. If he knew what hospital his mother was at he could go there or call her on the phone. Then he thought of trying to get back to the South Side and find James. That's what the feeling now was most like – feeling free on Saturdays, he and James going somewhere, maybe the Adelphi, sitting up in the balcony zinging flattened popcorn boxes through the projection beam, their shadows flying across the screen and everybody in the theatre shouting and laughing.

He jogged the streets for a long time, finally jaywalking through traffic to where a group of people crowded around a carryout stand. Some of them were Puerto Ricans, like the kids at his new school, talking rapidly in Spanish. He could hear the grease popping and his stomach turned over. He ordered a Polish sausage with everything on it and a chocolate malt. He ate half of it walking down the streets, walking till he found a doorway in a boarded-up store where he could relax. Pigeons landed and he tossed them pieces of bun till he had them eating out of his hand. Then it started to get chilly and little whirlpools of dust blew out at him from the corners of the doorway, so he left.

He kept checking the street signs and fronts of buses for names he recognized and watching for buildings that looked like hospitals. His earlier feeling of freedom had dissolved into an aimlessness that bordered on panic. Even though it was still daylight neon lights were blinking on in the fronts of stores. The sidewalks were already in shadow. He became more and more aware of losing his invisibility as the crowds thinned and he tried not to look at cops, but kept meeting their eyes. At an intersection he noticed a movie marquee flickering little yellow bulbs and wandered over to check out the advertisements.

Half the bulbs were burned out and so many letters were missing on the marquee that he couldn't tell what was playing. There were no pictures in the glass cases; the cases themselves were dirt-fogged and pocked with BB holes. But taped to the door was a torn black poster announcing in dripping red letters

VOODOO VAMPIRE
if you frighten easily
DO NOT enter this theatre!

He pushed one of his crumpled dollars through a slot in the glass booth and a faded violet ticket cranked out. An old junkie of an usher, one eye clouded pearl blue with a cataract, nodded at him as he tore the ticket in two. Calvin walked quickly across the empty tile lobby, through peeling arches and cracked pillars plastered with old posters of movies he'd never heard of, to a dim corner where an old woman sat behind a huge pile of popcorn heaped under a bare light bulb. He bought a box of popcorn and a box of Red Hots, then headed up the balcony stairs. The silence of the theatre made him uneasy – outside he'd imagined sitting among screaming gangs of kids like at the Adelphi. Finally he reached the top and entered through a dirty velvet curtain.

He stopped immediately and waited for his eyes to readjust. There was a bluish beam slanting directly overhead from the projectionist's slot and the sound of running film, but nothing onscreen. He couldn't even see the screen, as if a dense wall of blackness were being projected. Then he heard the far-off booming of surf and gulls trading calls.

Two disks flaring gold were emerging onscreen. Calvin made his way down the steps in the reflected glow, feeling along the backs of seats till his hand touched a face.

'Sorry,' he mumbled, veering to the other side of the aisle and stumbling into a lumpy stuffed seat amid an explosion of bird claws. At the same moment he became aware that the lights onscreen were actually the eyes of a black man watching the dawn.

Dawn broke all around the man now, his silhouette against pale golds and pinks, rocking in the bow of a longboat. He was chained like the others, all rowing in unison, while the whites sat in the stern, their muskets held ready. Raz, one of the other Africans called him, and he looked away from the horizon, where a square-rigger rode, towards where the man pointed to a green island jutting up from the sunrise-stained water.

The popcorn tasted a hundred years old, so stale it squeaked when he chewed it. Calvin sat there sucking the husks from his teeth, watching the movie: Raz and the rest of them marched through the jungle, were put to work in the cane fields. Calvin felt relieved and disappointed at the same time – the movie wasn't really frightening. About the only halfway-scary thing was the castle, which rose above everything, its dark stone draped in Spanish moss; women peered out from its shadowy balconies, elegant black women in hooped, billowing gowns, faces hidden by fans, holding their plumed floppy hats against the wind.

He let the popcorn box slide to the floor, then kicked it over, grinding the kernels under his feet. The floor seemed to attach itself to the soles of his gym shoes, slippery and sticky at the same time, as if the years had accumulated in layers of masticated caramel and decomposed Holloway bars. He sat unconsciously feeling stuck as he watched one of the slaves mired in quicksand. The man had been trying to escape through the swamps at night. He'd managed to grab on to a vine and had almost pulled himself free when the arms began shooting up through the slime all around him. Then came their heads – eyes without eyeballs, grey rotted flesh, tattered rags dripping and steaming in a ring of fox fire. The slave was screaming. Calvin could feel himself wanting to shout back like he would have, like everybody would have by now, at the Adelphi, but the theatre remained silent. There were only the screams and gurgling as the man was sucked under, the film clicking through the sprockets, and a low throbbing like an enormous heartbeat, which Calvin suddenly realized had been going on for some time, growing steadily louder, coming from the castle.

He opened the box of Red Hots. His legs felt cold and he drew them up under him on the seat. The throbbing speeded up, grew louder. Calvin could feel it in his teeth. Filled with tension, he bunched himself up, peering into the midnight of the screen, trying to brace himself for whatever was coming.

The women ran shrieking down the grassy slopes between the castle and slave shacks, their nightgowns streaming, eyes mad, lips curled back into fang-baring smiles.

Calvin could almost feel their breath. They were horrible and yet he was unable to look away. He kept telling himself it would be over soon and he would watch just a little more despite the part of him that knew already that watching this movie was a terrible mistake and that urged him to tear himself from his seat and leave the theatre now. He juxtaposed an inner image of himself against the huge images on the screen: he lay stiffened with fear in his bed while the women made their way down the hallway to his room.

Then it was over: Raz picking his way from shack to shack over the bodies of the men he'd landed with. They lay face up, smeared with blood, eye sockets empty, skin grey as if it had been drained of colour as well as of blood.

Calvin filled his mouth with Red Hots, wondering if the peppery candies could warm him up. The theatre kept getting colder, as if someone had turned the air conditioner on full blast. A wind seemed to be swirling under the seats.

'Ohhh God, ooohh God,' a voice was saying, then it gurgled off into a spasm of retching. At first Calvin tried to fit it in the film – the choking in between Raz's panting – but it seemed to come from directly behind him. Heaves like someone's insides were coming apart, so violent he was afraid to turn around. The Red Hots were gone and he started chewing the cardboard flaps of the box.

Raz had entered the castle. Scarlet draperies were flailing in a scarlet room. He moved past chandeliers and tapestries of wolves leaping at the throats of stags, through rooms lined with armour and weapons, across marble floors inlaid with strange symbols. A piano was playing a disjointed melody and he followed the sound till he came to the room where it stood, silent, no one at the keys.

An iron door swung slowly open. The women stood on the other side smiling. They filed out towards him, hands reaching out like claws in hideous supplication. He backed away, then suddenly whirled, seizing a sword from the wall and slashing it wildly before him, breaking through their circle, till he was through the door, pulling it shut against them.

He ran down a stone tunnel lined with fuming torches, up broken stone stairs, scattering rats, splashing through black puddles. The stairs spiralled higher and higher, curling back outside along the seaward wall of the castle, the waves smashing in far below, the wind howling through eaves. A skull-like moon sailed through smoking clouds. The stairs tapered into mere footholds, until at last he scaled the side of the highest turret, boosting himself in through a narrow window.

The moonlight streamed like a projectionist's beam through the window behind him. Sword poised, he stood silvered in the centre of a low, tilted chamber peering into the shadows. It looked empty, only the wind whistling in over ledges of stone. Then, mixed with the wind, came another sound, like the hissing of a snake. In the furthest corner the vampire was unfolding from his black cape. He hung from the ceiling like an enormous insect, his skin so white it was luminous, pulsing from within with the whiteness of maggots. His eyes were ringed by hollows of red and a gaping hole of a mouth curled back, revealing long yellow fangs and a scaly grey tongue that flicked as he hissed. He began to circle the walls, eyes liquid red like an albino rat's, grinning at Raz's paralysis. When he reached the window he crouched as if about to take flight, his body blotting out the moonlight. Then, with a shriek, he whirled and sprang at Raz, the sword arcing to meet him, both connected for a moment, and then his hands unclasped from Raz's throat, his torso collapsing into a deflated heap of silks and ashes while his head toppled backwards, rolling across the tilted floor.

It seemed to Calvin to roll out of the screen, to hang in midair even with the balcony, eyes still living, teeth gnashing and foaming up blood, flames starting to lick out of nostril and eye sockets, screaming over and over in a voice that shook the theatre, 'Kill Me! Kill Me!'

Calvin held to the sides of his seat as he felt it begin to whirl. For a moment the seat seemed to pitch backwards like a dentist's chair. His body had flinched as the head appeared to roll into space. He struggled like a dreamer half awakened from a nightmare of falling to regain his equilibrium and breath. The earsplitting screaming made him weak and nauseated; he couldn't understand how it could continue like a broken record. Where was the audience? Had the projectionist gone mad?

Calvin ducked his head between his knees and clapped his hands over his ears. He entered the world of the smell of the theatre floor, the spearmint wrappers, the rancid popcorn oil, old urine, stale sweet wine. Above him it went on as if it would never end.

He felt a bony hand lock on the back of his neck.

'Hey, boy,' the old usher said, his gums showing as he chuckled, 'it's just a movie.'

Calvin opened his eyes. The houselights were on, naked light bulbs dim among cobwebs, shining down from the filthy ornate dome of the empty theatre. He looked around at the curving rows of dilapidated seats, their backs wadded with hardened gum. The screen hung down below, dirty white, looking small and flabby like a piss-stained sheet. He pushed himself up and limped up the aisle. His foot had fallen asleep. The usher was still grinning and grinding his toothless jaws, rolling over popcorn with a carpet sweeper. In the last row a ragged figure slouched forward over the back of a seat, a strand of bilious vomit dripping from his mouth.

'A winehead,' the usher's voice said from a few rows below, tiny and unamplified in the empty expanse. 'They come in here all the time to die.'

Calvin turned to stare at him.

'Say, my man,' the usher said, his cataract twinkling, 'you ever had a gum job?'

'Huh?' Calvin said.

'A gum job, heh-heh!' He demonstrated, retracing his lips till his purple gums showed in a grin, munching softly together. 'Dig? You old enough to get it hard?' He set his sweeper aside and trudged up the aisle towards Calvin.

Calvin forced himself to walk until he reached the curtain, but as soon as he slipped through he was bounding down the stairs. He hurried through the lobby, instinctively braced for the bright sunlight after the darkness of the theatre. Night came as a shock, bringing the images he'd just seen back in a rush. All he could think of doing was getting away from the theatre.

He jogged down the sidewalks, past grated shop windows and padlocked doors, keeping to the best-lit streets, conserving his strength for sprints across dark alleys and doorways. The streetlights bounced above him as he ran, turning from time to time to check behind him, but the streets were empty except for a single figure blocks away.

He kept going till he came to a long viaduct. A train was *ding*ing, hissing out steam on the tracks above. Most of the bulbs in the tunnel were out and he stared through the darkness of crisscrossing girders, unable to see the other side.

The walls inside were cracked, the sidewalks strewn with hunks of concrete and broken bottles. He felt the presence of sewer rats sneaking along the gutters, of eyeless men moving towards him in stiff-legged strides. The train coupled overhead with a screech of metal wheels. Calvin spun and raced back out to the street. But the figure he'd seen blocks away was closer now, approaching, hunched under the streetlights.

He dashed down a dark side street where the streetlights seemed spaced farther apart, glowing down through a tangle of swaying branches. He ran a block and turned – nothing. But now he couldn't stop running. He had given the sign – his panic was an open admission of their existence. The movie informed the street like an after-image. He could feel the women clutch after him from doorways as he rushed by.

He hurdled across an alley. A car with only its orange parking lights burning glided out after him, its spotlight sweeping the walls and trees along his path.

'Stop right there!' a cop hollered out the squad-car window. Calvin cut down a gangway between two buildings, across a backyard, the dog in the next yard enraged, barking at him along the fence. He flipped a low gate and took off down the alley, zigzagging as he ran, tensed for the gunshot, wondering if he could throw himself down before the slug tore into his back, an image of a kid his age sprawled in a puddle of blood on a magazine cover and the caption KILLED BY PIGS at the centre of his mind. He made it to the intersection of the alley and a dark street lined with junkyards. He trotted low behind parked cars, avoiding the next street, which was well lit, knowing now he had to keep to the side streets with the cops looking for him. He was thinking again of the places they sent you – Audy Home, Good Counsel Orphanage, St Charles Reform School.

He crossed over between parked cars at the next street, unable to run any more, his side bursting and heart swollen so huge he was barely able to suck his breath past it. A bar's neon sign burned in the middle of the block. Music floated out down the street. Staring between parked cars, through the open door he could see people lined up drinking and shouting and a woman dancing on the bar in her underwear. A drunk groaned, passed out in a doorway. At the mouth of the next alley a man was bracing himself against a wall pissing and laughing at two other men. They had an enormous fat Puerto Rican woman tied to a phone pole with a shirt. Her face was smeared red with rouge and lipstick and she had a bloody nose. Their eyes met.

'Help,' she said in English. She didn't yell, she hardly said it, just kind of formed the word with her lips, looking straight at him with terrified made-up eyes. One of the men kicked her when she said it. It wasn't a violent kick – he brought his foot up like a punter into her breast, which flopped up and hit her in the chin.

'Ooowww,' she said, as if he had hurt her feelings.

'What are you looking at, man?' the guy pissing said to Calvin.

Calvin kept on going. He knew none of them were afraid he'd try to help her, that even she didn't really expect it, that they all knew you couldn't help anyone unless you were big enough to hurt someone. He couldn't run any more. He was shivering. The windshields of cars were fogged with vapour, their hoods wet as if it had rained. The streetlights had haloes; mist hung over a block of rubbled lots and half-wrecked houses.

He looked back and caught a glimpse of a figure several blocks away jumping into a doorway. Maybe the guy who was pissing had decided to follow him just in case, he thought. He started walking fast, listening for footsteps behind him. He turned around again. This time he was sure he'd seen the same figure leap out of sight behind a tree. He was feeling sick. His mouth tasted sour and he spat, fighting to keep from vomiting. He turned the next corner, stopped, and peeked around the building. He was coming! The same hunched figure he'd seen earlier that night, running towards him now, in and out of the shadows of trees. It was hard for him to start running again. His legs had gone stiff. Help me, help me, his mind kept repeating with each breath.

He turned corners, dodged through parked cars, racing

down the middle of empty streets, praying to see headlights, even the cops. At the end of a street a wall of high-rise housing projects reared up, lit in yellow. When he saw it he knew where he was and caught his second wind.

The street dead-ended and he ran through canyons of buildings, his gym shoes slapping in an echo chamber of walls. Yellow bulbs smouldered above green doors; everything looking locked, as if the world were hiding for the night. He could hear the wind knocking the wires against the flagpole. He leaped over a row of hedges, turning his head in midair as if suspended and glimpsing the figure still running behind him across the expanse of concrete, overcoat billowing, hair shining silver, then he hit the other side, staggering to regain his balance, back in stride, past swings and monkey bars, highfliers, teeter-totters, the playground floodlights projecting his giant fleeting shadow across a screen of concrete walls.

They were nearing the high cyclone fence that separated the playground from the street. All his efforts had been directed towards it since he'd seen the project. He knew where the mesh had been bent up at the bottom, just wide enough for him to roll under, but he didn't recognize the spot in the dark till he was right on it. He hit the ground, arms dragging the rest of his body clear, shirt hooked a fraction of a second till his momentum tore it loose, scrambling back up to run, his scraped knees on fire, then numb. Behind him he heard a body hit the fence so hard that the sound rang up and down the block. He glanced back and saw the figure spread-eagled against the mesh, clawing his way to the three strands of barbed wire at the top.

Calvin fled across the street, down the alley. He remembered having left the back door open, but realized it might be locked if someone had come home. He raced up the back stairs and pushed against the door; the doorknob turned and he was alone in the dark kitchen.

His hands were trembling so bad he could hardly lock the door. He slid down it and lay deafened by his own breathing and blood pounding through his head, trying to hear past it for footsteps climbing the back stairs. He fought to regain control, afraid his heaving would carry out into the alley.

Slowly he became aware of his body again: instead of a single throbbing pain it divided itself into many, his head, his chest and side, his shaking legs, knees. He touched his knees through the tears in his jeans. Part of the material seemed ground into the skin; his kneecaps felt sticky and his own touch like a sting. He still hadn't heard any footsteps.

He sat on the floor in the kitchen wondering what to do next, thinking of sneaking down the hallway to his bedroom, climbing into bed deep under the covers with the cross against his throat. But the thought continued beyond his stopping it like a runaway reel of film, images of himself cringing in the dark, waiting night after night for the terrors pacing the flat.

His legs kicked out on their own, knocking over a chair. At the instant it hit he thought he heard someone exclaim in the front of the apartment. He held very still – there had been a click like the opening of a door. He became aware of a draught along the floor as if the front door were open. And then he realized that while he lay here gasping and listening at the back stairs they could have fooled him, could have come stalking up the front way through the silent hallways, listening at doors for him, peering through the cracks.

He got to his feet and made his way along the stove to the drawer where the silverware was kept. He opened the drawer and felt along the utensils, his fingers trailing over can openers, ladles, the potato masher, until they located the heavy blade.

He picked out the butcher knife and felt it balance in his hand, testing the razor-sharp thinness of the edge growing into the heavy thickness of the blade. His fingers fitted perfectly along the wooden handle. It had taken him so long to pick it up and now he knew that he had always been right – to grasp it would be the final admission that everything was real. For a fraction of a moment he thought – suppose it was his mother, back from the hospital, moving down the hallway in her nightgown, or Earl, finally returned, but he knew it wasn't either. It was as if they had never existed.

He swung it gently in front of him, feeling the air swish by, slightly resisting the blade and turning it in his hand, feeling the strength its heavy momentum imparted to his arm as he swung it down again, cleaving the air before him, stepping into the long hallway, with each footstep cocking his arm and pumping, possessed by a new freedom as he hacked through darkness.

Chopin in Winter

The winter Dzia-Dzia came to live with us in Mrs Kubiac's building on Eighteenth Street was the winter that Mrs Kubiac's daughter, Marcy, came home pregnant from college in New York. Marcy had gone there on a music scholarship, the first person in Mrs Kubiac's family to go to high school, let alone college.

Since she had come home I had seen her only once. I was playing on the landing before our door, and as she came up the stairs we both nodded hi. She didn't look pregnant. She was thin, dressed in a black coat, its silvery fur collar pulled up around her face, her long blonde hair tucked into the collar. I could see the snowflakes on the fur turning to beads of water under the hall light bulb. Her face was pale and her eyes the same startled blue as Mrs Kubiac's.

She passed me almost without noticing and continued up the next flight of stairs, then paused and, leaning over the banister, asked, 'Are you the same little boy I used to hear crying at night?'

Her voice was gentle, yet kidding.

'I don't know,' I said.

'If your name is Michael and if your bedroom window is on the fourth floor right below mine, then you are,' she said. 'When you were little sometimes I'd hear you crying your heart out at night. I guess I heard what your mother couldn't. The sound travelled up.'

'I really woke you up?'

'Don't worry about that. I'm a very light sleeper. Snow falling wakes me up. I used to wish I could help you as long as we were both up together in the middle of the night with everyone else snoring.'

'I don't remember crying,' I said.

'Most people don't once they're happy again. It looks like you're happy enough now. Stay that way, kiddo.' She smiled. It was a lovely smile. Her eyes seemed surprised by it. 'Too-da-loo.' She waved her fingers.

'Too-da-loo.' I waved after her. A minute after she was gone I began to miss her.

Our landlady, Mrs Kubiac, would come downstairs for tea in the afternoons and cry while telling my mother about Marcy. Marcy, Mrs Kubiac said, wouldn't tell her who the child's father was. She wouldn't tell the priest. She wouldn't go to church. She wouldn't go anywhere. Even the doctor had to come to the house, and the only doctor that Marcy would allow was Dr Shtulek, her childhood doctor.

'I tell her, "Marcy, darling, you have to do something",' Mrs Kubiac said. ' "What about all the sacrifices, the practice, the lessons, teachers, awards? Look at rich people – they don't let anything interfere with what they want." '

Mrs Kubiac told my mother these things in strictest confidence, her voice at first a secretive whisper, but growing louder as she recited her litany of troubles. The louder she talked the more broken her English became, as if her worry and suffering were straining the language past its limits. Finally, her feelings overpowered her; she began to weep and lapsed into Bohemian, which I couldn't understand.

I would sit out of sight beneath the dining-room table, my plastic cowboys galloping through a forest of chair legs, while I listened to Mrs Kubiac talk about Marcy. I wanted to hear everything about her, and the more I heard the more precious the smile she had given me on the stairs became. It was like a secret bond between us. Once I became convinced of that, listening to Mrs Kubiac seemed like spying. I was Marcy's friend and conspirator. She had spoken to me as if I was someone apart from the world she was shunning. Whatever her reasons for the way she was acting, whatever her secrets, I was on her side. In daydreams I proved my loyalty over and over.

At night we could hear her playing the piano – a muffled rumbling of scales that sounded vaguely familiar. Perhaps I actually remembered hearing Marcy practising years earlier, before she had gone on to New York. The notes resonated through the kitchen ceiling while I wiped the supper dishes and Dzia-Dzia sat soaking his feet. Dzia-Dzia soaked his feet every night in a bucket of steaming water into which he dropped a tablet that fizzed, immediately turning the water bright pink. Between the steaming water and pink dye, his feet and legs, up to the knees where his trousers were rolled, looked permanently scalded.

Dzia-Dzia's feet seemed to be turning into hooves. His heels and soles were swollen nearly shapeless and cased in scaly calluses. Nails, yellow as a horse's teeth, grew gnarled from knobbed toes. Dzia-Dzia's feet had been frozen when as a young man he walked most of the way from Krakov to Gdansk in the dead of winter escaping service in the Prussian army. And later he had frozen them again mining for gold in Alaska. Most of what I knew of Dzia-Dzia's past had mainly to do with the history of his feet.

Sometimes my uncles would say something about him. It sounded as if he had spent his whole life on the move – selling dogs to the Igorot in the Philippines after the Spanish–American War; mining coal in Johnstown, Pennsylvania; working barges on the Great Lakes; riding the rails out West. No one in the family wanted much to do with him. He had deserted them so often, my uncle Roman said, that it was worse than growing up without a father.

My grandma had referred to him as Pan Djabel, 'Mr. Devil', though the way she said it sounded as if he amused her. He called her a *gorel*, a hillbilly, and claimed that he came from a wealthy, educated family that had been stripped of their land by the Prussians.

'Landowners, all right!' Uncle Roman once said to my mother. 'Besides acting like a bastard, according to Ma he actually *was* one in the literal sense.'

'Romey, shhh, what good's bitter?' my mother said.

'Who's bitter, Ev? It's just that he couldn't even show up to bury her, I'll never forgive that.'

Dzia-Dzia hadn't been at Grandma's funeral. He had disappeared again, and no one had known where to find him. For years Dzia-Dzia would simply vanish without telling anyone, then suddenly show up out of nowhere to hang around for a while, ragged and smelling of liquor, wearing his two suits one over the other, only to disappear yet again.

'Want to find him? Go ask the bums on skid row,' Uncle Roman would say.

My uncles said he lived in boxcars, basements, and abandoned buildings. And when, from the window of a bus, I'd see old men standing around trash fires behind billboards, I'd wonder if he was among them.

Now that he was very old and failing he sat in our kitchen, his feet aching and numb as if he had been out walking down Eighteenth Street barefoot in the snow.

It was my aunts and uncles who talked about Dzia-Dzia 'failing'. The word always made me nervous. I was failing, too – failing spelling, English, history, geography, almost everything except arithmetic, and that only because it used numbers instead of letters. Mainly I was failing penmanship. The nuns complained that my writing was totally illegible, that I spelled like a DP, and threatened that if I didn't improve they might have to hold me back.

Mother kept my failures confidential. It was Dzia-Dzia's they discussed during Sunday visits in voices pitched just below the level of an old man's hearing. Dzia-Dzia stared fiercely but didn't deny what they were saying about him. He hadn't spoken since he had reappeared, and no one knew whether his muteness was caused by senility or stubbornness, or if he'd gone deaf. His ears had been frozen as well as his feet. Wiry white tufts of hair that matched his horned eyebrows sprouted from his ears. I wondered if he would hear better if they were trimmed.

Though Dzia-Dzia and I spent the evenings alone together in the kitchen, he didn't talk any more than he did on Sundays. Mother stayed in the parlour, immersed in her correspondence courses in bookkeeping. The piano rumbled above us through the ceiling. I could feel it more than hear it, especially the bass notes. Sometimes a chord would be struck that made the silverware clash in the drawer and the glasses hum.

Marcy had looked very thin climbing the stairs, delicate, incapable of such force. But her piano was massive and powerful-looking. I remembered going upstairs once with my mother to visit Mrs Kubiac. Marcy was away at school then. The piano stood unused – top lowered, lid down over the keys – dominating the apartment. In the afternoon light it gleamed deeply, as if its dark wood were a kind of glass. Its pedals were polished bronze and looked to me more like pedals I imagined motormen stamping to operate streetcars.

'Isn't it beautiful, Michael?' my mother asked.

I nodded hard, hoping that Mrs Kubiac would offer to let me play it, but she didn't.

'How did it get up here?' I asked. It seemed impossible that it could fit through a doorway.

'Wasn't easy,' Mrs Kubiac said, surprised. 'Gave Mr Kubiac a rupture. It come all the way on the boat from Europe. Some old German, a great musician, brang it over to give concerts, then got sick and left it. Went back to Germany. God knows what happened to him – think he was a Jew. They auctioned it off to pay his hotel bill. That's life, huh? Otherwise who could afford it? We're not rich people.'

'It must have been very expensive anyway,' my mother said.

'Only cost me a marriage,' Mrs Kubiac said, then laughed, but it was forced. 'That's life too, huh?' she asked. 'Maybe a woman's better off without a husband?' And then, for just an instant, I saw her glance at my mother, then look away. It was a glance I had come to recognize from people when they caught themselves saying something that might remind my mother or me that my father had been killed in the war.

The silverware would clash and the glasses hum. I could feel it in my teeth and bones as the deep notes rumbled through the ceiling and walls like distant thunder. It wasn't like listening to music, yet more and more often I would notice Dzia-Dzia close his eyes, a look of concentration pinching his face as his body swayed slightly. I wondered what he was hearing. Mother had said once that he'd played the fiddle when she was a little girl, but the only music I'd even seen him show any interest in before was the 'Frankie Yankovitch Polka Hour', which he turned up loud and listened to with his ear almost pressed to the radio. Whatever Marcy was playing, it didn't sound like Frankie Yankovitch.

Then one evening, after weeks of silence between us,

punctuated only by grunts, Dzia-Dzia said, 'That's boogie-woogie music.'

'What, Dzia-Dzia?' I asked, startled.

'Music the boogies play.'

'You mean from upstairs? That's Marcy.'

'She's in love with a coloured man.'

'What are you telling him, Pa?' Mother demanded. She had just happened to enter the kitchen while Dzia-Dzia was speaking.

'About boogie-woogie.' Dzia-Dzia's legs jiggled in the bucket so that the pink water sloshed over on to the linoleum.

'We don't need that kind of talk in the house.'

'What talk, Evusha?'

'He doesn't have to hear that prejudice in the house,' Mom said. 'He'll pick up enough on the street.'

'I just told him boogie-woogie.'

'I think you better soak your feet in the parlour by the heater,' Mom said. 'We can spread the newspaper.'

Dzia-Dzia sat, squinting as if he didn't hear.

'You heard me, Pa. I said soak your feet in the parlour,' Mom repeated on the verge of shouting.

'What, Evusha?'

'I'll yell as loud as I have to, Pa.'

'Boogie-woogie, boogie-woogie, boogie-woogie,' the old man muttered as he left the kitchen, slopping barefoot across the linoleum.

'Go soak your head while you're at it,' Mom muttered behind him, too quietly for him to hear.

Mom had always insisted on polite language in the house. Someone who failed to say 'please' or 'thank you' was as offensive to her ears as someone who cursed.

'The word is "yes", not "yeah",' she would correct. Or 'If you want "hey", go to a stable.' She considered 'ain't' a form of laziness, like not picking up your dirty socks.

Even when they got a little drunk at the family parties that took place at our flat on Sundays, my uncles tried not to swear, and they had all been in the army and the marines. Nor were they allowed to refer to the Germans as Krauts, or the Japanese as Nips. As far as Mom was concerned, of all the misuses of languages, racial slurs were the most ignorant, and so the most foul.

My uncles didn't discuss the war much anyway, though whenever they got together there was a certain feeling in the room as if beneath the loud talk and joking they shared a deeper, sadder mood. Mom had replaced the photo of my father in his uniform with an earlier photo of him sitting on the running-board of the car they'd owned before the war. He was grinning and petting the neighbour's Scottie. That one and their wedding picture were the only photos that Mom kept out. She knew I didn't remember my father, and she seldom talked about him. But there were a few times when she would read aloud parts of his letters. There was one passage in particular that she read at least once a year. It had been written while he was under bombardment, shortly before he was killed.

When it continues like this without letup you learn what it is to really hate. You begin to hate them as a people and want to punish them all – civilians, women, children, old people – it makes no difference, they're all the same, none of them innocent, and for a while your hate and anger keep you from going crazy with fear. But if you let yourself hate and believe in hate, then no matter what else happens, you've lost. Eve, I love our life together and want to come home to you and Michael, as much as I can, the same man who left.

I wanted to hear more but didn't ask. Perhaps because everyone seemed to be trying to forget. Perhaps because I was afraid. When the tears would start in Mom's eyes I caught myself wanting to glance away as Mrs Kubiac had.

There was something more besides Mom's usual standards for the kind of language allowed in the house that caused her to lose her temper and kick Dzia-Dzia out of his spot in the kitchen. She had become even more sensitive, especially where Dzia-Dzia was concerned, because of what had happened with Shirley Popel's mother.

Shirley's mother had died recently. Mom and Shirley had

been best friends since grade school, and after the funeral, Shirley came back to our house and poured out the story.

Her mother had broken a hip falling off a curb while sweeping the sidewalk in front of her house. She was a constantly smiling woman without any teeth who, everyone said, looked like a peasant. After forty years in America she could barely speak English, and even in the hospital refused to remove her babushka.

Everyone called her Babushka, Babush for short, which meant 'granny', even the nuns at the hospital. On top of her broken hip, Babush caught pneumonia, and one night Shirley got a call from the doctor saying Babush had taken a sudden turn for the worse. Shirley rushed right over, taking her thirteen-year-old son, Rudy. Rudy was Babushka's favourite, and Shirley hoped that seeing him would instil the will to live in her mother. It was Saturday night and Rudy was dressed to play at his first dance. He wanted to be a musician and was wearing clothes he had bought with money saved from his paper route. He'd bought them at Smoky Joe's on Maxwell Street – blue suede loafers, electric-blue socks, a lemon-yellow, one-button, roll-lapel suit with padded shoulders and pegged trousers, and a parrot-green satin shirt. Shirley thought he looked cute.

When they got to the hospital they found Babush connected to tubes and breathing oxygen.

'Ma,' Shirley said, 'Rudy's here.'

Babush raised her head, took one look at Rudy and smacked her grey tongue.

'Rudish,' Babush said, 'you dress like nigger.' Then suddenly her eyes rolled; she fell back, gasped, and died.

'And those were her last words to any of us, Ev,' Shirley wept, 'words we'll carry the rest of our lives, but especially poor little Rudy – *you dress like nigger.*'

For weeks after Shirley's visit, no matter who called, Mom would tell them Shirley's story over the phone.

'Those aren't the kind of famous last words we're going to hear in this family if I can help it,' she promised more than once, as if it were a real possibility. 'Of course,' she'd sometimes add, 'Shirley always has let Rudy get away with too much. I don't see anything cute about a boy going to visit his grandmother at the hospital dressed like a hood.'

Any last words Dzia-Dzia had he kept to himself. His silence, however, had already been broken. Perhaps in his own mind that was a defeat that carried him from failing to totally failed. He returned to the kitchen like a ghost haunting his old chair, one that appeared when I sat alone working on penmanship.

No one else seemed to notice a change, but it was clear from the way he no longer soaked his feet. He still kept up the pretence of sitting there with them in the bucket. The bucket went with him the way ghosts drag chains. But he no longer went through the ritual of boiling water: boiling it until the kettle screeched for mercy, pouring so the linoleum puddled and steam clouded around him, and finally dropping in the tablet that fizzled furiously pink, releasing a faintly metallic smell like a broken thermometer.

Without his bucket steaming, the fogged windows cleared. Mrs Kubiac's building towered a storey higher than any other on the block. From our fourth-storey window I could look out at an even level with the roofs and see the snow gathering on them before it reached the street.

I sat at one end of the kitchen table, copying down the words that would be on the spelling test the next day. Dzia-Dzia sat at the other, mumbling incessantly, as if finally free to talk about the jumble of the past he'd never mentioned – wars, revolutions, strikes, journeys to strange places, all run together, and music, especially Chopin. 'Chopin,' he'd whisper hoarsely, pointing to the ceiling with the reverence of nuns pointing to heaven. Then he'd close his eyes and his nostrils would widen as if he were inhaling the fragrance of sound.

It sounded no different to me, the same muffled thumping and rumbling we'd been hearing ever since Marcy had returned home. I could hear the intensity in the crescendos that made the silverware clash, but it never occurred to me to care what she was playing. What mattered was that I could hear her play each night, could feel her playing just a floor above, almost as if she were in our apartment. She seemed that close.

'Each night Chopin – it's all she thinks about, isn't it?'

I shrugged.

'You don't know?' Dzia-Dzia whispered, as if I were lying and he was humouring me.

'How should I know?'

'And I suppose how should you know the "Grande Valse brillante" when you hear it either? How should you know Chopin was twenty-one when he composed it – about the same age as the girl upstairs. He composed it in Vienna, before he went to Paris. Don't they teach you that in school? What are you studying?'

'Spelling.'

'Can you spell *dummkopf*?'

The waves of the keyboard would pulse through the warm kitchen and I would become immersed in my spelling words, and after that in penmanship. I was in remedial penmanship. Nightly penmanship was like undergoing physical therapy. While I concentrated on the proper slant of my letters my left hand smeared graphite across the loose-leaf paper.

Dzia-Dzia, now that he was talking, no longer seemed content to sit and listen in silence. He would continually interrupt.

'Hey, Lefty, stop writing with your nose. Listen how she plays.'

'Don't shake the table, Dzia-Dzia.'

'You know this one? No? "Valse brillante".'

'I thought that was the other one.'

'What other one? The E flat? That's *"Grande Valse brillante"*. This one's A flat. Then there's another A flat – Opus 42 – called *"Grande Valse"*. Understand?'

He rambled on like that about A and E flat and sharps and opuses and I went back to compressing my capital *M*s. My homework was to write five hundred of them. I was failing penmanship yet again, my left hand, as usual, taking the blame it didn't deserve. The problem with *M* wasn't my hand. It was that I had never been convinced that the letters could all be the same widths. When I wrote, *M* automatically came out twice as broad as *N*, *H*, double the width of *I*.

'This was Paderewski's favourite waltz. She plays it like an angel.'

I nodded, staring in despair at my homework. I had made the mistake of interconnecting the Ms into long strands. They hummed in my head, drowning out the music, and I wondered if I had been humming aloud. 'Who's Paderewski?' I asked, thinking it might be one of Dzia-Dzia's old friends, maybe from Alaska.

'Do you know who's George Washington, who's Joe DiMaggio, who's Walt Disney?'

'Sure.'

'I thought so. Paderewski was like them, except he played Chopin. Understand? See, deep down inside, Lefty, you know more than you think.'

Instead of going into the parlour to read comics or play with my cowboys while Mom pored over her correspondence courses, I began spending more time at the kitchen table, lingering over my homework as an excuse. My spelling began to improve, then took a turn towards perfection; the slant of my handwriting reversed towards the right; I began to hear melodies in what had sounded like muffled scales.

Each night Dzia-Dzia would tell me more about Chopin, describing the preludes or ballads or mazurkas, so that even if I hadn't heard them I could imagine them, especially Dzia-Dzia's favourites, the nocturnes, shimmering like black pools.

'She's playing her way through the waltzes,' Dzia-Dzia told me, speaking as usual in his low, raspy voice as if we were having a confidential discussion. 'She's young but already knows Chopin's secret – a waltz can tell more about the soul than a hymn.'

By my bedtime the kitchen table would be shaking so much that it was impossible to practise penmanship any longer. Across from me, Dzia-Dzia, his hair, eyebrows, and ear tufts wild and white, swayed in his chair, with his eyes squeezed closed and a look of rapture on his face as his fingers pummelled the table top. He played the entire width of the table, his body leaning and twisting as his fingers swept the keyboard, left hand pounding at those chords that jangled silverware, while his right raced through runs across tacky oilcloth. His feet pumped the empty bucket. If I watched him, then closed my eyes, it sounded as if two pianos were playing.

One night Dzia-Dzia and Marcy played so that I expected at any moment that the table would break and the ceiling collapse. The bulbs began to flicker in the overhead fixture, then went out. The entire flat went dark.

'Are the lights out in there, too?' Mom yelled from the parlour. 'Don't worry, it must be a fuse.'

The kitchen windows glowed with the light of snow. I looked out. All the buildings down Eighteenth Street were dark and the streetlights were out. Spraying wings of snow, a snow-removal machine, its yellow lights revolving, disappeared down Eighteenth like the last blinks of electricity. There wasn't any traffic. The block looked deserted, as if the entire city was deserted. Snow was filling the emptiness, big flakes floating steadily and softly between the darkened buildings, coating the fire escapes, while on the roofs a blizzard swirled up into the clouds.

Marcy and Dzia-Dzia never stopped playing.

'Michael, come in here by the heater, or if you're going to stay in there put the burners on,' Mom called.

I lit the burners on the stove. They hovered in the dark like blue crowns of flame, flickering Dzia-Dzia's shadow across the walls. His head pitched, his arms flew up as he struck the notes. The walls and windowpanes shook with gusts of wind and music. I imagined plaster dust wafting down, coating the kitchen, a fine network of cracks spreading through the dishes.

'Michael?' Mother called.

'I'm sharpening my pencil.' I stood by the sharpener grinding it as hard as I could, then sat back down an went on writing. The table rocked under my point, but the letters formed perfectly. I spelled new words, words I'd never heard before, yet as soon as I wrote them their meanings were clear, as if they were in another language, one in which words were understood by their sounds, like music. After the lights came back on I couldn't remember what they meant and threw them away.

Dzia-Dzia slumped back in his chair. He was flushed and mopped his forehead with a paper napkin.

'So, you liked that one,' he said. 'Which one was it?' he asked. He always asked me that, and little by little I had begun recognizing their melodies.

'The polonaise,' I guessed. 'In A flat major.'

'Ahhh,' he shook his head in disappointment. 'You think everything with a little spirit is the polonaise.'

'The "Revolutionary" étude!'

'It was a waltz,' Dzia-Dzia said.

'How could that be a waltz?'

'A posthumous waltz. You know what "posthumous" means?'

'What?'

'It means music from after a person's dead. The kind of waltz that has to carry back from the other side. Chopin wrote it to a young woman he loved. He kept his feelings for her secret, but never forgot her. Sooner or later feelings came bursting out. The dead are as sentimental as anyone else. You know what happened when Chopin died?'

'No.'

'They rang the bells all over Europe. It was winter. The Prussians heard them. They jumped on their horses. They had cavalry then, no tanks, just horses. They rode until they came to the house where Chopin lay on a bed next to a grand piano. His arms were crossed over his chest, and there was plaster drying on his hands and face. The Prussians rode right up the stairs and barged into the room, slashing with their sabres, their horses stamping and kicking up their front hooves. They hacked the piano and stabbed the music then wadded up the music into the piano, spilled on kerosene from the lamps, and set it on fire. Then they rolled Chopin's piano to the window – it was those French windows, the kind that open out and there's a tiny balcony. The piano wouldn't fit, so they rammed it through, taking out part of the wall. It crashed three storeys into the street, and when it hit it made a sound that shook the city. The piano lay there smoking, and the Prussians galloped over it and left. Later, some of Chopin's friends snuck back and removed his heart and sent it in a little jewelled box to be buried in Warsaw'.

Dzia-Dzia stopped and listened. Marcy had begun to play again very faintly. If he had asked me to guess what she was playing I would have said a prelude, the one called the 'Raindrop'.

I heard the preludes on Saturday nights, sunk up to my ears in bathwater. The music travelled from upstairs through the plumbing, and resonated as clearly underwater as if I had been wearing earphones.

There were other places I discovered where Marcy's playing carried. Polonaises sometimes reverberated down an old trash chute that had been papered over in the dining room. Even in the parlour, provided no one else was listening to the radio or flipping pages of a newspaper, it was possible to hear the faintest hint of mazurkas around the sealed wall where the stovepipe from the space heater disappeared into what had once been a fireplace. And when I went out to play on the landing, bundled up as if I was going out to climb on the drifts piled along Eighteenth Street, I could hear the piano echoing down the hallways. I began to creep higher up the stairs to the top floor, until finally I was listening at Mrs Kubiac's door, ready to jump away if it should suddenly open, hoping I would be able to think of some excuse for being there, and at the same time almost wishing they would catch me.

I didn't mention climbing the stairs in the hallway, nor any of the other places I'd discovered, to Dzia-Dzia. He never seemed interested in any place other than the kitchen table. It was as if he were attached to the chair, rooted in his bucket.

'Going so early? Where you rushing off to?' he'd ask at the end of each evening, no matter how late, when I'd put my pencil down and begun buckling my books into my satchel.

I'd leave him sitting there, with his feet in his empty bucket, and his fingers, tufted with the same white hair as his ears, still tracing arpeggios across the tabletop, though Marcy had already stopped playing. I didn't tell him how from my room, a few times lately after everyone was asleep, I could hear her playing as clearly as if I were sitting at her feet.

*

Marcy played less and less, especially in the evenings after supper, which had been her regular time.

Dzia-Dzia continued to shake the table nightly, eyes closed, hair flying, fingers thumping, but the thump of his fingers against the oilcloth was the only sound other than his breathing – rhythmic and laboured as if he were having a dream or climbing a flight of stairs.

I didn't notice at first, but Dzia-Dzia's solos were the start of his return to silence.

'What's she playing, Lefty?' he demanded more insistently than ever, as if still testing whether I knew.

Usually now, I did. But after a while I realized he was no longer testing me. He was asking because the sounds were becoming increasingly muddled to him. He seemed able to feel the pulse of the music but could no longer distinguish the melodies. By asking me, he hoped perhaps that if he knew what Marcy was playing he would hear it clearly himself.

Then he began to ask what she was playing when she wasn't playing at all.

I would make up answers. 'The polonaise . . . in A flat major.'

'The polonaise! You always say that. Listen harder. Are you sure it's not a waltz?'

'You're right, Dzia-Dzia. It's the "Grande Valse".'

'The "Grande Valse" . . . which one is that?'

'A flat, Opus 42. Paderewski's favourite, remember? Chopin wrote it when he was twenty-one, in Vienna.'

'In Vienna?' Dzia-Dzia asked, then pounded the table with his fist. 'Don't tell me numbers and letters! A flat, Z sharp, Opus O, Opus 1,000! Who cares? You make it sound like a bingo game instead of Chopin.'

I was never sure if he couldn't hear because he couldn't remember, or couldn't remember because he couldn't hear. His hearing itself still seemed sharp enough.

'Stop scratching with that pencil all the time, Lefty, and I wouldn't have to ask you what she's playing,' he'd complain.

'You'd hear better, Dzia-Dzia, if you'd take the kettle off the stove.'

He was slipping back into his ritual of boiling water. The

kettle screeched like a siren. The windows fogged. Roofs and weather vanished behind a slick of steam. Vapour ringed the overhead light bulbs. The vaguely metallic smell of the fizzing pink tablets hung at the end of every breath.

Marcy played hardly at all by then. What little she played was muffled, far off as if filtering through the same fog. Sometimes, staring at the steamed windows, I imagined Eighteenth Street looked that way, with rings of vapour around the streetlights and headlights, clouds billowing from exhaust pipes and manhole covers, breaths hanging, snow swirling like white smoke.

Each night water hissed from the kettle's spout as from a blown valve, rumbling as it filled the bucket, brimming until it slopped over on to the warped linoleum.

Dzia-Dzia sat, bony calves half submerged, trousers rolled to his knees. He was wearing two suits again, one over the other, always a sure sign he was getting ready to travel, to disappear without saying goodbye. The fingers of his left hand still drummed unconsciously along the tabletop as his feet soaked. Steam curled up the arteries of his scalded legs, hovered over his lap, smouldered up the buttons of his two vests, traced his moustache and white tufts of hair until it enveloped him. He sat in a cloud, eyes glazed, fading.

I began to go to bed early. I would leave my homework unfinished, kiss Mother goodnight, and go to my room.

My room was small, hardly space for more than the bed and bureau. Not so small, though, that Dzia-Dzia couldn't have fitted. Perhaps, had I told him that Marcy played almost every night now after everyone was sleeping, he wouldn't have gone back to filling the kitchen with steam. I felt guilty, but it was too late, and I shut the door quickly before steam could enter and fog my window.

It was a single window. I could touch it from the foot of the bed. It opened on to a recessed, three-sided air shaft and faced the roof of the building next door. Years ago a kid my age named Freddy had lived next door and we still called it Freddy's roof.

Marcy's window was above mine. The music travelled down as clearly as Marcy said my crying had travelled up.

When I closed my eyes I could imagine sitting on the Oriental carpet beside her huge piano. The air shaft actually amplified the music just as it had once amplified the arguments between Mr and Mrs Kubiac, especially the shouting on those nights after Mr Kubiac had moved out, when he would return drunk and try to move back in. They'd argued mostly in Bohemian, but when Mr Kubiac started beating her, Mrs Kubiac would yell out in English, 'Help me, police, somebody, he's killing me!' After a while the police would usually come and haul Mr Kubiac away. I think sometimes Mom called them. One night Mr Kubiac tried to fight off the police, and they gave him a terrible beating. 'You're killing him in front of my eyes!' Mrs Kubiac began to scream. Mr Kubiac broke away and, with the police chasing him, ran down the hallways pounding on doors, pleading for people to open up. He pounded on our door. Nobody in the building let him in. That was their last argument.

The room was always cold. I'd slip, still wearing my clothes, under the goose-feather-stuffed *piersyna* to change into my pyjamas. It would have been warmer with the door open even a crack, but I kept it closed because of the steam. A steamed bedroom window reminded me too much of the winter I'd had pneumonia. It was one of the earliest things I could remember: the gurgling hiss of the vaporizer and smell of benzoin while I lay sunk in my pillows watching steam condense to frost on the pane until daylight blurred. I could remember trying to scratch through the frost with the key to a windup mouse so that I could see how much snow had fallen, and Mother catching me. She was furious that I had climbed out from under the warmth of my covers and asked me if I wanted to get well or to get sicker and die. Later, when I asked Dr Shtulek if I was dying, he put his stethoscope to my nose and listened. 'Not yet.' He smiled. Dr Shtulek visited often to check my breathing. His stethoscope was cold like all the instruments in his bag, but I liked him, especially for unplugging the vaporizer. 'We don't need this any more,' he confided. Night seemed very still without its steady exhaling. The jingle of snow chains and the scraping of shovels carried from Eighteenth Street. Maybe that was when I first heard Marcy practising scales. By then I had grown used to napping during the day and lying awake at night. I began to tunnel under my *piersyna* to the window and scrape at the layered frost. I scraped for nights, always afraid I would get sick again for disobeying. Finally, I was able to see the snow on Freddy's roof. Something had changed while I'd been sick – they had put a wind hood on the tall chimney that sometimes blew smoke into our flat. In the dark it looked as if someone was standing on the roof in an old-fashioned helmet. I imagined it was a German soldier. I'd heard Freddy's landlord was German. The soldier stood at attention, but his head slowly turned back and forth and hooted with each gust of wind. Snow drove sideways across the roof, and he stood banked by drifts, smoking a cigar. Sparks flew from its tip. When he turned completely around to stare in my direction with his faceless face, I'd duck and tunnel back under my *piersyna* to my pillows and pretend to sleep. I believed a person asleep would be shown more mercy than a person awake. I'd lie still, afraid he was marching across the roof to peer in at me through the holes I'd scraped. It was a night like that when I heard Mother crying. She was walking from room to room crying like I'd never heard anyone cry before. I must have called out because she came into my room and tucked the covers around me. 'Everything will be all right,' she whispered; 'go back to sleep.' She sat on my bed, towards the foot where she could look out the window, crying softly until her shoulders began to shake. I lay pretending to sleep. She cried like that for nights after my father was killed. It was my mother, not I, whom Marcy had heard.

It was only after Marcy began playing late at night that I remembered my mother crying. In my room, with the door shut against steam, it seemed she was playing for me alone. I would wake already listening and gradually realize that the music had been going on while I slept, and that I had been shaping my dreams to it. She played only nocturnes those last weeks of winter. Sometimes they seemed to carry over the roofs, but mostly she played so softly that only the air shaft made it possible to hear. I would sit huddled in my covers beside the window listening, looking out at the white dunes on Freddy's roof. The soldier was long gone, his helmet rusted off. Smoke blew unhooded; black flakes with sparking edges wafted out like burning snow. Soot and music and white gusts off the crests buffeted the pane. Even when the icicles began to leak and the streets to turn to brown rivers of slush, the blizzard in the air shaft continued.

Marcy disappeared during the first break in the weather. She left a note that read: 'Ma, don't worry.'

'That's all,' Mrs Kubiac said, unfolding it for my mother to see. 'Not even "love", not even her name signed. The whole time I kept telling her "do something", she sits playing the piano, and now she does something, when it's too late, unless she goes to some butcher. Ev, what should I do?'

My mother helped Mrs Kubiac call the hospitals. Each day they called the morgue. After a week, Mrs Kubiac called the police, and when they couldn't find Marcy, any more than they had been able to find Dzia-Dzia, Mrs Kubiac began to call people in New York – teachers, old roommates, landlords. She used our phone. 'Take it off the rent,' she said. Finally, Mrs Kubiac went to New York herself to search.

When she came back from New York she seemed changed, as if she'd grown too tired to be frantic. Her hair was a different shade of grey so that now you'd never know it had once been blonde. There was a stoop to her shoulders as she descended the stairs on the way to novenas. She no longer came downstairs for tea and long talks. She spent much of her time in church, indistinguishable among the other women from the Old Country, regulars at the morning Requiem Mass, wearing babushkas and dressed in black like a sodality of widows, droning endless mournful litanies before the side altar of the Black Virgin of Czestochowa.

By the time a letter from Marcy finally came, explaining that the entire time she had been living on the South Side in a Negro neighbourhood near the university, and that she had a son whom she'd named Tatum Kubiac – 'Tatum' after a famous jazz pianist – it seemed to make little difference. Mrs Kubiac visited once but didn't go back. People had already learned to glance away from her when certain subjects were mentioned – daughters, grandchildren, music. She had learned to glance away from herself. After she visited Marcy she tried to sell the piano, but the movers couldn't figure how to get it downstairs, nor how anyone had ever managed to move in it.

It took time for the music to fade. I kept catching wisps of it in the air shaft, behind walls and ceilings, under bathwater. Echoes travelled the pipes and wallpapered chutes, the bricked-up flues and dark hallways. Mrs Kubiac's building seemed riddled with its secret passageways. And, when the music finally disappeared, its channels remained, conveying silence. Not an ordinary silence of absence and emptiness, but a pure silence beyond daydream and memory, as intense as the music it replaced, which, like music, had the power to change whoever listened. It hushed the close-quartered racket of the old building. It had always been there behind the creaks and drafts and slamming doors, behind the staticky radios, and the flushings and footsteps and crackling fat, behind the wails of vacuums and kettles and babies, and the voices with their scraps of conversation and arguments and laughter floating out of flats where people locked themselves in with all that was private. Even after I no longer missed her, I could still hear the silence left behind.

The Apprentice

As always, the boy could smell the blood of animals in the rain. Drops pummelled the old wooden station wagon while a single wiper blade saluted feebly against the flooded windshield. This was not how he'd imagined the city, dark as a blackout, thunder overhead like bombers. Wolfgang, cringing in the back, wedged farther under the seat and began to whine.

'Can you believe a monster like that crying?' Uncle asked, and exploded into another coughing fit.

Uncle swung the wagon off the street, spitting out the window as rain blew in, gunning into an alley, up its clattering current of tin cans and rubbish. Waterfalls from rotted drainpipes sluiced through fire escapes as their headlights sped past.

When they stopped, the downpour flowed over them as if they were still speeding. Uncle killed the headlights, lit his snuffed-out cigar, and immediately began coughing again, smothering his face in his sleeve.

'This is it,' he rasped, checking the rearview mirror as he repeatedly did to make sure they weren't being followed.

'This is what, Uncle?'

'*What, Uncle?* The restaurant!'

Reaching past him, Uncle rolled the window down and forced the boy's head out. Rain immediately flattened his hair, streamed down his face like tears, choking his nostrils. He stared into a cavernous doorway lit by a tiny orange bulb that glowed beneath a madly *ping*ing metal shade. Its light reflected off a sheet-metal door across which was spray-painted SPANISH BLADES. There were other names, hearts, slogans, obscenities, chalked and fading, but before he could make them out Uncle yanked him back in.

'What did it say, Zoltán?' Uncle often called him Zoltán when something important was happening.

'Spanish Blades.'

'Like I told you. Now you know the secret. Where I make our deliveries. Where maybe someday you'll be a waiter. If anything happens to me, here's where you come.'

'What could happen to you, Uncle?'

'Getting old, Zoltán. Getting old in a city of old Nazis. Every day they track you down a little more.' He coughed and spat violently as if in final punctuation. 'Goddamn!' he cursed as the spit dribbled on the window he'd once again forgotten to roll down.

The boy wanted to ask why the restaurant was here, in an alley among warehouses and factories; to say he wasn't sure he wanted to be a waiter. Up till tonight he hadn't been sure there even was a restaurant – though he'd kept that from Uncle. Now, at least, he'd seen the name, Spanish Blades, although it wasn't glowing in blue neon the way he'd pictured it from Uncle's description: *An exclusive restaurant, a private club, for all those who'd been excluded and had finally made their way here, to this city of displaced persons. Displaced persons, DPs, who'd come from the corners of the earth evading politics and poverty; draft dodgers, deportees, drifters, illegal aliens, missing persons, personae non grata, refugees, revolutionaries, and émigré royalty, all orphans, mingling beneath the same ensign in a dining room where chandeliers rotated a crystalline light and blue poofs of flame erupted as waiters, tuxedoed like magicians, ignited food.*

'And Gypsy violins, Zoltán,' Uncle would say, eyes magnified wildly behind the cracked spectacles he'd found on the highway, his accent propelling a spray of saliva. 'Chefs! Gourmets! Einsteins of the belly – exiled like him – who would be lost without our deliveries! This is what we ride the highways for! But never tell anyone our secret mission!'

The city had not been what he'd expected, but after that night it was what he dreamed of. Oily streets dissolving ruby and emerald beneath traffic lights, a restaurant secret among warehouses, and finally the girl in the flicker of blue flames. Especially the girl.

He daydreamed of her for days afterwards as they resumed 'salvaging' the highways, Uncle behind the wheel, he and Wolfgang riding shotgun, scanning the flat road. It was a life he'd loved, the fields and woods emerging from mists, roosters breaking out of their cocoons of night, Uncle asking, 'What is a rooster?' as if it were a riddle to be solved anew each sunrise.

A twig fire.

A fallen star in a barnyard.

And the road littered with the driftwood of night. Animals whose eyes had turned to quartz in the hypnosis of headlights, steamlike souls still hovering around their bodies. Rabbits, possums, coons, squirrels, pheasants – like a single species of highway animal. Some crushed beyond recognition, even their pelts useless and so left behind. But most still limp, waiting to be collected with the other highway scrap – blown tyres like lizard skins, dropped mufflers, thrown hubcaps, lumber, hay bales, deposit bottles, anything that could fall off a tailgate or blow out of a car window.

There was always the hope of finding something special – once, a pistol that Uncle claimed was a murderer's because he could see fingerprints glowing on it in the dark. Another time the viola, still in its battered case, or, as Uncle insisted, its coffin. According to Uncle the viola in its coffin was an omen that they must bury their valuables. Everything was an omen to Uncle.

'Could you teach me to read omens?' the boy once asked.

'I have been all along,' Uncle replied.

Uncle interpreted dreams, foretold weather, could read the future in the entrails of certain animals. Uncle knew everything about animals. He could rebuild them as he had Wolfgang's broken hind legs.

They'd found Wolfgang in a drainage ditch along the road. The boy yelled for Uncle to stop, thinking it was a dead fawn. When Uncle saw what kind of dog it was he was reluctant.

'Those are Nazi dogs. That dog is an omen of Nazi things to come.'

But he'd given in to the boy's request. They carefully moved Wolfgang, splinted his legs, and Uncle made casts out of the papier-mâché he used for his models.

Uncle's skill came from rebuilding dead animals. His small taxidermy shop remained closed since his licence had been revoked, but Uncle continued to work. A week before the trip to the city, the boy had watched him create his masterpiece, a strange bird assembled from the parts of many birds – hawk, heron, owl, plumes of cock pheasant and peacock, cardinal red, jay blue.

'I wish I could give it songs,' Uncle said. 'What would we make it sing like?'

'Meadowlarks,' the boy said.

'Good. And whippoorwills, thrushes, doves.'

The bird, wearing a newspaper hood, balanced on the front seat between them the night they drove into the city.

'Hold it tight,' Uncle said as they roared down the alleys faster and faster, away from SPANISH BLADES. He hadn't turned on the headlights. They paused at the mouth of an alley to let a black-and-white sedan go by.

'*Polici*,' Uncle muttered.

The *polici* were something they worried about on the highways but seldom encountered. Uncle regarded the game wardens as a worse threat, especially a man named Kopf, who had been instrumental in closing his taxidermy shop. They took precautions. If they were stopped the boy was to be an idiot nephew, Malvolio the mute, and Uncle made him practice rolling his eyes and drooling. They also rehearsed throwing the army blanket over whatever they'd collected in the back of the De Soto, and muzzling Wolfgang.

'*Polici* are not necessarily our enemies.'

'Who are our enemies, Uncle?'

'*Who*? The same as those of all peoples. The *secret* police. The KGB of the soul, CIA of the brain, SS who think they are only harmless dogcatchers. Game wardens persecuting a man who do not know themselves they are a branch of the Gestapo. KKK, FBI, ICBM, DDT, initials! Initials are our enemies, Tadeusz.'

Uncle pulled the wagon into an abandoned lot behind a tattered billboard. They adjusted the hood over the bird and, holding newspapers over their heads, ran across the puddled street, leaving Wolfgang behind to cower and guard.

They shouldered open a warped door and stumbled up a crooked stairway. A string ran along the banister and when Uncle tugged it a light bulb swung on at the head of the stairs.

Uncle huffed and coughed more with each stair. At the top he stood swaying against the door, balancing the bird, its talons clutching his wrist as if perched.

A buxom woman in a kimono, make-up congealed in the wrinkles around her eyes, opened the door a crack and stared out at them. Her hair was dyed the colour of copper wire. Uncle presented the bird with a flourish, whisking off the newspaper cone it wore. She smiled, revealing gold teeth, and opened the door wider.

'My apprentice, Josef,' Uncle said, introducing him. The boy bowed.

The woman ignored him as they entered the room and said nothing about the girl who sat on a small rug near the space heater with an open book and spiral notebook. Blue flames from the space heater reflected in her eyes and flitted along her bare arms like butterflies.

Uncle was crouping, spitting up his sleeve. The woman set the bird on a round table draped with gold fringe. Her breasts swung exposed from her kimono as she stooped to arrange it. Uncle gaped. She winked and unbuttoned his shirt, putting an ear to his wheezing chest.

'A poultice,' she said, 'come,' leading Uncle into the kitchen.

Soon the house was full of the smell of lard and kerosene.

He stood listening to them laughing in the kitchen, watching the girl writing in the notebook.

The woman and Uncle came out arm in arm, Uncle pressing a towel to his chest. They went directly into the bedroom and closed the door.

There were new smells in the air – incense, rose water.

The girl was counting to herself, as if praying.

'I hate math,' she suddenly said.

The gas-blue butterflies of the space heater fluttered across her face. The Oriental carpet she sat on had designs like scarlet moths. The wings of moths had always reminded him of Oriental carpets and he wondered if moth wings hadn't inspired them. Nature was behind every invention, Uncle had taught him.

'What's your most unfavourite subject?' she asked.

'I don't go to school any more,' he said, then realized

Uncle had cautioned him never to reveal this and that the girl had already, so effortlessly, pried a secret from him. 'Don't tell anyone,' he said.

She smiled and made a crossed-finger sign over her lips and over her heart, where the open button of her blouse revealed budding breasts. 'I can keep secrets,' she said, 'can you?'

The blue butterflies were whirling about the room with its buckled ceiling and cracked plaster breaking through the wallpaper. The girl got up, showing her underpants as she did.

He noticed she wore small hooped earrings.

'Come in the closet,' she said, then opened a door that had been wallpapered over and disappeared among coats.

'Hurry,' she whispered, 'before they come out.'

He stood before the hanging coats. It looked like a display in a costume store – furs, boas, dressing gowns, umbrellas, the floor crowded with boots, tangled high heels, ballet slippers, galoshes.

'Where are you?' he whispered.

'Feel around.'

He could smell mothballs and lavender, and tried not to remember where he'd smelled a scent like that before. He reached into the closet, filling his arms with leopard-dyed rabbit fur, buried his face in a raccoon coat, thought for an instant of telling her about the dead coons on the highway, how their guts were always the cleanest, full of crayfish at certain times of the year, but knew he should say nothing, only press into the warmth, moving toward small moans, wondering if the faint scent was hers or faded perfume the lining had absorbed forty years ago when a woman like his mother might have worn such a coat. He held the coats to him, stroking fur, kissing collars and buttons, inserting his arms up sleeves, and being kissed and fondled back, a soft voice whispering *oh Joey*. But when he tried to separate her from the fur she slipped away like a silk lining, leaving him enfolding a Persian lamb. He could hear her giggling in the depths of the closet. The bedroom door opened.

'Hey, Stefan, let's go,' Uncle said.

The boy let go of the coat. The girl was nowhere to be seen.

The woman slouched against the doorway of the bedroom, mascara shaping her eyes like a cat's. Her powdered breasts hung pendulous in loose fabric. Uncle reeked of kerosene and rose water, camphor, and some subtle salmon scent.

'The bird is beautiful,' she said, spreading her arms within her billowy sleeves like wings so that her breasts rose nearly free of the kimono as the door closed.

They clumped down the stairs in the dark. 'Remorse, remorse,' Uncle kept repeating.

In the car Wolfgang growled, the engine groaned, and so did Uncle. He often groaned lately, as if oppressed by an invisible force. Groans he wasn't even aware of would build into a crescendo and everything he did would become loud – singing in a melancholy baritone, carrying on conversations with himself in strange languages, slurping soup, smacking lips, belching, farting, puffing, snorking, stomping, all accompanied by a constant droning groan.

'Dmitri, Dmitri,' he groaned as they drove, 'sometimes even an old man needs a mother's touch. And what about a poor boy who lives his life without it?'

The third morning after the trip to the city, they saw something they'd never seen before – the highways totally empty. They'd found little the two previous days: a dented hubcap, a flattened weasel, a torn sack at the end of a trail of lime. The boy wondered if his own dreaminess was now somehow responsible for their lack of luck.

Uncle was growing increasingly sullen, hunched behind the steering wheel, eyes squinting through cracked lenses, no longer coughing, but hardly talking either except for occasional grumbling in a foreign language. He still wore the scarf smelling of camphor and kerosene – the scents of rose water and salmon having evaporated.

'There are seasons on the highway too, Dupush,' Uncle mumbled. 'In spring woodchucks every few miles, in summer rabbits, coons, possum, now there should be pheasants, squirrels. We should be eating like gourmets. They must be disappointed with us at the restaurant.' He swigged from the cough-medicine bottle the woman had given him.

It glazed his eyes and left a sticky brown ring around his lips.

The fourth day, they arose earlier than they ever had before. Uncle said he wanted to make sure that scavengers had not invaded their territory, stripping the highways before them. Uncle made a distinction between scavengers and salvagers. He'd mounted a searchlight and swept it as they sped, alert for eyes glowing alongside the road. In the glaring headlights the highway appeared to be streaming, oil-splotched, skid-marked, and empty. Leaves gusted along curving shoulders.

At dawn, when the birches began to simmer with light, they spotted the crow. Wolfgang yelped and Uncle slammed to a gravel-skidding stop. The boy was out of the wagon before Uncle had both front wheels on the shoulder, running back towards the black body, wind inflating his burlap sack.

The crow rested on the centre stripe almost too perfectly: unmarked, wings poised as if it had gently floated down in mid-flight. He stuffed it in the sack and raced back, meaning to ask Uncle if birds suffered heart attacks.

Instead of spilling the crow into the cardboard box on the backseat, Uncle examined it while the engine idled. He spread its glossy dark wings; his fingers traced its scaly feet and opened the wizened eyelids. He had to use his jackknife to pry open the beak.

'Look.'

The tongue was black and split like a snake's.

'This bird talked.'

'You mean like a parrot?'

'No, Dupush. Parrots gab. Crows tell secrets. This one might have told what's happening. I saw it once before. In the Old Country, just before the war. The animals all disappeared. Some said they were starting to change. There were rumours of strange animals: a fox with the face of a monkey, hares with snouts of rats, chickens with teeth. Everything was changing for the worse. And now everything is in hiding again.

'From what? Another war?'

'What "another war"? You think the last one ended yet? The Nazis just moved over here. They know I know who they are. That's why they make trouble for me. Who do you think is doing these assassinations? Causing these race problems? Go back to your dreams, Nightstein.'

The boy could feel himself blushing as if Uncle had caught him at something secret, and looked out the window. The first truck of the day, a semi hauling hogs, rumbled by, and the De Soto vibrated. Uncle pulled on to the road and followed it.

'They called me Nightstein too when I was your age,' Uncle said in a softer voice. 'I know all about it. An old woman in the village offered to buy what the priests call "nocturnal emissions". She thought it was sinless seed, seed a boy could spill and still be innocent. No one talks even today about a boy's innocence. It's a taboo subject, one men are ashamed of and women know nothing about, but a boy has an innocence different but as delicate as a girl's. She wanted the seed of dreams . . . I thought I would be rich.'

'What happened?'

'Nothing happened. She became a joke.'

That was the last day they salvaged along the old, familiar highways. Uncle began to explore other roads, driving further into the backcountry, narrow blacktops twisting past fiery stands of maples, highways aging into potholed, buckled, one-lane macadam, dead-ending in tarred gravel. He drove erratically, eyes continually on the rearview mirror. Black roads cut through a countryside the boy had never seen before, where the fields sank into swamp and slough and gnarled trees stood among stumps in muddy water. Autumn was absent here among cattails and willows.

They rose earlier, in the pitch-black before dawn. The riddles changed.

What is a crow?

A mortician's musician.

What is a bat?

A meat butterfly.

Animals began to appear again. Muskrats, frogs and toads, lizards, turtles, water voles. Marsh birds flapped across the highway, rasped and hooted from a camouflage of rushes. Still, many of these were animals the boy knew Uncle could salvage. But each time he signalled to stop, Uncle ignored him. Totally confused, Wolfgang began to bark, and Uncle insisted they muzzle him.

Uncle sipped steadily from the medicine bottle, his lips stained a permanent syrupy brown as if they'd been charred, eyes red-rimmed and obsessed behind greasy glasses. Whereas once he'd cursed the carelessness of other drivers, he now swerved across the road as he fiddled with the radio, dialling it far right, hunting mazurkas among crackling static.

'Why aren't we stopping for anything, Uncle?'

'It's not what we're looking for, Tadeusz.'

'What are we looking for?'

'We'll know when we find it. A very special creature. One with the future in him, an animal with Wall Street ticker tape for guts, with golden ovaries, a carcass they'll pay a fortune for.'

It was nearing dusk and they were driving the long drive home from the swamp roads when they found the doll. At first, because of its size and blackness, the boy thought it might be another crow. He shouted stop, wondering if they would. Uncle *had* stopped once earlier that day for a porcupine and a frazzled radiator hose, which were now in the box in the backseat. The hose had protruded from the porcupine's skull like a trunk and Uncle had braked, thinking they'd found his special animal.

'It must have been eating the hose for the salt when it got hit.' Uncle had laughed when he'd seen what they'd really collected.

This time he braked so hard that Wolfgang slammed into the dashboard. The boy leaped from the wagon and ran back on to the road. She was lying staring up, arms crossed over her breast, and for the first time he understood what Uncle meant by an omen. Uncle said the feeling would simply emerge without any doubt to it and he could feel that now. The doll was a gift from the highway like the viola, but more. It was a gift he was meant to deliver to the girl.

It was a doll a girl like that could love: an elegant old woman dressed in black-crepe skirts, hatpins studded with pearls stuck about her throat like a necklace. Her skull was wisped with silver angel hair and her spidery legs ended in real shoes with spike heels and rhinestone buckles. He carefully gathered her into his sack. He could already visualize himself, dressed in his waiter's tuxedo, presenting the doll out of nowhere, like a magician. And the girl who thought his name was Joey would smile, though already he had forgotten the exact look of that smile, as if he'd worn out her image replaying it over and over.

In the wagon Uncle grabbed the sack and plucked out the doll.

'This is what you took so much time with? I thought maybe you'd found my animal for me.' He tossed it into the box with the porcupine and radiator hose. She seemed to nestle in the porcupine's paws, her dress absorbing blood.

The sun was setting along a line of skeletal trees. Uncle and the boy drove in silence.

'When do you think I could start at the restaurant, Uncle?'

'She has an evil eye – did you notice? Just like in the fable.'

'What fable?'

'Hah!' Uncle said to Wolfgang. 'Nightstein here never heard 'The Fable of the Doll''.'

Wolfgang flattened his dragon's ears.

'Yes, yes, I know it's frightening, but then everything's frightening to you.' Uncle uncorked the medicine bottle with his teeth, swigged, then began addressing the dog in a language of foreign words mixed with growls and barks, pausing to laugh uproariously as if it were a hilarious tale.

'Tell it in English, Uncle.'

A boy, studying to be a ventriloquist, finds a heartless-looking doll and tries to hide her. Don't ask from what. He puts her in a hatbox in the attic, but at night he hears a soprano voice repeating, 'I want my heart, I want my heart!' He goes up to the attic and when he opens the hatbox swallows swarm out from the nest they've pecked from the doll's straw. So he puts her in a steamer trunk and again hears the voice at night and when he opens the trunk mice skitter away. They have nibbled her plaster face. So this time he locks her in a wall safe behind a huge oil painting of a ship on a stormy sea, but once again, 'I want my heart, I want my heart,' and when he opens the safe she's spilling out sawdust, crawling with carpenter ants. Things are getting worse, so at dawn he takes her to a city park near where a water fountain has become a birdbath

*for sparrows. He digs a rectangular hole. It's not a grave, he
explains to her. He lines it with mirrors like a dressing room, and
inside arranges little doll furniture all made out of mirrors – chairs,
table, bureau, bookcase with mirror books, mirror candle, even a
mirror bed with mirror pillows and quilt. Leaves fall; their prophecy
of snow comes true. It settles deep, flat, silent. Then, at the edge
of spring, with snow crusting in sunlight, when he's long forgotten
the doll, he hears a muffled, screaky voice: 'My heart, my heart.'
He goes to the park, still white as the train of a bridal gown, and
there, everywhere, surrounding the birdbath burbling through ice,
are little doll arms and little doll legs, a garden flashing with mirror
rings and buckles, sprouting from the thawing earth.*

He woke from the dream. Everywhere mounted animals
gazed with their glass eyes, spreading wings, varnished feathers and fur, lacquered shells, scales, teeth, claws. Along
the bookshelves specimens stared from bottles. The small
taxidermist-shop window was lit, but Uncle wasn't there.

He could hear Caruso singing in the basement and slowly
descended the stairs. Until last year he hadn't been permitted
in Uncle's workroom, but now that Uncle was teaching him
to tan and preserve, it was allowed. He knew Uncle was
working. Uncle always played old opera records when he
worked.

The bare electric bulb dangled over the butcher block.
Uncle, wearing his eyeshade, and leather apron over long
underwear, was skinning the porcupine. The doll lay nearby
staring at the proceedings.

He watched Uncle artfully pare meat from bone, occasionally pausing to hose the block and toss scraps into a slop jar.

'So, Mr Alger, you are ready to go to the big city to meet
the maître d'.' Uncle heaped the diced stew pieces into a
marinade of bourbon.

'Do you think I'm ready, Uncle?'

'*Ridi Pagliaccio,*' Uncle sang in duet with Caruso while
mopping the block with operatic gestures. Then Uncle meth-
odically spread the doll out where the porcupine had been.
Paint from her face was flaked in her hair.

'Our delivery record has been too hot lately. Maybe it's
better to wait on the restaurant until we produce something

really marvellous for them,' Uncle said, sharpening his carving knife on the whetstone.

'What are you going to do with the doll?'

'How do you think she would look with the head of a porcupine stitched on?' Uncle tested the sharpness of the blade and winced. 'Or how would the porcupine look with the head and dress of a doll?'

The boy wasn't totally convinced Uncle was kidding. It was getting harder to tell lately. He shook his head no.

'No good, eh?' Uncle said. 'I know! I can stuff her, preserve her forever the way she looks now.'

'Uncle, she's stuffed already.'

'Ah! Good point. Well, what do *you* want to do with her?' he asked slyly.

'She might be rare, worth something,' the boy said.

'You think she's valuable maybe? Then there's only one thing we can do.'

'What's that?'

'Bury her!'

They both broke into laughter, then raced to the boxes heaped with clothing in the corner of the basement, tossing garments about as they tried on various outfits. There were full suitcases that had blown off cars, clothes that had tumbled from moving vans and laundry trucks, that had been discarded by lovers and hitchhikers, runaway clotheslines, entire wardrobes they'd picked out of branches along roadsides where abandoned farmhouses gaped, pillaged.

'How's this?' Uncle was modelling a motorcycle jacket that was ridiculously short on him, his arms sticking out. 'A good Nazi jacket.' He topped off his outfit with a frosted-blond wig.

The boy was enveloped by a rubber slicker he wore like a cape, a white life preserver around his neck, and a top hat they'd found one New Year's Eve.

'Don't forget the armbands, Uncle.'

They tied a strip of black satin around each other's arm.

Uncle noisily sorted through piles of scrap that had accumulated against the walls. 'We can bury her in this,' he called, holding up a bathroom medicine cabinet, its cracked shaving mirror revealing a cardboard backing. The boy handed over the doll.

'Wolfgang! Wolfgang!' they shouted, and when the dog bounded down the stairs he was fitted with a black wreath that must have been left on the highway by a funeral cortège.

They marched up the cellar stairs, the boy with the viola, Uncle with lantern and spade, carrying the medicine chest between them.

Outside, Uncle lit the lantern and they loaded the medicine chest and spade into a wheelbarrow, then harnessed it up to Wolfgang's wreath with clothesline.

'Don't trip,' Uncle cautioned, raising the lantern as they picked their way. The back of the house was littered with junked cars, appliances, gutted furniture. Makeshift tombstones struck up everywhere, marking the graves of mufflers and transmissions, the burial ground of broken radios, crates of magazines, animal bones. Ever since the game warden had confiscated his furs and equipment, and accused him of poaching, Uncle claimed he believed in keeping his valuables hidden – though, anything useful, like the viola, they dug up again a few days later.

The procession crossed a meadow, Uncle leading with the lantern, Wolfgang dragging the wheelbarrow, and the boy bringing up the rear, beating time on the drum skin of his life preserver.

They wound through an orchard that smelled faintly of fermenting apples. There was a trickle of stream he'd often played at, where morel mushrooms sprouted profusely in the spring. Uncle had brought him there to pick them long ago. His memory of that time when he first came to live with Uncle continued to be vague; it existed as a numbness the boy felt buried within him; whether unexpressed grief or love no longer mattered: he had remained faithful, even reverent to it. Uncle had once said that what had worried him most was the boy's refusing to cry. So he had tried to make the boy laugh instead, and that was something the boy could remember – Uncle holding him, rubbing a stubbly beard against his cheek, tickling him till he giggled, then whirling him upside down through the fragrance of apple blossoms. The boy was too old for that now, though they still gathered morels together in the spring. He remembered apple-picking contests, how life was when people still came to the taxidermy shop, before the game wardens had revoked Uncle's licence. Uncle had refused to explain to them how he'd acquired the pelts they'd found, refused to mention anything about salvaging the highways, and once he lost his licence, he became more secretive than ever. He was suspicious of everyone, convinced Kopf continued to spy on him. No one had come to visit them for a long time.

Uncle hung a lantern on a branch and began to dig, but after a few shovelfuls was so winded he had to sit down. They let Wolfgang finish, his huge paws scooping dirt between his legs. Then they lowered the medicine chest gently into the earth and covered it up. The boy knew exactly where the spot was. He'd come back in daylight and dig up the doll for the girl.

'Play a little something,' Uncle requested.

The boy cradled the viola against his collar and played 'Greensleeves', a bit out of tune but the only song he could play all the way through. As usual, it made Wolfgang howl.

'Ah, lovely! You can be a playing waiter. You'll make a fortune in tips, Kreisler.'

The flame fluttered in the lamp and faded out. They walked back through dead leaves together in the dark.

'It was a beautiful ceremony, don't you think?' Uncle asked.

Uncle shook him from a dreamless sleep, whispering, 'Wake up, Zoltán, but no light. Here, dress in your suit.'

'No highways today?'

'Don't ask so much – do what your uncle tells you. And hurry.'

The boy pulled on his good trousers under the quilt for warmth. Uncle's croup had returned, a smothered rattle. The man was packing the boy's clothes into a sack, huffing as if he'd been running.

'Uncle, is this an *escape*?'

'Bring your viola. Maybe they'll think it's a machine gun in the big city.' Uncle chuckled. 'I got mine.' He opened his coat. In the dark the boy could still make out the handle of the revolver tucked in his belt.

'You dug it up!'

'Me and Wolfgang. Digging all night while you snored, Nightstein,' Uncle explained as they moved through the darkened house. It seemed nearly stripped. Places where the boy instinctively balanced to bump past end tables were now only empty spaces. The stuffed animals that had loomed from walls and shelves – moosehead, antlers, hawks, owls – were gone. 'Hidden away like a squirrel's acorns,' Uncle whispered. 'When they come this time it will be just another abandoned house. Here.'

Uncle handed him a change purse. The boy could feel the weight of coins in it among crushed bills.

'What's this for?'

'You never know,' Uncle said. 'Something might happen to me. In case we get separated.'

Uncle had never given him money during any of their other escapes. Nor had he ever hidden things so thoroughly. Usually, the escapes were more like drills. Uncle would wake him in the middle of the night saying that Kopf was on the way, or the truant officer, or the dogcatcher, the Gestapo, the KKK, sometimes never exactly who. They would sneak from the house with their coats on over their nightclothes and ride around the back roads until Uncle felt it was safe to return home.

'I don't want us to get separated, Uncle.'

'It's always best to be prepared. Besides, I thought you were ready to go work at the restaurant.'

'Just to *work* there. I didn't mean to live there.'

Uncle hugged him in the dark, empty taxidermy shop. 'Don't worry, Dupush, you can live off the land. You're ready for anything.'

The boy could still smell the faint camphor scent about the old man, mixed with cigar smoke and the odd, herbal odour of the cough medicine. It reminded him of the night with the girl, of returning to the city where she lived, and of the doll he'd wanted to give her – there wasn't time now to dig it up. The doll would have to wait under the orchard until he got back. He wished they were merely going out to salvage. He'd never enjoyed the escape drills.

Uncle disconnected the little doorbell and they sneaked to where the De Soto was parked under birch trees. Wolfgang was already inside, shivering and wagging, wedging his head out from under the seat to lick their faces. Up close the boy could see that Uncle had not buried everything. The back of the wagon was stuffed with specimens – all the large birds and foxes, the lynx, antlers, a jumbled menagerie. The moosehead had been roped to the carriers on the roof of the car.

'Look what they did,' Uncle said, striking a match along the side of the station wagon. Finger-etched in the dirt on the door was a swastika.

They drove on to the interstate, towards the city, away from their usual routes. Semis passed, towing clattering, empty automobile trailers, diesel horns bellowing as their headlights illuminated the moosehead. Uncle kept exhorting the boy to see if they were being followed, convinced that Kopf, still suspecting them of poaching, would tail them into the city, trying to uncover Uncle's outlets for illegal fur and game.

'Those headlights have been following us all the way, haven't they, Zoltán?'

The boy tried to stay alert, but kept drowsing. As sometimes happened late at night, Uncle couldn't seem to stop talking, rambling from one subject to another, connecting facts in a web of increasingly distorted stories: Kopf's persecution of him, their hard luck on the highways, the blank road and evil omens – strange animals, the doll, how if one were to dig her up there'd be nothing but one's own reflection staring back from the earth, and how earlier that evening, after the burial, while trying to pick up Caruso singing faintly among the ghosts of polka stations, he'd tuned in on the sound of crows.

'Crows – they were on the radio. When I heard them I knew it was time to get the hell out. We'll try the city.'

All the while Uncle talked the boy fought sleep, jerking awake from half dreams confused with Uncle's phantoms: a recurring sensation of headlights passing through his body, of lead-soled running across railroad tracks to a highway where trucks rumbled in the white smoke of snow and he walked backward along the shoulder, hitchhiking in the exit-sign aura of flares.

He opened his eyes to a grey sky and pale streetlights still burning. They were cruising down a deserted street of apartment buildings, lined with parked cars, fog condensed on their windshields. Uncle, silent and haggard, turned into an alley.

'The restaurant?' the boy asked. He suddenly didn't want to see it in the daylight.

'No. I just wanted to lose anybody following us. Besides, we couldn't show up at the restaurant empty-handed after missing deliveries all week saying, "All right, get the tuxedo out for the kid". We need something special for them.' Uncle's voice was very hoarse.

They turned back on to a street. The boy knew the lighter it got, the more outlandish they looked. On top, beside the moosehead, Uncle had tied a lacrosse stick they'd once found poking from a beaver dam. In the backseat, Wolfgang sat perfectly still as if trying to blend in with the postured animals he was surrounded with. People, waiting on corners for buses to take them to work, stared as they drove by. Uncle tried to hum 'The Song of the Volga Boatman' and began to hack. The boy sank down in his seat with the uneasy feeling that Uncle was driving aimlessly.

'A couple DPs with nowhere to call home, eh?' Uncle said.

They were on an expressway in heavy traffic, crossing a suspension bridge over the river. Uncle turned off at the next exit, down a street of factories with broken windows, past towering grain elevators, where they bumped over railroad tracks, and finally down a cinder road winding among scrap yards. There were no longer any buildings. The skyline, in an industrial haze, rose jagged beyond the fields and river. But what dominated the boy's attention was the black railroad bridge they were driving towards. He'd noticed it down-river when they crossed the suspension bridge, and it had appeared massive even at that distance.

'What's it look like?' Uncle asked.

'Giant wings.'

'A Black Angel. Though some call it the Jackknife because of how it opens.'

Uncle parked the wagon off the rutted trail that had deteriorated to two muddy treads impressed by enormous tyres. Payscrapers and bulldozers rusted in fields like grazing prehistoric animals. Everything seemed gigantic and abandoned here. The boy felt vulnerable and vaguely afraid, but Uncle was grinning.

'How do you feel about climbing it?' he asked.

'The bridge! For what?'

'Pigeon eggs.'

The trampled towards the river through dry, blond weeds, dragging Wolfgang along on a clothesline leash.

'We might need him to scare off some of the maniacs around here,' Uncle said.

A freight train was clattering across the bridge, open boxcar doors making it look abandoned too. Thousands of glinting birds glided about its spans.

Uncle pointed. 'A sky full of squab.'

They followed a streambed lined with rusted cans and bottles. Rabbits bounced off; a hen pheasant broke. Despite the acrid breeze of chemicals and sewage the area seemed a wilderness, secret at the very heart of the city.

The bank curved by a blue mound of salt. Beneath the collapsed framework of an old wooden trestle stood a charred boxcar, its stovepipe chimney knocked askew, rough-cut windows and doors blackened.

'Goddamn!' Uncle said. 'They burned out Cookie John.'

'Who?'

'Always questions with you, Dupush. Cookie John. A tramp. A squatter. An old friend. Who does these things? It's always the same – other tramps, a gang of boys, *polici*, railroad dicks, some kind of Nazis!' Uncle sat down heavily and began to shake with coughing, gasping for breath between attacks. It brought tears to his eyes. When it was over he looked very old and drained in the bright sunlight.

'Uncle, I'm sorry. Sometimes I'm not sure what's real and what's a joke any more.'

'*Everything* used to be real to you, Dupush. Now you're starting to sort it out. Someday, when you understand about death, you'll answer your own question. Either everything's real or nothing's real. There's no in between. People who find an in between live foolish lives.'

Uncle stood. Wolfgang's muscles were twitching as if he were being swarmed by invisible flies. They had to tug him the rest of the way to the bridge, his hind legs dragging as if still broken. Uncle tied him to one of the dwarfed willows that grew horizontally out of the bank. A small rowboat, coated in a grey film of mud, had been pulled up among the trees on the narrow slope of shore. The dog began to whimper as they climbed in and Uncle shoved them off.

'Tell him something soothing,' Uncle said.

'We'll be right back,' the boy told the dog. 'Don't worry.'

But Wolfgang continued to strain at the leash, snapping back on it, dancing up on his hind legs.

Uncle poled them around the huge concrete abutment with a long pole, hooked at one end like a shepherd's crook, while the boy tried to paddle with a stubby oar that seemed better suited as a ladle. The river smelled of tar, like a hot highway. It flowed sluggishly, feculent, a surface of oil slicks and brown suds. Water seeped into the bottom of the boat and he tried not to get his shoes wet; Uncle said men had died from letting it come in contact with an open sore. Wolfgang was barking wildly from shore.

'Well, anybody interested knows we're here now,' Uncle said. 'I should have bit off his tail. That's what happens when you let their tails grow. Keep an eye open for railroad dicks. They carry pepper guns.'

'What's that?'

'Shotguns loaded with rock salt instead of buckshot.'

The had floated under the deep shadows of the bridge and it was suddenly chilly. The boy looked up through the black, ponderous latticework of beams and trusses, railroad track and spans, semaphores, and flame-blue autumn sky leaking light through uncountable angles. From below, the structure of the bridge made no sense at all. Uncle hooked a rusty rung in the concrete and moored the boat, and they clambered up the rung ladder.

The girders were just wide enough to walk on, studded with rivets, slippery with grease and crusted pigeon droppings. The boy felt clumsy climbing in his suit, trying to keep it clean. They climbed level by level, ascending a series of narrow metal ladders. The river flowed torpidly below, though the higher they climbed, the more it sparkled. He could see circles bursting on the surface almost as if fish, impossibly alive in the poisoned current, were feeding. Wind twanged in the overhead struts.

'Where are the nests?'

'In the upper girders, tucked in the trusses.' Uncle still carried the long, hooked pole, using it to boost himself along. He was breathing heavily, wheezing, and when they reached the railroad tracks he had to stop to catch his breath.

'I can't make it further, Zoltán. You have to get up there alone from here. They're out there over the middle of the river. Here, take this.' Uncle handed him a sack shaped like a wind sock, made from cheesecloth like a butterfly net. 'Put the eggs in this. Be very careful,' Uncle cautioned, mussing the boy's hair.

The ladders had ended. He climbed the latticework of girders that rose over the tracks in towering cantilevered wings, glancing back at each level for Uncle's hand signals. The tar smell of the river had been replaced by a smell of the bridge itself – of grease, corrosion, iron, and damp feathers. Finally, at the proper height, Uncle, far below, directed him out over the river. The boy inched along a girder, peeking down, though trying not to, at the shimmering, increasingly narrow-looking river. He'd never been higher. The entire city spread out in a haze. He breathed deeply and allowed himself the view.

Noon patinaed the downtown skyscrapers. Smokestacks fumed among copper green church steeples and an endless assortment of water towers. Overhead, an airliner droned, and he wondered if anyone could see him – a boy on a bridge with a white sack blowing like a pennant. His mind seemed clearer than it ever had before, as if he were seeing in a new way. His life spread out before him like the cityscape, suspended in time, rather than the dark, speeding blur it had been on the highways. This was a landscape he was the centre of, completely alone, though surrounded by a city. The dreams were over. Out there under plumes of smoke in some glinting neighbourhood the girl sat in a classroom over a math book. Between them was a distance greater than between foreign countries. He could actually *see* from the bridge that in escaping to the city Uncle had merely substituted one kind of isolation for another. And with an intensity of feeling that surprised him, he knew that it didn't matter if the doll in the orchard were ever dug up – he would never see the girl again. The doll had been his first omen, but he had misinterpreted it. Rather than a gift the doll was a warning. The doll could have been anything – a shoe, a hubcap, a bottle. His mind had never put things together so easily. Uncle had kept telling him there would be a breakthrough, that insight would come in a flash, and even as the boy began to understand he wanted the understanding to stop, wanted to tell Uncle he didn't want any more experience with omens. It was better to live without them than to be so wrong, than to realize suddenly as he just had that the girl was no more possible than the restaurant for which he had climbed a bridge to gather pigeon eggs.

He started back along the girder, looking for Uncle below, wanting to signal that he was coming down. But Uncle was no longer there.

A gust of wind almost knocked him off balance. Between gusts an eerie cooing reverberated like waves of a tuning fork. From where he stood he could survey the length of the bridge. Leaning out over the river, he glimpsed the rowing boat still moored to the abutment, but couldn't spot Wolfgang among the scrub trees along the bank. Pigeons flapped like laundry among the girders. Inflated males strutted along beams, swivelling iridescent heads. He began finding nests tucked in the latticed trusses – ancient-looking constructions of weeds, rags, foil, paper. The pigeons are salvagers too, he thought. He couldn't resist gathering eggs. Panicked birds flailed past his head as he reached into nests. The footing was treacherous with droppings, but he continued edging further out over the river, towards the opposite shore, plundering the small white eggs, handfuls splattering on the girders and tumbling through updrafts as he angrily stuffed the sack.

He was more than halfway to the other side when he heard

the first shot. It boomed amplified through the superstructure, launching flurries of birds like secondary explosions. The boy grabbed a girder and held on as they beat around him. He frantically scanned the bridge for Uncle, spotting two men instead, approaching from below, jogging along the railroad tracks. He glanced from them back across the river, checking for the De Soto. It was still there, windshield flaring on a rise beyond the blue mountain of salt. From the bridge the station wagon appeared the size of a toy, but he could clearly make out the black-and-white markings of the squad car parked beside it.

'Uncle,' he tried yelling, 'Uncle,' but his voice was swept away by wind. Another shot propelled the birds into frenetic circles. Its echoes ricocheted among the girders so that he couldn't tell what direction it had come from. The *polici* on the tracks dropped to a crouch. He could see their blue uniforms but not whether they'd drawn their guns. They didn't seem to be doing the shooting.

Bells were ringing insistently upriver and down. He tried to move but his legs were locked and his hands clutched a girder in a knuckle-aching grip. A horn blasted, its deep vibration travelling the iron beams into his bones. A floating junkyard was moving towards the bridge – cabled barges heaped with scrap cars, pushed by a tug. He felt a rumbling tremor and slid to his knees as the landscape began to tilt. The bridge was opening.

Pigeons continued to wheel, gulls, starlings, and grackles screaming in their midst. The two *polici* on the tracks, trying to scramble back before the bridge opened completely, lunged to either side as Wolfgang, clothesline streaming, hurtled past them. The dog's rangy body compressed and expanded with each pumping stride, and as if possessed by terror and his own velocity, he leaped the gap between the expanding black spans of the bridge, arcing slow-motion through midair, and for a moment the boy thought the dog might make it, then he looked away as Wolfgang plunged.

When the boy opened his eyes barges were passing below. He began working hand over hand down the elevated girders towards the base of the bridge, using the rivets as toe holds. His suit was torn, grease-slathered, smeared with yolk and feathers from the egg sack he'd knotted to his belt. Tears were running down his face though he didn't feel that he was crying. He felt numb – the bridge was too massive for tears to mean anything. Across the gulf of its gaping wings he saw where Uncle had been hiding from the *polici*. Crouched in the latticework of girders beneath the railroad tracks, Uncle was gesturing wildly to him. Sunlight flashed off the revolver in Uncle's hand, and the boy guessed it had been Uncle firing earlier in an effort to attract his attention to the barges before the bridge opened. Uncle continued to signal. The barges with their mangled cars slid like endless highway wrecks beneath thousands of screeching birds. Warning bells clanged. Finally the boy raised his arm. Through swirling birds he waved goodbye.

Lights

In summer, waiting for night, we'd pose against the after-glow on corners, watching traffic cruise through the neigh-bourhood. Sometimes, a car would go by without its head-lights on and we'd all yell, 'Lights!'

'Lights!' we'd keep yelling until the beams flashed on. It was usually immediate – the driver honking back thanks, or flinching embarrassed behind the steering wheel, or gunning past, and we'd see his red taillights blink on.

But there were times – who knows why? – when drunk or high, stubborn, or simply lost in that glide to somewhere else, the driver just kept driving in the dark, and all down the block we'd hear yelling from doorways and storefronts, front steps, and other corners, voices winking on like fireflies: 'Lights! Your *lights*! Hey, lights!'

Blight

During those years between Korea and Vietnam, when rock and roll was being perfected, our neighbourhood was proclaimed an Official Blight Area.

Richard J. Daley was mayor then. It seemed as if he had always been, and would always be, the mayor. Ziggy Zilinsky claimed to have seen the mayor himself riding down Twenty-third Place in a black limousine flying one of those little purple pennants from funerals, except his said WHITE SOX on it. The mayor sat in the backseat sorrowfully shaking his head as if to say 'Jeez!' as he stared out the bulletproof window at the winos drinking on the corner by the boarded-up grocery.

Of course, nobody believed that Zig had actually seen the mayor. Ziggy had been unreliable even before Pepper Rosado had accidentally beaned him during a game of 'it' with the bat. People still remembered as far back as third grade when Ziggy had jumped up in the middle of Mass yelling, 'Didya see her? She nodded! I asked the Blessed Virgin would my cat come home and she nodded yes!'

All through grade school the statues of saints winked at Ziggy. He was in constant communication with angels and the dead. And Ziggy sleepwalked. The cops had picked him up once in the middle of the night for running around the bases in Washtenaw Playground while still asleep.

When he'd wake up, Ziggy would recount his dreams as if they were prophecies. He had a terrible recurring nightmare in which atomic bombs dropped on the city the night the White Sox won the pennant. He could see the mushroom cloud rising out of Comiskey Park. But Zig had wonderful dreams, too. My favourite was the one in which he and I and Little Richard were in a band playing in the centre of St Sabina's roller rink.

After Pepper brained him out on the boulevard with a bat – a fungo bat that Pepper whipped like a tomahawk across a twenty-yard width of tulip garden that Ziggy was trying to hide behind – Zig stopped seeing visions of the saints. Instead, he began catching glimpses of famous people, not movie stars so much as big shots in the news. Every once in a while Zig would spot somebody like Bo Diddley going by on a bus. Mainly, though, it would be some guy in a Homburg who looked an awful lot like Eisenhower, or he'd notice a reappearing little grey-haired fat guy who could turn out to be either Nikita Khrushchev or Mayor Daley. It didn't surprise us. Zig was the kind of kid who read newspapers. We'd all go to Potok's to buy comics and Zig would walk out with the *Daily News*. Zig had always worried about things no one else cared about, like the population explosion, people starving in India, the world blowing up. We'd be walking along down Twenty-second and pass an alley and Ziggy would say, 'See that?'

'See what?'

'Major Daley scrounging through garbage.'

We'd all turn back and look but only see a bag lady picking through cans.

Still, in a way, I could see it from Ziggy's point of view. Mayor Daley *was* everywhere. The city was tearing down buildings for urban renewal and tearing up streets for a new expressway, and everywhere one looked there were signs in front of the rubble reading:

SORRY FOR THE INCONVENIENCE
ANOTHER IMPROVEMENT
FOR A GREATER CHICAGO
RICHARD J. DALEY, MAYOR

Not only were there signs everywhere, but a few blocks away a steady stream of fat, older, bossy-looking guys emanated from the courthouse on Twenty-sixth. They looked like a corps of Mayor Daley doubles, and sometimes, especially on election days, they'd march into the neigbourhood chewing cigars and position themselves in front of the flag-draped barbershops that served as polling places.

But back to blight.

That was an expression we used a lot. We'd say it after going downtown, or after spending the day at the Oak Street Beach, which we regarded as the beach of choice for sophisticates. We'd pack our towels and, wearing our swimsuits under our jeans, take the subway north.

'North to freedom,' one of us would always say.

Those were days of longing without cares, of nothing to do but lie out on the sand inspecting the world from behind our sunglasses. At the Oak Street Beach the city seemed to realize our dreams of it. We gazed out nonchalantly at the white-sailed yachts on the watercolour-blue horizon, or back across the Outer Drive at the lake-reflecting glass walls of high rises as if we took it all for granted. The blue, absorbing shadow would deepen to azure, and a fiery orange sun would dip behind the glittering buildings. The crowded beach would gradually empty, and a pitted moon would hover over sand scalloped with a million footprints. It would be time to go.

'Back to blight,' one of us would always joke.

I remember a day shortly after blight first became official. We were walking down Rockwell, cutting through the truck docks, Zig, Pepper, and I, on our way to the viaduct near Douglass Park. Pepper was doing his Fats Domino impression, complete with opening piano riff: *Bum-pah-da-bum-pa-da-dummmmm . . .*

> Ah foun' mah thrill
> Ahn Blueberry Hill . . .

It was the route we usually walked to the viaduct, but since blight had been declared we were trying to see our surroundings from a new perspective to determine if anything had been changed, or at least appeared different. Blight sounded serious, biblical in a way, like something locusts might be responsible for.

'Or a plague of gigantic, radioactive cockroaches,' Zig said, 'climbing out of the sewers.'

'Blight, my kabotch,' Pepper said, grabbing his kabotch and shaking it at the world. 'They call this blight? Hey, man, there's weeds and trees and everything, man. You shoulda seen it on Eighteenth Street.'

We passed a Buick somebody had dumped near the railroad tracks. It had been sitting there for months and was still crusted with salt-streaked winter grime. Someone had scraped WASH ME across its dirty trunk, and someone else had scrawled WHIP ME across its hood. Pepper snapped off the aerial and whipped it back and forth so that the air whined, then slammed it down on a fender and began rapping out a Latin beat. We watched him smacking the hell out of it, then Zig and I picked up sticks and broken hunks of bricks and started clanking the headlights and bumpers as if they were bongos and congas, all of us chanting out the melody to 'Tequila'. Each time we grunted out the word *tequila*, Pepper, who was dancing on the hood, stomped out more windshield.

We were revving up for the viaduct, a natural echo chamber where we'd been going for blues-shout contests ever since we'd become infatuated with Screamin' Jay Hawkins's 'I Put a Spell on You'. In fact, it was practising blues shouts together that led to the formation of our band, the No Names. We practised in the basement of the apartment building I lived in: Zig on bass, me on sax, Pepper on drums, and a guy named Deejo who played accordion, though he promised us he was saving up to buy an electric guitar.

Pepper could play. He was a natural.

'I go crazy', was how he described it.

His real name was Stanley Rosado. His mother sometimes called him Stashu, which he hated. She was Polish and his father was Mexican – the two main nationalities in the neighbourhood together in one house. It wasn't always an easy alliance, especially inside Pepper. When he got pissed he was a wild man. Things suffered, sometimes people, but always things. Smashing stuff seemed to fill him with peace. Sometimes he didn't even realize he was doing it, like the time he took flowers to Linda Molina, a girl he'd been nuts about since grade school. Linda lived in one of the well-kept two-flats along Marshall Boulevard, right across from the Assumption Church. Maybe it was just that proximity to the church, but there had always been a special aura about her.

Pepper referred to her as 'the unadulterated one'. He finally worked up the nerve to call her, and when she actually invited him over, he walked down the boulevard to her house in a trance. It was late spring, almost summer, and the green boulevard stretched like an enormous lawn before Linda Molina's house. At its centre was a blazing garden of tulips. The city had planted them. Their stalks sprouted tall, more like corn than flowers, and their colours seemed to vibrate in the air. The tulips were the most beautiful thing in the neighbourhood. Mothers wheeled babies by them; old folks hobbled for blocks and stood before the flowers as if they were sacred.

Linda answered the door and Pepper stood there holding a huge bouquet. Clumps of dirt still dangled from the roots.

'For you,' Pepper said.

Linda, smiling with astonishment, accepted the flowers; then her eyes suddenly widened in horror. 'You didn't – ?' she asked.

Pepper shrugged.

'Lechon!' the Unadulterated One screamed, pitching a shower of tulips into his face and slamming the door.

That had happened a year before and Linda still refused to talk to him. It had given Pepper's blues shouts a particularly soulful quality, especially since he continued to preface them, in the style of Screamin' Jay Hawkins, with the words 'I love you'. *I love you! Aiiyyaaaaaa!!!*

Pepper even had Screamin' Jay's blues snork down.

We'd stand at the shadowy mouth of the viaduct, peering at the greenish gleam of light at the other end of the tunnel. The green was the grass and trees of Douglass Park. Pepper would begin slamming an aerial or board or chain off the girders, making the echoes collide and ring, while Ziggy and I clonked empty bottles and beer cans, and all three of us would be shouting and screaming like Screamin' Jay or Howlin' Wolf, like those choirs of unleashed voices we'd hear on 'Jam with Sam's' late-night blues show. Sometimes a train streamed by, booming overhead like part of the song, and we'd shout louder yet, and I'd remember my father telling me how he could have been an opera singer if he hadn't ruined his voice as a kid imitating trains. Once, a gang of black kids appeared on the Douglass Park end of the viaduct and stood harmonizing from bass through falsetto just like the Coasters, so sweetly that though at first we tried outshouting them, we finally shut up and listened, except for Pepper keeping the beat.

We applauded from our side but stayed where we were, and they stayed on theirs. Douglass Park had become the new boundary after the riots the summer before.

'How can a place with such good viaducts have blight, man?' Pepper asked, still rapping his aerial as we walked back.

'Frankly, man,' Ziggy said, 'I always suspected it was a little fucked up around here.'

'Well, that's different,' Pepper said. 'Then let them call it an Official Fucked-Up Neighbourhood.'

Nobody pointed out that you'd never hear a term like that from a public official, at least not in public, and especially not from the office of the mayor who had once promised, 'We shall reach new platitudes of success.'

Nor did anyone need to explain that Official Blight was the language of revenue, forms in quintuplicate, grants, and federal aid channelled through the Machine and processed with the help of grafters, skimmers, wheeler-dealers, an army of aldermen, precinct captains, patronage workers, their relatives and friends. No one said it, but instinctively we knew we'd never see a nickel.

Not that we cared. They couldn't touch us if we didn't. Besides, we weren't blamers. Blight was just something that happened, like acne or old age. Maybe declaring it official mattered in that mystical world of property values, but it wasn't a radical step, like condemning buildings or labelling a place a slum. Slums were on the other side of the viaduct.

Blight, in fact, could be considered a kind of official recognition, a grudging admission that among blocks of factories, railroad tracks, truck docks, industrial dumps, scrapyards, expressways, and the drainage canal, people had managed to wedge in their everyday lives.

Deep down we believed what Pepper had been getting at: blight had nothing to do with ecstasy. They could send in the building inspectors and social workers, the mayor could drive through in his black limo, but they'd never know about the music of viaducts, or churches where saints winked and nodded, or how right next door to me our guitar player, Joey 'Deejo' DeCampo, had finally found his title, and inspired by it had begun the Great American Novel, *Blight*, which opened: 'The dawn rises like sick old men playing on the rooftops in their underwear.'

We had him read that to us again and again.

Ecstatic, Deejo rushed home and wrote all night. I could always tell when he was writing. It wasn't just the wild, dreamy look that overcame him. Deejo wrote to music, usually the *1812* Overture, and since only a narrow gangway between buildings separated his window from mine, when I heard bells and cannon blasts at two in the morning I knew he was creating.

Next morning, bleary-eyed, sucking a pinched Lucky, Deejo read us the second sentence. It ran twenty ballpoint-scribbled loose-leaf pages and had nothing to do with the old men on the rooftops in their underwear. It seemed as though Deejo had launched into a digression before the novel had even begun. His second sentence described an epic battle between a spider and a caterpillar. The battle took place in the gangway between our apartment buildings, and that's where Deejo insisted on reading it to us. The gangway lent his voice an echoey ring. He read with his eyes glued to the page, his free hand gesticulating wildly, pouncing spiderlike, fingers jabbing like a beak tearing into green caterpillar guts, fist opening like a jaw emitting shrieks. His voice rose as the caterpillar reared, howling like a damned soul, its poisonous hairs bristling. Pepper, Ziggy, and I listened, occasionally exchanging looks.

It wasn't Deejo's digressing that bothered us. That was how we all told stories. But we could see that Deejo's inordinate fascination with bugs was surfacing again. Not that he was alone in that, either. Of all our indigenous wildlife – sparrows, pigeons, mice, rats, dogs, cats – it was only bugs that suggested the grotesque richness of nature. A lot of kids had, at one time or another, expressed their wonder by torturing them a little. But Deejo had been obsessed. He'd become diabolically adept as a destroyer, the kind of kid who would observe an ant hole for hours, even bait it with a Holloway bar, before blowing it up with a cherry bomb. Then one day his grandpa Tony said, 'Hey, Joey, pretty soon they're gonna invent little microphones and you'll be able to hear them screaming.'

He was kidding, but the remark altered Deejo's entire way of looking at things. The world suddenly became one of an infinite number of infinitesimal voices, and Deejo equated voices with souls. If one only listened, it was possible to hear tiny choirs that hummed at all hours as on a summer night, voices speaking a language of terror and beauty that, for the first time, Deejo understood.

It was that vision that turned him into a poet, and it was really for his poetry, more than his guitar playing, that we'd recruited him for the No Names. None of us could write lyrics, though I'd tried a few takeoffs, like the one on Jerry Lee Lewis's 'Great Balls of Fire':

> My BVDs were made of thatch,
> You came along and lit the match,
> I screamed in pain, my screams grew higher,
> Goodness gracious! My balls were on fire!

We were looking for a little more soul, words that would suggest Pepper's rages, Ziggy's prophetic dreams. And we might have had that if Deejo could have written a bridge. He'd get in a groove like 'Lonely Is the Falling Rain':

> Lonely is the falling rain,
> Every drop
> Tastes the same,
> Lonely is the willow tree,
> Green dress draped
>   Across her knee,
> Lonely is the boat at sea . . .

Deejo could go on listing lonely things for pages, but he'd never arrive at a bridge. His songs refused to circle back on themselves. They'd just go on and were impossible to memorize.

He couldn't spell, either, which never bothered us but created a real problem when Pepper asked him to write something that Pepper could send to Linda Molina. Deejo came up with 'I Dream', which, after several pages, ended with the lines:

> I dream of my arms
> Around your waste.

Linda mailed it back to Pepper with those lines circled and in angry slashes of eyebrow pencil the exclamations: *!LECHON! !!ESTÚPIDO!! !PERVERT!*

Pepper kept it folded in his wallet like a love letter.

But back to *Blight*.

We stood in the gangway listening to Deejo read. His seemingly nonstop sentence was reaching a climax. Just when the spider and caterpillar realized their battle was futile, that neither could win, a sparrow swooped down and gobbled them both up.

It was a parable. Who knows how many insect lives had been sacrificed in order for Deejo to have finally scribbled those pages?

We hung our heads and muttered, 'Yeah, great stuff, Deej, that was good, man, no shit, keep it up, be a best-seller.'

He folded his loose-leaf papers, stuffed them into his back pocket, and walked away without saying anything.

Later, whenever someone would bring up his novel *Blight*, and its great opening line, Deejo would always say, 'Yeah, and it's been all downhill from there.'

As long as it didn't look as if Deejo would be using his title in the near future, we decided to appropriate it for the band. We considered several variations – Boys from Blight, Blights Out, the Blight Brigade. We wanted to call ourselves Pepper and the Blighters, but Pepper said no way, so we settled on just plain Blighters. That had a lot better ring to it than calling ourselves the No Names. We had liked being the No Names at first, but it had started to seem like an advertisement for an identity crisis. The No Names sounded too much like one of the tavern-sponsored softball teams the guys back from Korea had formed. Those guys had been our heroes when we were little kids. They had seemed like legends to us as they gunned around the block on Indians and Harleys while we walked home from grade school. Now they hung out at corner taverns, working on beer bellies, and played softball a couple of nights a week on teams that lacked both uniforms and names. Some of their teams had jerseys with the name of the bar that sponsored them across the back, but the bars themselves were mainly named after beers – the Fox Head 400 on Twenty-fifth Street, or the Edelweiss Tap on Twenty-sixth, or down from that the Carta Blanca. Sometimes, in the evenings, we'd walk over to Lawndale Park and watch one of the tavern teams play softball under the lights. Invariably some team calling itself the Damon Demons or the Latin Cobras, decked out in gold-and-black uniforms, would beat their butts.

There seemed to be some unspoken relationship between being nameless and being a loser. Watching the guys from Korea after their ball games as they hung around under the buzzing neon signs of their taverns, guzzling beers and flipping the softball, I got the strange feeling that they had acually chosen anonymity and the loserhood that went with it. It was something they looked for in one another, that held them together. It was as if Korea had confirmed the choice in them, but it had been there before they'd been drafted. I could still remember how they once organized a motorcycle club. They called it the Motorcycle Club. Actually, nobody ever called it that. It was the only nameless motorcycle gang I'd ever heard of.

A lot of those guys had grown up in the housing project that Pepper and Ziggy lived in, sprawling blocks of row houses known simply as 'the projects', rather than something ominous sounding like Cabrini-Green. Generations of nameless gangs had roamed the projects, then disappeared, leaving behind odd, anonymous graffiti – unsigned warnings, threats, and imprecations without the authority of a gang name behind them.

It wasn't until we became Blighters that we began to recog-

nize the obscurity that surrounded us. Other neighbourhoods at least had identities, like Back of the Yards, Mar-
quette Park, Logan Square, Greektown. There were places
named after famous intersections, like Halsted and Taylor.
Everyone knew the mayor still lived where he'd been born,
in Bridgeport, the neighbourhood around Sox Park. We
heard our area referred to sometimes as Zone 8, after its
postal code, but that never caught on. Nobody said, 'Back
to Zone 8.' For a while Deejo had considered *Zone 8* as a
possible title for his novel, but he finally rejected it as sounding too much like science fiction.

As Blighters, just walking the streets we became suddenly
aware of familiar things we didn't have names for, like the
trees we'd grown up walking past, or the flowers we'd
always admired that bloomed around the blue plastic shrine
of the Virgin in the front yard of the Old Widow. Even the
street names were mainly numbers, something I'd never
have noticed if Debbie Weiss, a girl I'd met downtown,
hadn't pointed it out.

Debbie played sax, too, in the band at her all-girls high
school. I met her in the sheet-music department of Lyon &
Healy's music store. We were both flipping through the same
Little Richard songbooks. His songs had great sax breaks,
the kind where you roll on to your back and kick your feet
in the air while playing.

'Tenor or alto?' she asked without looking up from the
music.

I glanced around to make sure she was talking to me. She
was humming 'Tutti Frutti' under her breath.

'Tenor,' I answered, amazed we were talking.

'That's what I want for my birthday. I've got an alto, an
old Martin. It was my Uncle Seymour's. He played with
Chick Webb.'

'Oh, yeah,' I said, impressed, though I didn't know exactly
who Chick Webb was. 'How'd you know I played sax?' I
asked her, secretly pleased that I obviously looked like someone who did.

'It was either that or you've got weird taste in ties. You
always walk around wearing your neck strap?'

'No, I just forgot to take it off after practising,' I explained, effortlessly slipping into my first lie to her. Actually, I had taken to wearing the neck strap for my saxophone sort of in the same way that the Mexican guys in the neighbourhood wore gold chains dangling outside their T-shirts, except that instead of a cross at the end of my strap I had a little hook, which looked like a mysterious Greek letter, from which the horn was meant to hang.

We went to a juice bar Debbie knew around the corner from the music store. I had a Coco-Nana and she had something with mango, papaya, and passion fruit.

'So how'd you think I knew you played sax? By your thumb callus?' She laughed.

We compared the thumb calluses we had from holding our horns. She was funny. I'd never met a girl so easy to talk to. We talked about music and saxophone reeds and school. The only thing wrong was that I kept telling her lies. I told her I played in a band in Cicero in a club that was run by the Mafia. She said she'd never been to Cicero, but it sounded like really the pits. 'Really the pits' was one of her favourite phrases. She lived on the North Side and invited me to visit. When she wrote her address down on a napkin and asked if I knew how to get there, I said, 'Sure, I know where that is.'

North to Freedom, I kept thinking on my way to her house the first time, trying to remember all the bull I'd told her. It took over an hour and two transfers to get there. I ended up totally lost. I was used to streets that were numbered, streets that told you exactly where you were and what was coming up next. 'Like knowing the latitude,' I told her.

She argued that the North Side had more class because the streets had names.

'A number lacks character, David. How can you have a feeling for a street called Twenty-second?' she asked.

She'd never been on the South Side except for a trip to the museum.

I'd ride the Douglass Park B train home from her house and pretend she was sitting next to me, and as my stop approached I'd look down at the tarpaper roofs, back porches, alleys, and backyards crammed between factories and try to imagine how it would look to someone seeing it for the first time.

At night, Twenty-second was a streak of coloured lights, electric winks of neon glancing off plate glass and sidewalks as headlights surged by. The air smelled of restaurants – frying burgers, pizza parlours, the cornmeal and hot-oil blast of *taquerías*. Music collided out of open bars. And when it rained and the lights on the oily street shimmered, Deejo would start whistling 'Harlem Nocturne' in the back seat.

I'd inherited a '53 Chevy from my father. He hadn't died, but he figured the car had. It was a real Blightmobile, a kind of mustardy, baby-shit yellow where it wasn't rusting out, but built like a tank, and rumbling like one, too. That car would not lay rubber, not even when I'd floor it in neutral, then throw it into drive.

Some nights there would be drag races on Twenty-fifth Place, a dead-end street lined with abandoned factories and junkers that winos dumped along the curb. It was suggested to me more than once that my Chevy should take its rightful place along the curb with the junkers. The dragsters would line up, their machines gleaming, customized, bull-nosed, raked, and chopped, oversize engines revving through chrome pipes; then someone would wave a shirt and they'd explode off, burning rubber down an aisle of wrecks. We'd hang around watching till the cops showed up, then scrape together some gas money and go riding ourselves, me behind the wheel and Ziggy fiddling with the radio, tuning in on the White Sox while everyone else shouted for music.

The Chevy had one customized feature: a wooden bumper. It was something I was forced to add after I almost ruined my life forever on Canal Street. When I first inherited the car all I had was my driver's permit, so Ziggy, who already had his licence, rode with me to take the driving test. On the way there, wheeling a corner for practice, I jumped the curb on Canal Street and rumbled down the sidewalk until I hit a no-parking sign and sent it flying over the bridge. Shattered headlights showered the windshield and Ziggy was choking on a scream caught in his throat. I swung a U and fled back to the neighbourhood. It took blocks before

Ziggy was able to breathe again. I felt shaky, too, and started to laugh with relief. Zig stared at me as if I were crazy and had purposely driven down the sidewalk in order to knock off a no parking sign.

'Holy Christ! Dave, you could have ruined your life back there forever,' Zig told me. It sounded like something my father would have said. Worries were making Ziggy more nervous that summer than ever before. The Sox had come from nowhere to lead the league, triggering Zig's old night-mare about atom bombs falling on the night the White Sox won the pennant.

Besides the busted headlights, the sign pole had left a perfect indentation in my bumper. It was Pepper's idea to wind chains around the bumper at the point of indentation, attach the chains to the bars of a basement window, and floor the car in reverse to pull out the dent. When we tried it the bumper tore off. So Pepper, who saw himself as mechanically inclined, wired on a massive wooden bumper. He'd developed a weird affection for the Chevy. I'd let him drive and he'd tool down alleys clipping garbage cans with the wooden front end in a kind of steady bass-drum beat: *boom boom boom*.

Pepper reached the point where he wanted to drive all the time. I understood why. There's a certain feeling of freedom you can get only with a beater, that comes from being able to wreck it without remorse. In a way it's like being indestruc-tible, impervious to pain. We'd cruise the neighbourhood on Saturdays, and everywhere we looked guys would be waxing their cars or tinkering under the hoods.

I'd honk at them out the window on my sax and yell, 'You're wasting a beautiful day on that hunk of scrap.'

They'd glance up from their swirls of simonize and flip me the finger.

'Poor, foolish assholes,' Pepper would scoff.

He'd drive with one hand on the wheel and the other smacking the roof in time to whatever was blaring on the radio. The Chevy was like a drum-set accessory to him. He'd jump out at lights and start bopping on the hood. Since he was driving, I started toting along my sax. We'd pull up to a bus stop where people stood waiting in a trance and Pepper would beat on a fender while I wailed a chorus of 'Hand Jive'; then we'd jump back in the Chevy and grind off, as if making our getaway. Once the cops pulled us over and frisked us down. They examined my sax as if it were a weapon.

'There some law against playing a little music?' Pepper kept demanding.

'That's right, jack-off,' one of the cops told him. 'It's called disturbing the peace.'

Finally, I sold Pepper the Chevy for twenty-five dollars. He said he wanted to fix it up. Instead, he used it as a battering ram. He drove it at night around construction sites for the new expressway, mowing down the blinking yellow barricades and signs that read: SORRY FOR THE INCONVENIENCE . . .

Ziggy, who had developed an eye twitch and had started to stutter, refused to ride with him any more.

The Sox kept winning.

One night, as Pepper gunned the engine at a red light on Thirty-ninth, the entire transmission dropped out into the street. He, Deejo and I pushed the car for blocks and never saw a cop. There was a slight decline to the street and once we got it moving, the Chevy rolled along on its own momentum. Pepper sat inside steering. With the key in the ignition the radio still played.

'Anybody have any idea where we're rolling to?' Deejo wanted to know.

'To the end of the line,' Pepper said.

We rattled across a bridge that spanned the drainage canal, and just beyond it Pepper cut the wheel and we turned off on to an oiled, unlighted cinder road that ran past a foundry and continued along the river. The road angled downhill, but it was potholed and rutted and it took all three of us grunting and struggling to keep the car moving.

'It would have been a lot easier to just dump it on Twenty-fifth Place,' Deejo panted.

'No way, man,' Pepper said. 'We ain't winos.'

'We got class,' I said.

The road was intersected by railroad tracks. After half an hour of rocking and heaving we got the Chevy on to the tracks and from there it was downhill again to the railroad bridge. We stopped halfway across the bridge. Pepper climbed on to the roof of the car and looked out over the black river. The moon shone on the oily surface like a single, intense spotlight. Frankie Avalon was singing on the radio.

'Turn that simp off. I hate him,' Pepper yelled. He was peeing down on to the hood in a final benediction.

I switched the radio dial over the late-night mush-music station – Sinatra singing 'These Foolish Things' – and turned the volume up full blast. Pepper jumped down, flicked the headlights on, and we shoved the car over the bridge.

The splash shook the girders. Pigeons crashed out from under the bridge and swept around confusedly in the dark. We stared over the side half expecting to see the Chevy bob back up through the heavy grease of the river and float off in the moonlight. But except for the bubbles on the surface, it was gone. Then I remembered that my sax had been in the trunk.

A week later, Pepper had a new car, a red Fury convertible. His older cousin Carmen had co-signed. Pepper had made the first payment, the only one he figured on making, by selling his massive red-sparkle drum set – bass, snare, tom-tom, cymbals, high hat, bongos, conga, cowbell, woodblock, tambourine, gong – pieces he'd been accumulating on birthdays, Christmases, confirmation, graduation, since fourth grade, the way girls add pearls to a necklace. When he climbed behind those drums, he looked like a mad king beating his throne, and at first we refused to believe he had sold it all, or that he was dropping out of school to join the marines.

He drove the Fury as gently as a chauffeur. It was as if some of the craziness had drained out of him when the Chevy went over the bridge. Ziggy even started riding with us again, though every time he'd see a car pass with a GO GO sox sign he'd get twitchy and depressed.

Pennant fever was in the air. The city long accustomed to losers was poised for a celebration. Driving with the top down brought the excitement of the streets closer. We were part of it. From Pepper's Fury the pace of life around us seemed different, slower than it had from the Chevy. It was as if we were in a speedboat gliding through.

Pepper would glide repeatedly past Linda Molina's house, but she was never out as she'd been the summer before, sunning on a towel on the boulevard grass. There was a rumour that she'd gotten knocked up and had gone to stay with relatives in Texas. Pepper refused to believe it, but the rest of us got the feeling that he had joined the marines for the same reason Frenchmen supposedly joined the foreign legion.

'Dave, man, you wanna go by that broad you know's house on the North Side, man?' he would always offer.

'Nah,' I'd say, as if that would be boring.

We'd just drive, usually further south, sometimes almost to Indiana, where the air smelled singed and towering foundry smokestacks erupted shooting sparks, like gigantic Roman candles. Then, skirting the worst slums, we'd head back through the dark neighbourhoods broken by strips of neon, the shops grated and padlocked, but bands of kids still out splashing in the water of open hydrants, and guys standing in the light of bar signs, staring hard as we passed.

We toured places we'd always heard about – the Fulton produce mart with its tailgate-high sidewalks, Midway Airport, skid row – stopped for carryout ribs, or at shrimp houses along the river, and always ended up speeding down the Outer Drive, along the skyline-glazed lake, as if some force had spun us to the inner rim of the city. That was the summer Deejo let his hair get long. He was growing a beard, too, a Vandyke, he called it, though Pepper insisted it was really trimmings from other parts of Deejo's body pasted on with Elmer's glue.

Wind raking his shaggy hair, Deejo would shout passages from his dog-eared copy of *On the Road*, which he walked around reading like a breviary ever since seeing Jack Kerouac on *The Steve Allen Show*. I retaliated in a spooky Vincent Price voice, reciting poems off an album called *Word Jazz* that Deej and I had nearly memorized. My favourite was 'The Junkman', which began:

In a dream I dreamt that was no dream,
In a sleep I slept that was no sleep,
I saw the junkman in his scattered yard . . .

Ziggy dug that one, too.

By the time we hit downtown and passed Buckingham Fountain with its spraying, mulicoloured plumes of light, Deejo would be rhapsodic. One night, standing up in the backseat and extending his arms towards the skyscraper we called God's House because of its glowing blue dome – a blue the romantic, lonely shade of runway lights – Deejo blurted out, 'I dig beauty!'

Even at the time, it sounded a little extreme. All we'd had were a couple of six-packs. Pepper started swerving, he was laughing so hard, and beating the side of the car with his fist, and for a while it was as if he was back behind the wheel of the Chevy. It even brought Ziggy out of his despair. We rode around the rest of the night gaping and pointing and yelling, 'Beauty ahead! Dig it!'

'Beauty to the starboard!'

'Coming up on it fast!'

'Can you dig it?'

'Oh, wow! I am digging it! I'm digging beauty!'

Deejo got pimped pretty bad about it in the neighbourhood. A long time after that night, guys would still be asking him, 'Digging any beauty lately?' Or introducing him: 'This is Deejo. He digs beauty.' Or he'd be walking down the street and from a passing car someone would wave, and yell, 'Hey, Beauty-Digger!'

The last week before the Fury was repoed, when Pepper would come by to pick us up, he'd always say, 'Hey, man, let's go dig some beauty.'

A couple of weeks later, on a warm Wednesday night in Cleveland, Gerry Staley came on in relief with the bases loaded in the bottom of the ninth, threw one pitch, a double-play ball, Aparicio to Kluszewski, and the White Sox clinched their first pennant in forty years. Pepper had already left on the bus for Parris Island. He would have liked the celebration. Around 11 p.m. the air-raid sirens all over the city began to howl. People ran out into the streets in their bath-robes crying and praying, staring up past the roofs as if trying to catch a glimpse of the mushroom cloud before it blew the neighbourhood to smithereens. It turned out that Mayor Daley, a lifelong Sox fan, had ordered the sirens as part of the festivities.

Ziggy wasn't the same after that. He could hardly get a word out without stammering. He said he didn't feel reprieved but as if he had died. When the sirens started to wail, he had climbed into bed clutching his rosary which he still had from grade-school days, when the Blessed Mother used to smile at him. He'd wet the bed that night and had continued having accidents every night since. Deej and I tried to cheer him up, but what kept him going was a book by Thomas Merton called *The Seven Storey Mountain*, which one of the priests at the parish church had given him. It meant more to Zig than *On the Road* did to Deejo. Finally, Ziggy decided that since he could hardly talk anyway, he might be better off in the Trappists like Thomas Merton. He figured if he just showed up with the book at the monastery in Gethsemane, Kentucky, they'd have to take him in.

'I'll be taking the vow of silence,' he stammered, 'so don't worry if you don't hear much from me.'

'Silence isn't the vow I'd be worrying about,' I said, still trying to joke him out of it, but he was past laughing and I was sorry I'd kidded him.

He, Deejo, and I walked past the truck docks and railroad tracks, over to the river. We stopped on the California Avenue Bridge, from which we could see a succession of bridges spanning the river, including the black railroad bridge we had pushed the Chevy over. We'd been walking most of the night, past churches, under viaducts along the boulevard, as if visiting the landmarks of our childhood. Without a car to ride around in, I felt like a little kid again. It was Zig's last night, and he wanted to walk. In the morning he intended to leave home and hitchhike to Kentucky. I had an image of him standing along the shoulder holding up a sign that read GETHSEMANE to the oncoming traffic. I didn't want him to go. I kept remembering things as we walked along and then not mentioning them, like that dream he'd had about him and me and Little Richard. Little Richard had found religion and been ordained a preacher, I'd read, but I didn't think he had taken the vow of silence. I had a fantasy of all the monks with their hoods up, meditating in total silence, and suddenly Ziggy letting go with an ear-splitting, wild, howling banshee blues shout.

The next morning he really was gone.

Deejo and I waited for a letter, but neither of us heard anything.

'He must have taken the vow of silence as far as writing, too,' Deejo figured.

I did get a postcard from Pepper sometime during the winter, a scene of a tropical sunset over the ocean, and scrawled on the back the message 'Not diggin' much beauty lately'. There was no return address, and since Pepper's parents had divorced and moved out of the projects I couldn't track him down.

There was a lot of moving going on. Deejo moved out after a huge fight with his old man. Deej's father had lined up a production-line job for Deejo at the factory where he'd worked for twenty-three years. When Deej didn't show up for work the first day his father came home in a rage and tried to tear Deejo's beard off. So Deej moved in with his older brother, Sal, who'd just gotten out of the navy and had a bachelor pad near Old Town. The only trouble for Deejo was that he had to move back home on weekends, when Sal needed more privacy.

Deejo was the last of the Blighters still playing. He actually bought a guitar, though not an electric one. He spent a lot of time listening to scratchy old 78s of black singers whose first names all seemed to begin with either Blind or Sonny. Deejo even cut his own record, a paper-thin 45 smelling of acetate, with one side blank. He took copies of it around to all the bars that the guys from Korea used to rule and talked the bartenders into putting his record on the jukebox. Those bars had quietened down. There weren't enough guys from the Korean days still drinking to field the corner softball teams any more. The guys who had become regulars were in pretty sad shape. They sat around, endlessly discussing baseball and throwing dice for drinks. The jukeboxes that had once blasted The Platters and Buddy Holly had filled up with polkas again and with Mexican songs that sounded suspiciously like polkas. Deejo's record was usually stuck between Frank Sinatra and Ray Charles. Deej would insert a little card handprinted in ballpoint pen: HARD-HEARTED WOMAN BY JOEY DECAMPO.

It was a song he'd written. Deejo's hair was longer than ever, his Vandyke had filled in, and he'd taken to wearing sunglasses and huaraches. Sometimes he would show up with one of the girls from Loop Junior College, which was where he was going to school. He'd bring her into the Edelweiss or the Carta Blanca, usually a wispy blonde with scared eyes, and order a couple of drafts. The bartender or one of us at the bar would pick up Deejo's cue and say, 'Hey, how about playing that R5?' and feed the jukebox. 'Hard-hearted Woman' would come thumping out as loud as the 'She's-Too-Fat Polka', scratchy as an old 78, Deejo whining through his nose, strumming his three cords.

> Hard-hearted woman,
> Oh yeah, Lord,
> She's a hard-hearted woman,
> Uuuhhh . . .

Suddenly, despite the Delta accent, it would dawn on the girl that it was Deejo's voice. He'd kind of grin, shyly admitting that it was, his fingers on the bar tapping along in time with the song, and I wondered what she would think if she could have heard the one I wished he had recorded, the one that opened:

> The dawn rises,
> Uuuhhh,
> Like sick old men,
> Oh, Lord,
> Playing on the rooftops in their underwear,
> Yeah . . .

Back to blight.

It was a saying that faded from my vocabulary, especially

after my parents moved to Berwyn. Then, some years later, after I quit my job at UPS in order to hide out from the draft in college, the word resurfaced in an English Lit survey class. Maybe I was just more attuned to it than most people ordinarily would be. There seemed to be blight all through Dickens and Blake. The class was taught by a professor nicknamed 'the Spitter'. He loved to read aloud, and after the first time, nobody sat in the front rows. He had acquired an Oxford accent, but the more excitedly he read and spat, the more I could detect the South Side of Chicago underneath the veneer, as if his *th*'s had been worked over with a drill press. When he read us Shelley's 'To a Skylark', which began 'Hail to thee, blithe spirit', I thought he was talking about blight again until I looked it up.

One afternoon in spring I cut class and rode the Douglass Park B back. It wasn't anything I planned. I just wanted to go somewhere and think. The draft board was getting ready to reclassify me and I needed to figure out why I felt like telling them to get rammed rather than just saying the hell with it and doing what they told me to do. But instead of thinking, I ended up remembering my early trips back from the North Side, when I used to pretend that Debbie Weiss was riding with me, and when I came to my stop on Twenty-second Street this time it was easier to imagine how it would have looked to her – small, surprisingly small in the way one is surprised returning to an old grade-school classroom.

I hadn't been back for a couple of years. The neighbourhood was mostly Mexican now, with many of the signs over the stores in Spanish, but the bars were still called the Edelweiss Tap and the Budweiser Lounge. Deejo and I had lost touch, but I heard that he'd been drafted. I made the rounds of some of the bars looking for his song on the jukeboxes, but when I couldn't find it even in the Carta Blanca, where nothing else had changed, I gave up. I was sitting in the Carta Blanca having a last, cold *cerveza* before heading back, listening to 'CuCuRuCuCu Paloma' on the jukebox and watching the sunlight streak in through the dusty wooden blinds. Then the jukebox stopped playing, and through the open door I could hear the bells from three different churches tolling the hour. They didn't quite agree on the precise moment. Their rings overlapped and echoed one another. The streets were empty, no one home from work or school yet, and something about the overlapping of those bells made me remember how many times I'd had dreams, not prophetic ones like Ziggy's, but terrifying all the same, in which I was back in my neighbourhood, but lost, everything at once familiar and strange, and I knew if I tried to run, my feet would be like lead, and if I stepped off a curb, I'd drop through space, and then in the dream I would come to a corner that would feel so timeless and peaceful, like the Carta Blanca with the bells fading and the sunlight streaking through, that for a moment it would feel as if I'd wandered into an Official Blithe Area.

Bijou

The film that rumour has made the dernier cri of this year's festival is finally screened.

It begins without credits, challenging the audience from its opening frame. Not only has it been shot in black and white, but the black and white do not occur in usual relationships to one another. There is little grey. Ordinary light has become exotic as zebras.

Perhaps in the film's native country they are not familiar with abstract reductions such as black and white. There even vanilla ice cream is robin's egg blue, and liquorice almost amethyst when held to the sun. No matter what oppressive regime, each day vibrates with the anima of primitive paintings – continual fiesta! As ambulances siren, they flash through colour changes with the rapidity of chameleons. In the modern hospital, set like a glass mural against the sea, ceiling fans oscillate like impaled wings of flamingos above the crisp rhythm of nurses.

Black and white are not native to these latitudes. And grey requires the opaque atmosphere of Antwerp or Newcastle, Pittsburgh or Vladivostok, requires the industrial revolution, laissez-faire, imperialism, Seven Year Plan, Great Leap Forward, pollution, cold war, fallout, PCB, alienation . . .

Nor does the film appear to be alluding to the classic black-and-white films of Fritz Lang, King Vidor, Orson Welles. Nor to the social realism of the forties or neorealism of the fifties. In fact, the only acknowledged influence is an indirect one, that of an obscure poem by Victor Guzman, the late surrealist dentist of Chilpancingo.

Trees, for example, are blinding white, rather than the darknesses so often etched against a dying sky.

Shade is white.

Fruit is white.

Asphalt roads are white.

It is the windowpanes through which one sees them that

are black. Smoked with kerosene or smeared with shoe polish for secrecy or air-raid blackouts, who can determine?

It is true that at times the film closely resembles a negative – the moon a sooty zero in a silver nitrate night. But the gimmick of shooting in negative is used with restraint. It's obvious that the filmmakers are after something beyond the simple reversal of the values of light.

Take the clouds – plumed, milky black in an albino, noon sky. But are they clouds? Or the smoke from a burning village, bombs, an erupting volcano?

In another sequence, an execution, there is a close-up of bullets being x'd to make the heads dumdum. The lead is white. And later, when the flour sack hoods are removed from the prisoners, the wounds are white. The camera pans along the riddled convent wall. In the distance, mountains rise tipped with anthracite. To put it another way, black is not meant to define white, nor vice versa.

The first colour goes almost unnoticed.

The pink washrag of a cat's tongue as it grooms in the bleached shadow of the jail.

Almost unnoticed – but a subconscious shock registers through the theatre.

Gradually, it becomes apparent that tongues, only tongues, are assuming colour: dogs panting in the dust of traffic, snakes and geckos flicking from drainpipes, colour licking and poking from a thousand tiny caves.

Even tongues ordinarily colourless take on brilliance: the black lash of the butterfly uncoils azure at the flower; the cow masticating its cud lolls a tongue suddenly crimson as black jeeps siren past down the alabaster highway to the interior.

There, the guerrillas have been ambushed, surrounded, betrayed. A chopper flattens palms as it drops in CIA advisers. The camera pans the faces of the rebels in macro lens close-ups as if a boil or a louse swelling among beads of sweat might reveal a man's character; or as if white hairs sprouting from a mole, or a childhood scar beneath a stubble beard might tell his past.

And it is here that the tongues begin to obsess the camera, that the realistic soundtrack of bird caws, gunshots, shouting, machinery, is intercut with the whispered litany of Guzman's lines from *Laughing Gas: gold-dust tongues, ochre tongues eating earth, walking tongue, candy tongue, milky tongue, sleeper's tongue, passion's tongues, cankered tongues, tongues tinctured yellow, flaming tongue, hovering tongues of epiphany* . . .

The screen is nearly technicolour with tongues.

Canisters of nerve gas explode.

Then, in a sequence more excruciating than any since *The Battle of Algiers*, the guerrillas are captured. Scene follows scene documenting torture in the modern military state. Cattle prods are used for confessions, electrodes taped to eyelids, tongues, genitals.

At night, out by the black fire, the guards have begun to drink. Soon they cannot tolerate the refined torments of electricity. Fists, truncheons, empty bottles, boots pummel bone.

The prisoners refuse to talk.

Near dawn, in a drunken rage, the guards take them one by one and mock their silence by tearing out their tongues with wire snips. They are forced to kneel, mouths wedged open with a wooden stake, and tongues forceped out in a scream and dark gush of blood – blue, green, yellow, orange, violet, red tongues. The tongues are collected in a coffee can the way ears are sometimes collected, and stored on the colonel's desk. Each new victim stares at the can as he is questioned for the final time. The tongues brim over and flop to the floor and the guards pass out from drunkenness, their own tongues gaping from snoring jaws.

'Raspberry tongues,' Guzman wrote, 'the entrails of a clown.'

The audience stares in silence. Some have turned away; there have been gasps. But, on the whole, they have been conditioned to accept, almost to expect, this violence on screen. They have watched blood spurt and limbs dismembered in Peckinpah's choreographed slow motion, brains sprayed across a wall, bodies explode, monks topple in flaming gasoline, eyes gouged, chain saws buzzing through bone, decapitations in 3–D. They are not at the festival to censor but to discern: where is violence statement and where merely further exploitation? When does Art become carnography? Is this perhaps the Cinema of Cruelty?

They watch as the next morning a young private is assigned to clean up the night's excesses. He takes the coffee can to bury in the old graveyard behind the cathedral while bells chime through an intermittent hiss of wind and mewing of gulls. His shovel bites dirt and he breathes louder with every scoopful he flings over his shoulder into the blurred eye of climbing sun. He sweats, his breath becomes panting, then gagging, and suddenly he's doubled over retching into the hole, mumbling the Lord's Prayer in between spasms. Still heaving, he rises, kicks the can in, frantically raking over loose dirt, smacking it down with the flat of the shovel, raining down blows as if he were killing a snake.

The sound track cuts off.

The whump of the shovel is the last sound, though on screen the soldier continues to beat the earth.

Now the screen seems even more unrelievedly black and white – no more background strumming of guitars, no mountain flutes, birdcalls, wind, distant thunder of gunfire. Not even the unavoidable drone of a jet overhead on its way to another country. A world of action suddenly mute as Griffith's galloping Klan, as Méliès blasting off for the moon, as Chaplin twirling a cane. There is only the faint, nearly subliminal metronome of ticking sprockets audible from the projection booth in the now-silent theatre. But as the silence continues, the steady clack seems increasingly obtrusive, and the suspicion begins to arise that the racket of sprockets *is* the sound track. There's something too rickety about its clatter – a sound that evokes, perhaps by design, evenings long ago, when after the supper dishes were cleared, a father, who served as director, would set up a projector with tinny spools while children removed pictures from a wall to transform it into a screen, and then the lights would be extinguished and home movies would beam into unsteady focus – silent, unedited, the mugging face of each family member plainer than memory, appearing as they once were, startlingly young, innocent of time.

Subtitles begin to appear. Too fast to read. Partially telegraphed messages. Single words or parts of words flashed on screen: AWE DIS KER.

Static as the words, a progression of freeze-frames the bled tones of tabloid photos dissolve one into another: peasants on their way to market, slum children, children with rickets, a beggar with yaws, fruit loaders sweating at an outdoor market of gutted fish, piled monkey skulls, tourists.

In churches and universities, on corners beneath bug-clouded lights, people are opening their mouths to speak, but everywhere it appears the mouths are black, gaping holes. There is only continual silence, intercut dissolves, subtitles flashing on and off, sometimes like fading neon signs, sometimes like a collage, commenting on the action (WHERE THERE IS NO FREEDOM WORDS FILL THE MOUTH WITH BLOOD).

The footage continues running faster, almost blurred, as if a documentary were being filmed from a speeding train – assassinations, bombed motorcades, bombed restaurants, bombed schools, strikes, soldiers firing into a crowd, smouldering bodies, mothers in mourning, black coffins, black flags, the revolt of students, the revolt of the army, newspaper offices ransacked by Blackshirts, presses smashed, mobs, fires, men hauled out into the street and lynched from lampposts before the shattered windows of the capitol, streets littered with books from the gutted library, and all the while a sound rising from underground as if the clatter of sprockets has become a subway train roaring down a tunnel, its brake shoe scraping metal from track, metal on metal whining into a siren-pitched screech (EVEN THE HANGED HAVE NO TONGUES TO PROTRUDE!).

The house lights flick on. The audience, many of them North Americans, is stunned. Some talk as if making sure they still can. Some weep. Others leave the theatre cursing – what? The film? The oppressors? It isn't clear. Someone in the balcony shouts, 'Bravo!' And another in front, 'Long live the revolution!' People are up from their seats and applauding as if it were a live presentation.

'The ultimate praise for a film,' one critic is heard to remark on his way to the lobby, 'is to treat it as if it were a play deserving curtain calls, to confuse celluloid images with flesh and blood, to transcend the isolated private dream state of the movie theatre by merging with the mass in simple applause.'

Tomorrow the Arts sections will carry rave reviews: *'a new and daring fusion of avant-garde technique with documentary sensibility . . .'*

A journalist for the *Voice* will write: 'Uncompromisingly powerful, it demands to be seen, though a film like this might be better kept secret, protected from the corrupting influence of the Hollywood glamour and promotion machine, the invidious American penchant for reducing substance to marketable style.'

While another reviewer, writing for a more conservative publication, will comment: 'This looks like the year for Terrorist Cinema. Another fad pretending to usher in a change of consciousness but lacking the moral imperative of the civil rights movement and peace marches that launched the 60s.'

The audience files out through the mirrored lobby, backs turned on the posters of stars, out under the winking marquee, squinting at the pink smoulder of dusk. Behind them, on the silver screen in the houselit theatre, a final frame hovers like the ghost image phenomena sometimes haunting TV screens, a blown-up image that could only have been shot by a camera implanted in a mouth, of an indigo tongue working at a husk of popcorn stuck in a gold-capped molar.

And across this image a delayed rolling of credits begins: the names of actors, writers, cameramen, assistant director, director, producer, editors, sound, music, make-up, gaffers, soldiers, officers, generals, politicians – a cast of thousands – workers, students, peasants, the audience, the victims, the maimed, the maddened, the myriad names of the dead.

Nighthawks

SILHOUETTES

The alley became a river in the rain – a river with currents of clattering cans and a floe of cardboard. The boy would wake to the headlights of lightning spraying the walls of his small room, and lie listening to the single note of drops pinging the metal hood of a blue bulb that glowed above a garage door. Finally, he'd go to the window and look down.

The blue bulb gave the rain a bluish gleam. Rotted drainpipes gushed like dislocated fountains. Flooded tar roofs seemed to tilt, spilling waterfalls through sluices of fire escapes.

At the mouth of the alley, a streetlight swirled, slowly disappearing down the whirlpool of a sewer. And beyond the aura of the streetlight, on a street whose name and numbers had been washed away, shadows moved aimlessly through rain. Tonight, they had their collars raised. He could catch glimpses of them passing by the mouth of the alley. Even when he couldn't see them, he could sense their presence: shapes that he'd named *silhouettes*, shadows that threw shadows, that inhabited the hourless times of night stolen from dreams when it seemed to the boy as if he'd been summoned awake only to lie there wondering for what reason he'd been summoned. He couldn't remember when he'd become aware of their presence, or when he first thought of them as silhouettes. He had never thought of them as anything else – not ghosts, or spirits. Silhouettes were enough to haunt him.

Others had their own names for shadows. Downstairs, the Ukrainian kid who practised the violin slept with his arms extended in the shape of a cross to ward off the dead. Across the alley, in a basement flat, a Puerto Rican girl played as if begging before a vigil candle flickering the picture of the Virgin on her bureau, and sometimes the smell of the coal furnace behind the grate that opened on purgatory would fade into a faint scent of roses. There were guys who carried knives taped inside their socks to school, who still slept at the edges of their beds in order to leave room for their guardian angels. There were girls who wore mascara like a mask, who swore they'd seen Niña, the beautiful high school girl who had plunged from a roof one summer night. Niña had sneaked out that night to meet her boyfriend, Choco, a kid who played the conga and had gone AWOL to see her. Choco, his conga drum strapped over his shoulder, had led her up a fire escape to the roof where he slept on an old mattress. They took angel dust, which made the moon seem near enough to step on to from the roof. The girls said that on moonlit nights music would wake them – a song whose beat they all recognized, though none of them could hum back its melody – and they would see a *fantasma*, Niña, her hair flying and blouse billowing open, falling past their windows, but falling so slowly that it seemed as if it might take forever for her to hit the street.

And there were apparitions in broad daylight: the mute knife grinder pushing his screeching whetstone up alleys; the pedlars with clothesline whips flicking blinded horses as their wagons rumbled by tottering under jumbled loads of uprooted cellars and toppled attics; the hunchbacked woman who walked bent from the waist as if doubled over by the weight of the lifetime's length of filthy grey hair that streamed from her bowed head and swept the pavement before her.

They seemed part of the streets. If anyone noticed, it was only to glance away, but the boy secretly regarded them as if he were witnessing refugees from a cruel fairy tale groping their way through the ordinary world. He wondered where they disappeared to, where they slept at night, and what they dreamed.

Beside the daytime apparitions, the silhouettes seemed nearly invisible, camouflaged by night, shadows who'd broken their connections to whatever had thrown them and now wandered free, like dreams escaped from dreamers. They emerged from viaducts on nights when viaducts exhaled fog and manhole covers steamed. Where they stood in dripping doorways, they made the doorways darker. When they stepped into the open – shadows, but shadows no longer supported by walls or trailed along pavement – the rain, slanting through the glow of streetlights and shop signs, beaded off them like molten electricity. Oncoming headlights bent around them; flashes of lightning traced their outlines. The boy could sense them moving along the street and wondered if tonight was the night for which he'd been summoned awake, when the silhouettes would finally come up the alley, past the guardian streetlight now swirling and sinking, and assemble below his window, looking up at his face pressed against the spattered pane, their eyes and mouths opened on to darkness like the centres of guitars.

Love, it's such a night, laced with running water, irreparable, riddled with a million leaks. A night shaped like a shadow thrown by your absence. Every crack trickles, every overhang drips. The screech of nighthawks has been replaced by the splash of rain. The rain falls from the height of streetlights. Each drop contains its own blue bulb.

LAUGHTER

I knew a girl who laughed in her sleep. She had been in the States only a year and I wondered if being foreign didn't have something to do with her laughing that way. Her eyes were a gold-flecked green more suited to cats, and ringed with the longest lashes I'd ever seen. In the right light her half-lowered lashes threw small shadows across her face. She didn't look American yet. Once I woke her and asked what was so funny. She seemed confused and a little embarrassed, and I never asked her again.

We met at the ice-cream factory where I worked the summer between high school and college. She was the first girl I was *serious* about. I felt too young to be serious – a feeling I kept secret.

She kept me a secret from her Uncle Tassos.

Her uncle was the one who had brought her over and got her the job at the ice-cream factory. She worked on the bar tank line with the other, mostly foreign women, sitting before a conveyor belt and packing Popsicles, Fudgsicles, Creamsicles, and Dreamsicles into freezer cartons. At the end of the day her hands were stiff with cold and her fingers stained the colours of whatever flavours had been run.

Her Uncle Tassos worked on the ore boats out of Calumet Harbour. He would be away for two-week runs, and then off work for five days straight. When he was back home the only place I would get to see her was at the factory. I was still living with my parents and began to feel ashamed for not having my own place to take her. When Uncle Tassos left with the barges again – as safely off somewhere around Petoskey as if he'd sailed for Peloponnesus – she'd sneak me up to her one-room apartment that overlooked Halsted Street.

It was an old neighbourhood that Mayor Daley, despite his campaign promises, was preparing to demolish to make way for a new university. But life went on that summer as it always had – daily newspapers printed in strange alphabets; nuts, cheeses, dried cod sold in the streets; the scent of crushed lemons from the bakery that made lemon ice; Greek music skirling from the restaurant downstairs. And once she'd let me in I wouldn't leave until morning, but sometimes, in the middle of the night, I'd have to get up and pace while the dark room filled with laughter.

EVERYTHING

A couple of months after he'd married Joan, the phone rang in the middle of the night. The phone was in the kitchen and seemed to ring through the dark apartment like an alarm. He had always been afraid of phone calls at that hour. They triggered a dread in him that something terrible had happened, and he almost believed that if he didn't answer, whatever catastrophe had occurred might be undone by morning. But this time he leapt to answer. It was better to get the news first hand than to listen to his new wife answer the phone and then break into sobs.

'Hello,' he said, trying to sound composed.

'Yellow. Guess who?'

'I know who.'

'Guess what?'

'I give.'

'I'm tripping on MDA.'

'Oh.'

"Ecstasy", you know, the "Love Drug". Whatsamatter? You don't read *Newsweek* and keep up?'

'My subscription ran out.'

'It's a body rush. Incredibly erotic. I'm so horny – climbing the walls.'

'Nice of you to call and let me know.'

'It heightens memory, too. Hey, I'm still a little nuts about you. Is that Joanie flushing the toilet?'

'Yes.'

'She probably wants to know who's on the phone.'

'Exactly right.'

'That's why you're talking to me in that funny flat voice. So quiet. Not saying my name. You didn't used to be such a monosyllabic type of guy. Well, at least say something.'

'Like what?'

'Like what are you wearing? Cute little seersucker pyjamas?'

'Look, I should hang up.'

'You're supposed to talk people down when they're tripping. I could be in terrible trouble here. Remember that one time we did mushrooms? The night you said I turned into Cleopatra. You said it was the pinnacle.'

'We were in college, for chrissake.'

'I thought I'd try something like that one more time, you know, like they shout at the end of Basie's "April in Paris" – One more time!' – a tribute to the old days. I liked myself better then. Liked you better, too.'

'I don't want to be the one to hang up, OK?'

'You never did. Guess what I'm wearing? Guess how I look on the other end of this telephone line. Listen, I'll rub the phone down my body. See if you can hear . . . did you hear anything?'

'No.'

'Well, press your ear against the receiver. You didn't hear that? You didn't hear hair? What part of my body do you think you're talking to right now? Say something soft and breathy. Blow warm air into the phone. Pretend you're a mad breather.'

'It's late. You should go to sleep.'

'Come over.'

'I can't.'

'Baby, come see me. Tell her it's a buddy with a flat tyre.'

'I can't.'

'Baby, oh baby, I need you so much tonight. Baby, you gotta fix my flat tyre.'

'It's 3 a.m.'

'Please. Don't make me beg. Come over . . . we'll do *everything*.'

'How many other people have you called besides me?'

'Only one.'

KILLING TIME

Between job interviews, I'd wander around the Art Institute, killing time. The Art Institute was on the park side of Michigan Avenue, across the street from the towering office buildings in which the employment agencies were situated. It felt soothing to drift among the paintings. Several had begun to feel like old friends. Visiting them beat sitting over a lukewarm coffee in some greasy spoon, spending another afternoon studying not only the Want Ads, but the faces of the others at the counter who sat nursing their coffees as they grimly studied the Want Ads, too. By now, I spotted their faces everywhere. I'd become aware of an invisible army armed with Want Ads, pounding the pavement, knocking on doors, hoping opportunity would answer. It was an army without the consolation of camaraderie. I'd learned to recognize its unconscious salutes, its uniforms and ranks and outposts – personnel offices, coffee shops, and stands of public phones – from which its lonely campaigns were launched. I'd been looking for a job for a month and was beginning to feel desperate.

The Art Institute was my base of operations. Its public phones were usually empty, and its restroom was modern and clean with a full-length mirror perfect for last minute inspections before heading out on an interview.

My first couple weeks of job hunting I'd hung out at the Public Library. Unlike the Art Institute, admission to the library was free. But the longer I'd gone without work, the more an old dread crept back into me: a feeling from high school, a memory of dreary Saturdays when, loaded with note cards for research papers that I was hopelessly behind on, I'd enter the Public Library only to end up wandering around lost, wasting the day. I remembered how, the summer before I'd started high school, my father had insisted that I spend a week at the Library researching professions and the biographies of successful tycoons so that I'd have some sense of direction during my high school years and not live up to his nickname for me: The Dreamer. And I recalled how rather than doing what he'd asked, I'd only pretended to go to the Library and instead had used the money he'd given me on movies and record shops. Now, his dire predictions seemed to be coming true. My money was running out; I couldn't find a job. After a week of hanging around the Library, I began to recognize the same set of regulars – people who carried their possessions in bags, or wore them all at once, who seemed to be living in the library stacks. Soon I expected them to begin winking at me, giving me secret greetings I didn't want to recognize.

The public phones in the Public Library were always busy. In the old restrooms fluids pooled on the cracked terrazzo, and the homeless hung around inside, smoking, sometimes washing out their clothes in the plugged sinks. Even on the brightest days I began to notice the grey, gloomy cast of the marble corridors and flights of stairs. The reading rooms, dominated by the glow of green-shaded desk lamps, seemed worn as old railroad stations. There was a smell of musty pulp, of thumbed cloth covers, of too much print. At the long reading tables I could spot the displaced and dispossessed drowsing over enormous tomes or reading aloud to themselves as if engaged in debates with the complete works of Marx and Engels, Spengler, Tolstoy, Schopenhauer, while outside the windows cooing pigeons paced back and forth along the crusted slate ledges.

The Art Institute, by contrast, seemed flooded with light – not merely the light streaming from skylights or the track lights focused on paintings. The paintings themselves appeared to throw an internal light the way that oaks and maples seem aflame in fall, from the inside out. My favourite painters were the Impressionists. On days when it seemed as if I'd never find a job, when I was feeling desperate, I'd stand before their paintings and stare at them until it seemed I could almost step into their world, that if I closed my eyes and then opened them I'd find myself waking under the red coverlet in Van Gogh's *Bedroom at Arles*. I would open my eyes in a room of pastel light to find that one of Degas' dancers, who had been sleeping beside me, had discarded her chemise and was stepping into her morning bath. Or I would awaken already strolling without a care in and out of patches of precise shade, one of the Sunday crowd along the river on the island of *La Grande Jatte*. I wanted to be some-where else, to be a dark blur waiting to board the Normandy train in the smoke-smudged *Saint-Lazare* station; I wanted a ticket out of my life, to be riding a train whose windows slid past a landscape of haystacks in winter fields. It might be taking me to the beach of *Saint-Adresse* where the fishing boats have been drawn up on to the sand and a man with a telescope and his daughter by his side looks out to sea, or to *Pourville* where the wind gusts along the cliff walk and a woman opens an orange parasol while white sails hardly taller than the white capped waves pitch on the blue-green sea.

Yet, I would always end my walk through the paintings standing before the diner in Edward Hopper's *Nighthawks*. Perhaps I needed its darkness to balance the radiance of the other paintings. It was night in Hopper's painting; the diner illuminated the dark city corner with a light it didn't seem capable of throwing on its own. Three customers sat at the counter as if waiting, not for something to begin, but rather to end, and I knew how effortless it would be to open my eyes and find myself waiting there, too.

INSOMNIA

There is an all-night diner to which, sooner or later, insom-niacs find their way. In winter, when snow drifts over curbs, they cross the trampled intersections until they come upon footprints that perfectly fit their shoes and lead them there. On nights like this in summer, the diner's lighted corner draws them to its otherwise dark neighbourhood like moths.

They come from all over the city and beyond – from farm towns in Ohio, Iowa, and Indiana, crossing the unlit prairie, arriving at vacant train stations and bus terminals, then making their way towards that illuminated corner as if it's what they left home to find – a joint that asks no questions and never closes, a place to sit awhile for the price of a cup of coffee.

From the size of the two nickel-plated urns, the place must serve a lot of coffee. And yet it looks almost deserted now – only a couple, stretching out the night, at one end of the counter, and Ray, the blond counterman, bending to rinse out a cup, and a guy in a hat sitting alone with his back to the window. It never gets crowded. They file in and out – the night shift, cabbies, drunks, sometimes a cop, loners mostly – there's never telling who might step through the door.

Earlier this evening, when most of the stools were taken, a woman in heels and a summer dress stopped outside and stood peering in as if looking for someone. At least it seemed that way at first, before it became clear that she'd only stopped to fix her make-up in the reflection of the plate glass. There were mostly men at the counter, and they pretended not to watch as she stroked a comb through her hair. She seemed so unconscious of their presence that watching her would have been like spying on a woman before her own bedroom mirror. Yet, though they didn't stare, the men on the other side of the glass wondered about her; they wondered who it was she had stopped to make herself still prettier for, or if she'd just been with someone and was on her way back to someone else. When she stepped away from the window, the reflection of the lipstick she'd applied seemed to remain hovering on the glass like the impression of a kiss. The men in the diner pretended to ignore this, too, although in its way the reflected kiss was no less miraculous than the tears rolling down the cheeks of a parish church's plaster Virgin, that crowds will line up for blocks to see. The woman stepped beyond the light of the diner and disappeared down a street of shadowy windows. After a while, the reflected kiss disappeared too – who knows where – simply dissolving into darkness, or perhaps reappearing blocks away on the glass door of a corner phone booth, where an AWOL soldier named Choco, disoriented by grief as if it were a drug, has wedged inside with his conga drum because he has nowhere else to go. He sits dazed, as if waiting for an oracle to call, and doesn't notice the kiss on the glass door among the graffitied lipsticked initials and eyebrow-pencilled numbers. And when he begins to beat the booth, his open palm becom-ing a bloody handprint on cracked glass, the kiss vanishes again. Perhaps the kiss crosses the city, riding the blurred window of a subway, or of a cab running red lights down a boulevard of black glass . . .

That couple, stretching out the night at the end of the counter, has been in here before. They sit side by side like lovers, and yet there's something detached enough about them so that they could pass for strangers. It might be the way they sit staring ahead rather than looking at each other, or that their hands on the counter-top don't quite touch, but it's passion, not indifference, that is responsible for that. Tonight, at this late hour, they've wandered in feeling empty, a little drained by the mutual obsession that keeps them awake. The insomnia they share is the insomnia of desire. Walking here along deserted streets. they noticed this neigh-bourhood of shadowy windows was missing a moon, and so they began to make up a moon between them: solid as a cue ball; translucent and webbed with fine cracks, like bone china; cloudy, the bleached white of a bra tumbling in a dryer. Now, under a fluorescence that makes her arms appear too bare and her dress shimmer from rose to salmon to shades of red for which there's no approximation, they've fallen silent. He's smoking. She dreamily studies a match-book from some other place where they sat like this together killing time.

And Ray, he's been working here long enough to seem like part of the decor. The white of his uniform intensifies the lighting. He keeps the coffee urns gleaming and the counter swabbed. The cocky angle of the white paper cap perched on his blond head makes him look like a kid, but he's older than people take him for; friendly, but as much a loner as anyone he serves. Working nights might seem to grant him an immunity from insomnia, but job or not, he's here like the rest of them, awake. What he does during the day is anybody's guess. He disappears behind one of those shadowed, black, upper-storey windows, draws the shade, and the rising sun beats it gold. The restless sound of traffic carries up to him from the street. Perhaps it's something other than insomnia, to lie listening to children yelling as if they've re-created light; to try to dream, but succeed only in remembering; to toss and sweat in a dirty paste of sheets, while the drone of a ball game is gradually replaced by the buzz of a fly – a fly buzzing like the empty frequencies between stations as its shadow grows enormous between the shade and windowpane. Is it insomnia for a man to wad his ears with the cotton from a pill bottle, to mask his eyes with blinders, and press a stale pillow over his head, praying for another day to burn down, so he can wake into another night?

The guy with his back to the window has been sitting there a long time nursing his mug of java. Ray, stooping to rinse out a cup, avoids looking in his direction. There's something about the way the guy's hat shadows his face, about his shoulders, hunched as if braced for another blow, about his eyes plumbing the depths of his coffee, that discourages conversation. It would be like trying to make small talk with a hit man. Besides, the guy has been mumbling to himself, his mouth moving as if chewing something too bitter to swallow. If he's thinking about women, he must be counting up all the times they've cheated on him. If he's thinking about work, he's adding up the brutal ways of saying they're taking your job: *fired*, *canned*, *sacked*, *axed*, *terminated*. He's dwelling on the *lost* in 'lost his job' – *lost* – as if the eight hours of sweat at the heart of each day could be misplaced. Why call it *lost* if it's been taken from you? *Lost* is a lie, and without such lies the streets would be crowded with assassins. But his incessant tallies, his lists of lies and grievances, his roll call of betrayals, have added up to nothing but insomnia. Insomnia is a private score he has, so far, settled only with himself; it's the time he does each night for his own betrayals, his own petty offences of failure, hard luck, desperation. And insomnia is also the threat of unnamed crimes still more menacing. After dark, he carries it beside his heart, concealed like a weapon. His back is turned, he keeps his hat brim lowered, to hide the bloodshot fire of insomnia raging in his eyes.

And finally, what about the empty water glass set on the counter before an empty stool? No tip beside it. Not that anyone but Ray paid any attention to the person who sat there and ordered merely water. Only Ray recognized immediately that a sleepwalker had entered the diner. They wander in occasionally, and Ray has learned to recognize their habits – how they order nothing but water, and never tip. At first, Ray would serve them only what they asked for, but now sometimes he buys them a coffee on the house. He isn't sure himself whether he does it out of kindness or cruelty. He'd like to think it's kindness, that if it were he who was wandering the streets asleep, he'd be grateful to anyone who tried to help. But Ray's not certain. He's heard it can be dangerous to tamper with sleepwalkers, that their souls can leave their bodies, and so Ray always braces for that moment when the steaming coffee first touches their lips and they wake.

The sleepwalker's eyes roll open. He glances around wildly as if he doesn't realize what's happened or even that he is awake. Fluorescence scalds his pupils as the coffee did his lips. The diner seems frozen in the blinding pop of a flash-bulb that refuses to fade – a glare as stark as the illumination of certain dreams, brighter for being framed by night. In that paralysing light, the sleepwalker sees the lovers at the other end of the counter, with their bleached-out, hawk-featured faces staring straight ahead as if they're in a trance; and Ray, glancing away, caught in the act of dunking a cup under the counter as if disposing of evidence; and the hit man in the shadowy hat, mumbling to no one, his eyes smouldering like cinders. Stunned as he is, the sleepwalker can feel the paralysis of the diner drawing him in as if he belongs there, too. With a half spin, he shoves away from the counter, rises from his stool and, leaving no tip, staggers for the door. And as he pushes out, something snaps him fully awake – maybe the night air, or the slap of a patty hitting the grill, or his soul returning to him from shadows. He stands outside the diner, within the perimeter of its aura, and stares down a street of dark windows, wondering which way he's come from, which way to go. In the diner's almost phosphorescent glow, the deserted street looks like pavement might on the moon. Above the roofs, he can see the moon the lovers at the end of the counter left behind, no longer newly minted, surrounded by the same aura as the diner, waiting faithfully like a dog for them to re-emerge. In their absence, it's gone through phases, diminishing like a stalled traffic light in the rearview mirror of a taxi. Now it's less than a crescent, less than a smudged thumbprint of mother-of-pearl – only a shimmer like the glint of neon on the surface of a cup of black coffee. The bitter taste of coffee still burns his tongue. He can feel his nerves jumping and his heart starting to race as if that mere sip in the diner has stoked him with the stamina of caffeine, and converted him from sleepwalking to insomnia. From somewhere in the sky above the diner, he hears the screech of a single nighthawk, and suddenly he's happy. It seems to him enough to simply be awake like that bird soaring in the darkness that sleepers have abandoned, to be walking away from the lighted corner, down the empty, silent streets they've left to him, whistling as he passes dark windows, not sure where he's going, and in no hurry to find out. It's the middle of the night, and tomorrow seems as if it's still 93 million miles away.

GOLD COAST

They wake simultaneously in a hotel room on the thirty-seventh floor, neither of them sure of the time, both still a little drunk, a little numb from the silence that has grown between them.

'Look at the sky! Look at the light!' she exclaims.

He's already seen it – how could he not? The enormous bed faces a wall of windows. They've left the drapes open. The wall of windows now seems like a wall of sky, almost indigo, shot with iridescence as if veins of a newly discovered precious mineral have been exposed. It isn't dawn yet. It's still a gradation of night, but night with tomorrow already luminous behind it like the silver behind the glass of a cobalt mirror.

He can see the sky reflected in the windows of all the surrounding buildings that tower up to form the glass cliffs of the gold coast they've drifted to. He knows that every city has such strips, and he distrusts them. No matter how authentically elegant they might appear, he thinks of them as illusory, removed from the real life of cities, as places that are really no place, reflections floating like illuminated scum on the surface of a river. He remembers how, as teenagers, he and a buddy spent their nights exploring the gold coast in the city they'd grown up in, and the mixture of awe and contempt they'd felt towards it.

He no longer feels superior to gold coasts. He wonders how many of his fellow sleepers are sitting up as he is, silently peering out of high-rise rooms in which the drapes have been drawn open on tremendous windows, windows for giants, scaled to encompass the winking horizon of the city. He both envies those still sleeping peacefully and pities them for missing this nameless, early sky which he knows already will be more unforgettable than any dawn he's ever seen. He wonders which of those two emotions the future will reveal as the more accurate. Once, shortly after they'd become lovers, she told him, 'I'm not sure if meeting you has been the most lucky or unlucky thing that's ever happened to me.'

He had laughed.

'I wasn't kidding,' she said.

'I know,' he said. 'I'm only laughing because that's exactly what I was thinking about meeting you.'

'See. Maybe that's what happens when it's fate. One always feels what the other is feeling, at the same time, together.' She laughed too.

'Kind of emotional telepathy, eh?'

' "Emotional" makes it sound too *glandular*,' she said, rolling her eyes, speaking in the teasing way she had that made for private jokes between them. 'I'm not talking about something in the *glands;* I'm talking about something in the stars.'

Now, beside him in bed, she whispers, 'Why did we have to see this together?' It isn't said cruelly. He understands what she means. She means they've seen this unsuspected sky only because of each other; that it's something more between them to remember. And he knows that he doesn't need to answer, that it's as if he's merely overheard her speaking to herself, almost as if he isn't there any longer, as if she's awakened alone, at an unknown hour, along a gold coast.

TRANSPORT

A kiss crosses the city. It rides a glass streetcar that showers blue electric sparks along the ghost of a track – a track paved over in childhood – the line that she and her mother used to take downtown.

A kiss crosses the city, revolves through a lobby door into a rainy night, catches a cab along a boulevard of black glass, and, running red lights, dissolves behind the open fans of wiper blades.

Rain spirals colourlessly out of the dark, darkens all it touches and makes it gleam.

Her kiss crosses the city, enters a subway tunnel that descends at this deserted hour like a channel through an underground world. It's timeless there, always night, as if the planet doesn't turn below the street. At the mouth of the station stands a kid who's gone AWOL and now has nowhere else to go, a young conga drummer, a *congacero*, wearing a fatigue jacket and beating his drum. He has the pigeons up past their bedtime doing the mambo. He leaves his cap of small change behind him on the pavement and steps on to an escalator that carries him down in time to the tock of his drum. The more fervently the *congacero* drums, the deeper the escalator conveys him. He has it doing a rumba, a cha-cha-cha, a *guanguanco*, and finally, possessed, unable to fold back upon itself, the escalator becomes a staircase flowing like quicksilver, a shimmering waterfall, an anaconda slithering through the kingdom of sleep. It will transport him deeper than sleep, deeper than dreams, than nightmares, than the nod of junkies, than comas, until he steps off on to the platform where the newly dead, their souls still shaped like their bodies, mill about in confusion, waiting to be taken to their next destination.

'Is anyone in charge here?' the *congacero* asks, the way a foreigner in a city seeks directions. Despite the mob of souls, his voice echoes as if he's called into a void. He drums now to invoke whatever spirit governs this place, a beat so compelling that the arhythmic dead begin to sway as if they feel the accompaniment of their own hearts again.

'*Iku la tigwa un bai bai*,' he chants over his drumbeat, magic words in an ancient tongue that, he's been taught, will beckon the *iku*, his dead ancestors, who might intercede for him. But the only response is the hollow silence that his drum continues to punctuate.

The loss of the woman he has descended here to find has taught him that eternity is not a presence, but an absence. His drum shapes silence into time, keeping time where there is none to keep. Time is his song and his power. Draughts from the tunnels swirl about him. In spite of the bone-deep dampness, he's begun to sweat. Sweat, impossible here as tears, patters the drumskin that he leans above with his eyes closed and drumming hands nearly invisible.

The dead file by dancing jerkily like marionettes, but he doesn't notice. They stream around him like a rush-hour crowd past a street musician, a musician so absorbed in his intricate rhythms that he's forgotten the street, and worse, has forgotten how dangerous losing one's street sense can be. Possessed by his own drumming, he's become infused with forgetfulness. He has forgotten to drum in supplication to whatever spirit governs this place. He has forgotten to drum for the *iku*. He has forgotten to dedicate his drumming to his patron saint and guardian, Elleggua, whose necklace of sacred cowrie shells he wears under his fatigue jacket, entangled with his dog tags.

It is for Elleggua, the trickster, Master of Doors and Crossroads, that he should be drumming. Instead, he now drums solely for his lost love, the girl, who, legends say, falls endlessly. One of her perfumed black nylons is knotted around

his head like a sweatband. He has refused to allow his longing for her to turn to grief. The rhythm he weaves for her
has never been played before – a slap and swipe of fingertips
and palms on the drumskin that evokes the sounds their
sweating bodies made against one another. Its ebb and flow
is like the lilt of a melody.

His drum song is amplified by the tunnels. Its echoes
return delayed almost as if someone far off is at last respond-
ing. His conga answers its own echoes. His blurred hands
pound still faster and the echoes multiply, first, into a trio
of sacred *bata* drummers, and then into a corps of drummers.
He disperses his drum corps in search of her. Their frenzied
drumming reverberates down every tunnel as if time is pulsing through the underground like blood, and finally, still
dazed, she steps summoned from shadow.

He leads her back from the underground. She follows each
beat of his conga as if retracing the footprints of a complicated
dance step. The way they walk to the rhythm makes it look
as if their hips are leading them. Death has not disfigured
her beauty, and yet she wears her youthfulness like a mask.
Beneath it, her eyes seem glazed, gazing inward as if completely self-absorbed in her still new, utter lack of self. She
is serene and silent as he's never seen her. What's been done
to you already? he wants to cry, but says nothing. Having
glanced at her once, he can't look back at her again until
they have returned to the world of sunlight and substance –
a world where sparrows twitter in the sapling that has
insisted on sprouting from the rubble of a vacant lot, and
the only shadows are those of green awnings unfurled above
stands of fruits and flowers.

Even in high heels, she floats so lightly that her footfalls
aren't audible above the scurrying of rats. Yet, he can't look
back to be sure she is following, perhaps because with each
step her renunciation of death makes her more terrifyingly
beautiful. Or perhaps he doesn't dare to meet her inwardly
gazing eyes for fear they will distract him from the steady,
urgent domination of his beat. If his faith in his power to
keep time here in the confines of eternity is shaken and his
beat disrupted for even a moment they will both be lost.

Think only of light, little dove, he wishes to tell her. Open your memory as if you've just awakened and are slowly drawing a window shade up on noon. You'll return to who you were that moment when I first saw you standing in a doorway, sunlight streaming through your dress, illuminating your legs, the lace petals of your underclothes. In broad daylight, I could see the shadows of your breasts as if my eyes had special power.

But when they reach the knot of tunnels, the confluence of steel and slime where subway track and sewers interconnect, he stops. Still drumming, he stands otherwise motionless at the junction where sinkholes bottom out, and dry wells, abandoned mine shafts, and caverns intersect, then burrow off in all directions. The corridors are dark, a labyrinth of catacombs dropping into chasms and black canyons. His drumbeats collide with blind alleys and dead ends, and the cacophony of so many ricocheting echoes overwhelms him. Suddenly, his hands are confused; he's not aware at first that they've dropped silently to his sides. The drumming continues without him – incessant, chaotic, shattering time rather than keeping it. Where is his guardian, Elleggua, Master of Crossroads, who should have been his guide? If one's patron saint is a trickster, must his blessing be a trick? He looks back to tell her he's lost, but she's no longer there behind him. And when he turns again, she is standing before him as if she has been leading them, as if she is the one who has led them here. He follows her now, his drum dragging behind him, his eyes on her back as they move off deeper into the twisting passageways. Slowly, he begins to realize that from the start he has not been the one who has done the summoning.

The kiss, blurred on the window of a subway car, rockets by them down a tunnel lit by cobalt switches. The tunnel walls are stained with seepage where the train crosses beneath the river. The conductor's voice of rattling static calls out the stops where memories disembark and passion and desire are left behind. The walls of the stations the train rushes by are graffitied with names, dates, and epitaphs. The train hurtles past the station where those who died before their time now stand patiently waiting, and past the station of those who waited too long to die. It passes the station of those who died for love, and the jammed station of those who died for lack of love. A cavalcade of shadows open their eyes an instant and reach out to touch the kiss, to catch it on their extended fingertips – fingertips from which the prints have vanished – but the train is already gone, leaving them behind. Tonight, there's no stopping for loneliness or grief. The third rail, stretched thin, tuned like the string of a violin, senses the ineffable weight of the kiss and seems to shoot forward. Charged with current, the third rail does not belong to the kingdom of the dead, and the kiss follows its path as if tracing a silver thread out of a maze.

A kiss crosses the city. It travels along streets named for coasts – North Shore, Lakeside, Waveland, Surf – that echo as if paved with wet tile. Above the streetlights, nighthawks wheel, yiping like gulls. Beneath windowsills, the shadowy mark of the last tide fades like an impression of elastic on a bare waist.

The kiss crosses the city, floating facedown like a reflection over the dreamers gazing up from a neighbourhood of flooded basements and attics. Behind grated shop windows, the mannequins are mermaids; each night they re-enter the sea as if drawing a zipper down the spine of a blue-green gown.

Her kiss crosses the city along a bridge arched like the bluest note of a saxophone, an unfinished bridge extending out over a night sea of sweet water. The beacon revolving at its end may be the dome of a squad car or the lantern of a fisherman. Trailing less shadow than a fish, her kiss slips undetected past lamps, past the flashlights of night-watchmen, past gates, alarms, curfews. Not even the lips it's meant for feel the secret entry of her tongue, the scrape of her teeth, or, when she pulls away, the clinging thread of briny spit.

THE RIVER

In the rain, the alley becomes a river that winds through sleepers. Lovers listen to it flow through the dark – or so a man unable to sleep imagines. He can almost hear the river too, although he knows that listening for it may merely be a way of occupying his mind, which should be dreaming.

There may be no lovers at all. Even if there are, they may be asleep with mouths opened and backs turned to each other.

It wouldn't be the first time he's measured his life by imagining lovers. He remembers, on a morning when he was younger, standing at the window of the copy room in the high-rise office building in which he worked, and gazing across the busy avenue at the shade-drawn windows of an old hotel that still retained its elegance. Even now he recalls the surprising rush of emotions when it occurred to him as if he could *sense* it that, while he stood listening to the clatter of Xerox machines, lovers were waking just across the street. Perhaps he'd only imagined the lovers then as well, but at that moment their presence behind the shade-drawn windows seemed so palpable that his own life felt insubstantial beside it, and he was filled with an ache for something he couldn't name but knew was missing. If they were only a daydream, then it was the kind of daydream that sometimes precedes a revelation. That was the morning he'd become certain that he wasn't right for an office job and needed to change the direction of his life while there was still time. A week later, he had quit and returned to school.

Tonight, he senses their presence again. He'd rather feel the presence of lovers, imaginary though they may be, than the absence of the woman he's separated from. If only for a night, they're a respite from the conversation he carries on without her, addressing her as if she can hear him. The lovers are silent. They lie listening to the river, and with his eyes closed he can almost hear it as they must: a high-pitched echo of sewers, a sound of darkness laced with flowing water. Every crack trickles, every overhang drips. Each drop encases its own separate note, the way each drop engulfs its own blue pearl of light.

Between wakefulness and dreaming, with his eyes closed, he can see the light reflected by the falling river of rain: fogged streetlamps and taillights streaked along the Outer Drive, a downtown of dimmed office buildings and glowing hotel lobbies, acetylene sparking behind blue factory windows, racks of vigil candles in the cathedral always kept open, across the street from the neon-lit bus terminal. If he were to rise and walk along the river, he'd see the shades raised and curtains parted, and find himself in a neighbour-hood where the dark buildings, as he's always suspected, are populated by lovers. Their silhouettes stand undressing, framed in windows, naked and enigmatic like the lovers on a tarot card – men and women, men and men, women and women, embracing. Lovers in the present appear super-imposed over lovers from the past so that it's impossible for him to tell who is a shadow of whom. The rooms, parked cars, all the sites of their private histories, glimmer as if their memories have become luminous as spirits. Even the loners are visible beneath single bulbs, appraising their desire in mirrors. The El clatters by above the roofs, its lighted win-dows like a strip of blue movie.

Nearly asleep, the man listens to the clatter of the El train, fading over viaducts, merging, as it grows distant, with the sounds of sporadic traffic and occasional sirens, all swept along together in the rush of the river. Listening to the river is another way of thinking about the woman. He's drifting on a flood of night thoughts – thoughts he may try to dismiss in daylight, the way dreams are renounced and forgotten, but his restless nights have begun to inform his days. Almost dreaming, with the river flowing beside his ear, he under-stands why the lovers have been summoned: because the memory of the woman is becoming a shadow, one he carries like a secret, close to his heart; because beside this memory he has grown insubstantial. It draws him along behind it like a shadow – a shadow of a shadow. It has made him dark and incomprehensible even to himself. The lovers from the present have appeared, as they did when he was younger, to remind him that there is only so much time to change the direction of a life. The lovers from the past have appeared because it may already be too late, because it may be time to release his memories so that they can begin to assume a life of their own.

And what about the memory of the boy left at the window, staring out past his own spattered reflection? The boy could disappear behind a single breath fogged on the glass, then wiped away. The room has fallen asleep behind him; the bed, without his weight, is light enough to levitate. Down-stairs, the Ukrainian kid, a maestro now, has begun to fiddle a nocturne to pacify the dead. Across the alley, prayers rise like an attar of roses from a basement flat. Love, rain has replaced nighthawks. It drums on the helmet of a blue light. Each drop contains its own blue bulb, and when they shatter they collect into a blue river that continues to gleam. The river, the same river sweeping them both away, is all that connects the boy and the man. It flows through the inland city, down streets it submerges, to the slick highways that bank a black sea of prairie. It empties by the piers where the rusty barges are moored along the ghostly coastline. From his window overlooking the alley that has become a river, the boy can see this. He can see the blue of that single bulb diffused in the sheen of breakwaters and distant winks of pumping stations, in the vague outlines of freighters far out on what, come morning, will be a horizon. He could glimpse the future passing, reflected in the current, if he weren't watching the streetlight slowly sinking as it swirls into the vortex of a sewer, if he weren't still waiting for the silhouettes to come for him. He doesn't realize – he won't ever know – that, like them, he's become a shadow.

NIGHTHAWKS

The moon, still cooling off from last night, back in the sky – a bulb insects can't circle. Instead, they teem around a corner streetlight, while down the block air conditioners crank, synchronized with katydids.

There's a light on in a garage where a man's legs, looking lonely, stick out from under a Dodge. What is it that's almost tender about someone tinkering with a car after midnight? The askew glare of the extension lamp propped in the open engine reminds me of how once, driving through the dark in Iowa, I saw a man and woman outlined in light, kissing in a wheat field. They stood pressed against each other before the blazing bank of headlamps from a giant combine. It must have been threshing in the dark, for dust and chaff hung smouldering in the beams, making it seem as if the couple stood in smoke or fog.

I was speeding down a gravel-pinging road and caught only a glimpse of them, but took it as an omen to continue

following the drunken divorcée I'd met earlier in a roadside
bar and grill where I'd stopped for a coffee on my way back
to Chicago. *Divorcée* was her word, the way she'd introduced
herself. 'I'm celebrating becoming an official, gay divorcée,'
she'd told me. I must have looked a little surprised because
she quickly added, as if I'd gotten the wrong idea, 'You
know, not *gay* like with other women, but gay, like, you
know, wild.' We had several drinks, danced to the jukebox,
and ended up in the parking lot, necking in her pickup.
When I started to unbutton her blouse, she asked, 'You
intend to sit out here all night like teenagers or do you want
to follow me home?'

I didn't know the countryside. I followed her down highways, one veering into another, so many turns that I thought
she must be taking a shortcut. I had the windows rolled
down, hoping the streaming night air would clear my head.
Beyond the narrow beams of my headlights, I could feel the
immensity of prairie buoying us up, stretching in the dark
without the limit of a horizon, and I felt suddenly lost in its
vastness in a way I'd only felt before on the ocean, rocking
at night in a small boat. She kept driving faster, and I could
imagine the toe of her high heel pressing down hard on the
workboot-size gas pedal of her truck. I wasn't paying attention to where she was leading me and couldn't have kept
track if I'd tried. Unlit blacktop tunnelled through low hanging trees. By the time we hit the dirt roads she was driving
like a maniac, bouncing over railroad crossings and the
humps of drainage pipes, dust swirling behind her so that
her taillights were only red pinpoints, and I wondered what
radio station she must be listening to, wondered if she was
drunker than I'd realized and she thought that we were
racing, or if she'd had a sudden change of heart and was
trying to lose me on those back roads, and I wondered if I
ought to let her.

Tonight, a lot of people are still up watching the nighthawks hunt through the streetlights. The white bars on their
wings flash, as they dip through the lights, then glide off
against the dark trees that line the street. The trees seem
more like shadows, except where the inverted cones of light
catch their leaves and heighten their green. And despite all

the people still up, unable to let go of the evening, leaning from windows, smoking on steps or rocking on front porches, it's quiet – no small talk, or gossip, no stories, or lullabies – only the whir of insects and the stabbing cries of birds, as if we all know we should be sleeping now, leaving the nighthawks to describe the night.

Hot Ice

SAINTS

The saint, a virgin, was uncorrupted. She had been frozen in a block of ice many years ago.

Her father had found her half-naked body floating face-down among water lilies, her blonde hair fanning at the marshy edge of the overgrown duck pond people still referred to as the Douglass Park Lagoon.

That's how Eddie Kapusta had heard it.

Douglass Park was a black park now, the lagoon curdled in milky green scum as if it had soured, and Kapusta didn't doubt that were he to go there they'd find his body floating in the lily pads too. But sometimes in winter, riding by on the California Avenue bus, the park flocked white, deserted, and the lagoon frozen over, Eddie could almost picture what it had been back then: swans gliding around the small, wooded island at the centre, and rowboats plying into sun-light from the gaping stone tunnels of the haunted-looking boathouse.

The girl had gone rowing with a couple of guys – some said they were sailors, neighbourhood kids going off to the war – nobody ever said who exactly or why she went with them, as if it didn't matter. They rowed her around to the blind side of the little island. Nobody knew what happened there either. It was necessary for each person to imagine it for himself.

They were only joking at first was how Kapusta imagined it, laughing at her broken English, telling her to be friendly or swim home. One of them stroked her hair, gently undid her bun, and as her hair fell cascading over her shoulders surprising them all, the other reached too suddenly for the buttons on her blouse; she tore away so hard the boat rocked violently, her slip and bra split, breasts sprung loose, she dived.

Even the suddenness was slow motion the way Kapusta imagined it. But once they were in the water the rest went through his mind in a flash – the boat capsizing, the sailors thrashing for the little island, and the girl struggling alone in that sepia water too warm from summer, just barely deep enough for the bullheads, with a mud bottom kids said was quicksand exploding into darkness with each kick. He didn't want to wonder what she remembered as she held her last breath underwater. His mind raced over that to her father wading out into cattails, scooping her half-naked and still limp from the resisting water lilies, and running with her in his arms across the park crying in Polish or Slovak or Bohemian, whatever they were, and then riding with her on the streetcar he wouldn't let stop until it reached the icehouse he owned, where crazy with grief he sealed her in ice.

'I believe it up to the part about the streetcar,' Manny Santora said that summer when they told each other such stories, talking often about things Manny called *weirdness* while pitching quarters in front of Buddy's Bar. 'I don't believe he hijacked no streetcar, man.'

'What you think, man, he called a cab?' Pancho, Manny's older brother, asked, winking at Eddie as if he'd scored.

Every time they talked like this Manny and Pancho argued. Pancho believed in everything – ghosts, astrology, legends. His nickname was Padrecito, which went back to his days as an altar boy when he would dress up as a priest and hold Mass in the backyard with hosts punched with bottle caps from stale tortillas and real wine he'd collected from bottles the winos had left on door-steps. Eddie's nickname was Eduardo, though the only person who called him that was Manny, who had made it up. Manny wasn't the kind of guy to have a nickname – he was Manny or Santora.

Pancho believed if you played certain rock songs backwards you'd hear secret messages from the devil. He believed in devils and angels. He still believed he had a guardian angel. It was something like being lucky, like making the sign of the cross before you stepped into the batter's box. 'It's why I don't get caught even when I'm caught,' he'd say when the cops would catch him dealing and not take him in. Pancho believed in saints. For a while he had even belonged to a gang called the Saints. They'd tried to recruit Manny too, who, though younger, was tougher than Pancho, but Manny had no use for gangs. 'I already belong to the Loners,' he said.

Pancho believed in the girl in ice. In sixth grade, Sister Joachim, the ancient nun in charge of the altar boys, had told him the girl should be canonized and that she'd secretly written to the pope informing him that already there had been miracles and cures. 'All the martyrs didn't die in Rome,' she'd told Pancho. 'They're still suffering today in China and Russia and Korea and even here in your own neighbour-hood.' Like all nuns she loved Pancho. Dressed in his surplice and cassock he looked as if he should be beatified himself, a young St Sebastian or Juan de la Cruz, the only altar boy in the history of the parish to spend his money on different-coloured gym shoes so they would match the priest's vestments – red for martyrs, white for feast days, black for requiems. The nuns knew he punished himself during Lent, offering up his pain for the poor souls in purgatory.

Their love for Pancho had made things impossible for Manny in the Catholic school. He seemed Pancho's opposite in almost every way and dropped out after they'd held him back in sixth grade. He switched to public school, but mostly he hung out on the streets.

'I believe she worked miracles right in this neighbourhood, man,' Pancho said.

'Bullshit, man. Like what miracles?' Manny wanted to know.

'OK, man, you know Big Antek,' Pancho said.

'Big Antek the wino?'

They all knew Big Antek. He bought them beer. He'd been a butcher in every meat market in the neighbourhood, but drunkenly kept hacking off pieces of his hands, and finally quit completely to become a full-time alchy.

Big Antek had told Pancho about working on Kedzie Avenue when it was still mostly people from the Old Country and he had found a job at a Czech meat market with sawdust on the floor and skinned rabbits in the window. He wasn't there a week when he got so drunk he passed out in the freezer and when he woke the door was locked and everyone was gone. It was Saturday and he knew they wouldn't open again until Monday and by then he'd be stiff as a two-by-four. He was already shivering so badly he couldn't stand still or he'd fall over. He figured he'd be dead already except that his blood was half alcohol. Parts of him were going numb and he started staggering around, bumping past hanging sides of meat, singing, praying out loud, trying to let the fear out before it became panic. He knew it was hopeless, but he was looking anyway for some place to smash out, some plug to pull, something to stop the cold. At the back of the freezer, behind racks of meat, he found a cooler. It was an old one, the kind that used to stand packed with blocks of ice and bottles of beer in taverns during the war. And seeing it, Big Antek suddenly remembered a moment from his first summer back from the Pacific, discharged from the hospital in Manila and back in Buddy's lounge on Twenty-fourth Street, kitty-corner from a victory garden where a plaque erroneously listed his name among the parish war dead. It was an ordinary moment, nothing dramatic like his life flashing before his eyes, but the memory filled him with such clarity that the freezer became dreamlike beside it. The ball game was on the radio over Buddy's Bar, DiMaggio in centre again, while Bing Crosby crooned from the jukebox, which was playing at the same time. Antek was reaching into Buddy's cooler up to his elbow in ice water feeling for a beer, while looking out through the open tavern door that framed Twenty-fourth Street as if it were a movie full of girls blurred in brightness, slightly overexposed blondes, a movie he could step into any time he chose now that he was home; but right at this moment he was taking his time, stretching it out until it encompassed his entire life, the cold bottles bobbing away from his fingertips, clunking against the ice, until finally he grabbed one, hauled it up dripping, wondering what he'd grabbed – a Monarch or Yusay pilsner or Fox Head 400 – then popped the cork in the opener on the side of the cooler, the foam rising as he tilted his head back and let it pour down his throat, privately celebrating being alive. That moment was what drinking had once been about. It was a good thing to be remembering now when he was dying with nothing else to do about it. He had the funny idea of climbing inside the cooler and going to sleep to continue the memory like a dream. The cooler was thick with frost, so white it seemed to glow. Its lid had been replaced with a slab of dry ice that smoked even within the cold of the freezer, reminding Antek that as kids they'd always called it hot ice. He nudged it aside. Beneath it was a block of ice as clear as if the icemen had just delivered it. There was something frozen inside. He glanced away but knew already, immediately, it was a body. He couldn't move away. He looked again. The longer he stared, the calmer he felt. It was a girl. He could make out her hair, not just blonde but radiating gold like a candle flame behind a window in winter. Her breasts were bare. The ice seemed even clearer. She was beautiful and dreamy looking, not dreamy like sleeping, but the dreamy look DPs sometimes get when they first come to the city. As long as he stayed beside her he didn't shiver. He could feel the blood return; he was warm as if the smouldering dry ice really was hot. He spent the weekend huddled against her, and early Monday morning when the Czech opened the freezer he said to Antek, 'Get out . . . you're fired.' That's all either one of them said.

'You know what I think,' Pancho said. 'They moved her body from the icehouse to the butcher shop because the cops checked, man.'

'You know what I think,' Manny said, 'I think you're doing so much shit that even the winos can bullshit you.'

They looked hard at one another, Manny especially looking bad because of a beard he was trying to grow that was mostly stubble except for a black knot of hair frizzing from the cleft under his lower lip – a little lip of beard like a jazz musician's – and Pancho covered in crosses, a wooden one dangling from a leather thong over his open shirt, and small gold cross on a fine gold chain tight about his throat, and a tiny platinum cross in his right earlobe, and a faded India-ink cross tattooed on his wrist where one would feel for a pulse.

'He got a cross-shaped dick,' Manny said.

'Only when I got a hard-on, man,' Pancho said, grinning, and they busted up.

196

'Hey, Eddie, man,' Pancho said, 'what you think of all this, man?'

Kapusta just shrugged as he always did. Not that he didn't have any ideas exactly, or that he didn't care. That shrug *was* what Kapusta believed.

'Yeah. Well, man,' Pancho said, 'I believe there's saints, and miracles happening everywhere only everybody's afraid to admit it. I mean like Ralph's little brother, the blue baby who died when he was eight. He knew he was dying all his life, man, and never complained. He was a saint. Or Big Antek who everybody says is a wino, man. But he treats everybody as human beings. Who you think's more of a saint – him or the president, man? And Mrs Corillo who everybody thought was crazy because she was praying loud all the time. Remember? She kneeled all day praying for Puerto Rico during that earthquake – the one Roberto Clemente crashed on the way to, going to help. Remember that, man? Mrs Corillo prayed all day and they thought she was still praying at night and she was kneeling there dead. She was a saint, man, and so's Roberto Clemente. There should be like a church, St Roberto Clemente. Kids could pray to him at night. That would mean something to them.'

'The earthquake wasn't in Puerto Rico, man,' Manny told him, 'and I don't believe no streetcar'd stop for somebody carrying a dead person.'

AMNESIA

It was hard to believe there ever were streetcars. The city back then, the city of their fathers, which was as far back as a family memory extended, even the city of their childhoods, seemed as remote to Eddie and Manny as the capital of some foreign country.

The past collapsed about them – decayed, bulldozed, obliterated. They walked past block-length gutted factories, past walls of peeling, multicoloured doors hammered up around flooded excavation pits, hung out in half-boarded storefronts of groceries that had shut down when they were kids, dusty cans still stacked on the shelves. Broken glass collected everywhere, mounding like sand in the little, sunken front yards and gutters. Even the church's stained-glass windows were patched with plywood.

They could vaguely remember something different before the cranes and wrecking balls gradually moved in, not order exactly, but rhythms: five-o'clock whistles, air-raid sirens on Tuesdays, Thursdays when the stockyards blew over like a brown wind of boiling hooves and bone, at least that's what people said, screwing up their faces: 'Phew! They're making glue today!'

Streetcar tracks were long paved over; black webs of trolley wires vanished. So did the victory gardens that had become weed beds taking the corroded plaques with the names of neighbourhood dead with them.

Things were gone they couldn't remember but missed: and things were gone they weren't sure ever were there – the pickle factory by the railroad tracks where a DP with a net worked scooping rats out of the open vats, troughs for ragmen's horses, ragmen and their wooden wagons, knife grinders pushing screeching whetstones up alleys hollering 'Scissors! Knives!' hermits living in cardboard shacks behind billboards.

At times, walking past the gaps, they felt as if they were no longer quite there themselves, half-lost despite familiar street signs, shadows of themselves superimposed on the present except there was no present – everything either rubbled past or promised future – and they were walking as if floating, getting nowhere as if they'd smoked too much grass.

That's how it felt those windy nights that fall when Manny and Eddie circled the county jail. They'd float down California past the courthouse, Bridwell Correctional, the car pound, Communicable Disease Hospital, and then follow the long, curving concrete wall of the prison back towards Twenty-sixth Street, sharing a joint, passing it with cupped hands, ready to flip it if a cop should cruise by, but one place you could count on not to see cops was outside the prison.

Nobody was there; just the wall, railroad tracks, the river, and the factories that lined it – boundaries that remained intact while neighbourhoods came and went.

Eddie had never noticed any trees, but swirls of leaves

scuffed past their shoes. It was Kapusta's favourite weather, wild, blowing nights that made him feel free, flagpoles knocking in the wind, his clothes flapping like flags. He felt both tight and loose, and totally alive even walking down a street that always made him sad. It was the street that followed the curve of the prison wall, and it didn't have a name. It was hardly a street at all, more a shadow of the wall, potholed, puddled, half-paved, rutted with rusted railroad tracks.

'Trains used to go down this street,' Manny said.

'I seen tanks going down this street.'

'Tank cars?'

'No, army tanks,' Kapusta said.

'Battleships too, Eduardo?' Manny asked seriously.

Then the wind ripped a laugh from his mouth that was loud enough to carry over the prison wall.

Kapusta laughed loud too. But he could remember tanks, camouflaged with netting, rumbling on flatcars, their cannons outlined by the red lanterns of the dinging crossing gates that were down all along Twenty-sixth Street. It was one of the first things he remembered. He must have been very small. The train seemed endless. He could see the guards in the turrets on the prison wall watching it, the only time he'd ever seen them facing the street. 'Still sending them to Korea or someplace,' his father had said, and for years after Eddie believed you could get to Korea by train. For years after, he would wake in the middle of the night when it was quiet enough to hear the trains passing blocks away, and lie in bed listening, wondering if the tanks were rumbling past the prison, if not to Korea then to some other war that tanks went to at night; and he would think of the prisoners in their cells locked up for their violence with knives and clubs and cleavers and pistols, and wonder if they were lying awake, listening too as the netted cannons rolled by their barred windows. Even as a child Eddie knew the names of men inside there: Milo Hermanski, who had stabbed some guy in the eye in a fight at Andy's Tap; Billy Gomez, who set the housing project on fire every time his sister Gina got gang-banged; Ziggy's uncle, the war hero, who one day blew off the side of Ziggy's mother's face while she stood ironing her slip during an argument over a will; and other names of people he didn't know but had heard about – Benny Bedwell, with his 'Elvis' sideburns, who may have killed the Grimes sister; Mafia hit men; bank robbers; junkies; perverts; murderers on death row – he could sense them lying awake listening, could feel the tension of their sleeplessness, and Pancho lay among them now as Eddie and Manny walked outside the wall.

They stopped again as they'd been stopping and yelled together: 'Pancho, Panchooooooo,' dragging out the last vowel the way they had as kids standing on the sidewalk calling up at one another's windows, as if knocking at the door were not allowed.

'Pancho, we're out here, brother, me and Eddie,' Manny shouted. 'Hang tough, man, we ain't forgetting you.'

Nobody answered. They kept walking, stopping to shout at intervals the way they had been doing almost every night.

'If only we knew what building he was in,' Eddie said.

They could see the upper storeys of the brick buildings rising over the wall, their grated windows low lit, never dark, floodlights on the roof glaring down.

'Looks like a factory, man,' Eddie said. 'Looks like the same guy who planned the Harvester foundry on Western did the jail.'

'You rather be in the army or in there?' Manny asked.

'No way they're getting me in there,' Eddie said.

That was when Eddie knew Pancho was crazy, when the judge had given Pancho a choice at the end of his trial.

'You're a nice-looking kid,' the judge had said, 'too nice for prison. What do you want to do with your life?'

'Pose for holy cards,' Pancho said, 'St Joseph is my specialty.' Pancho was standing there wearing the tie they had brought him wound around his head like an Indian headband. He was wearing a black satin jacket with the signs of the zodiac on the back.

'I'm going to give you a chance to straighten out, to gain some self-respect. The court's attitude would be very sympathetic to any signs of self-direction and patriotism, joining the army, for instance.'

'I'm a captain,' Pancho told him.

'The army or jail, which is it?'

'I'm a captain, man, *soy capitan, capitan,*' Pancho insisted, humming 'La Bamba' under his breath.

'You're a misfit.'

Manny was able to visit Pancho every three weeks. Each time it got worse. Sometimes Pancho seemed hardly to recognize him, looking away, refusing to meet Manny's eyes the whole visit. Sometimes he'd cry. For a while at first he wanted to know how things were in the neighbourhood. Then he stopped asking, and when Manny tried to tell him the news Pancho would get jumpy, irritable, and lapse into total silence. 'I don't wanna talk about out there, man,' he told Manny. 'I don't wanna remember that world until I'm ready to step into it again. You remember too much in here you go crazy, man. I wanna forget everything, like I never existed.'

'His fingernails are gone, man,' Manny told Eddie. 'He's gnawing on himself like a rat, and when I ask him what's going down all he'll say is "I'm locked in hell, my angel's gone, I've lost my luck" – bullshit like that, you know? Last time I seen him he says, "I'm gonna kill myself, man, if they don't stop hitting on me." '

'I can't fucking believe it. I can't fucking believe he's in there,' Eddie said. 'He should be in a monastery somewhere; he should've been a priest. He had a vocation.'

'He had a vocation to be an altar boy, man,' Manny said, spitting it out as if he was disgusted by what he was saying, talking down about his own brother. 'It was that nuns-and-priests crap that messed up his head. He was happy being an altar boy, man, if they'd've let him be an altar boy all his life he'd still be happy.'

By the time they were halfway down the nameless street it was drizzling a fine, misty spray, and Manny was yelling in Spanish, *Estamos contigo, hermano! San Roberto Clemente te ayudará!'*

They broke into 'La Bamba', Eddie singing in Spanish too, not sure exactly what he was singing, but it sounded good: *'Yo no soy marinero, soy capitan, capitan, ay, ay Bamba! ay, ay, Bamba!'* He had lived beside Spanish in the neighbourhood all his life, and every so often a word got through, like *juilota,* which was what Manny called pigeons when they used to hunt them with slingshots under the railroad bridges. It seemed a perfect word to Eddie, one in which he could hear both their cooing and the whistling rush of their wings. He didn't remember any words like that in Polish, which his grandma had spoken to him when he was little, and which, Eddie had been told, he could once speak too.

By midnight they were at the end of their circuit, emerging from the unlighted, nameless street, stepping over tracks that continued to curve past blinded switches. Under the streetlights on Twenty-sixth the prison wall appeared rust stained, oozing at the cracks. The wire spooled at the top of the wall looked rusty in the wet light, as did the tracks as if the rain were rusting everything overnight.

They stopped on the corner of Twenty-sixth where the old icehouse stood across the nameless street from the prison. One could still buy ice from a vending machine in front. Without realizing it, Eddie guarded his breathing as if still able to detect the faintest stab of ammonia, although it had been a dozen years since the louvred fans on the icehouse roof had clacked through clouds of vapour.

'Padrecitooooo!' they both hollered.

Their voices bounced back off the wall.

They stood on the corner by the icehouse as if waiting around for someone. From there they could stare down Twenty-sixth – five dark blocks, then an explosion of neon at Kedzie Avenue: taco places, bars, a street plugged in, winking festive as a pinball machine, traffic from it coming towards them in the rain.

The streetlights surged and flickered.

'You see that?' Eddie asked. 'They used to say when the streetlights flickered it meant they just fried somebody in the electric chair.'

'So much bullshit,' Manny said. '*Compadre, no te rajes!*' he yelled at the wall.

'Whatcha tell him?'

'It sounds different in English,' Manny said.' "Godfather, do not give up." It's words from an old song.'

Kapusta stepped out into the middle of Twenty-sixth and stood in the misting drizzle squinting at Kedzie through cupped hands, as if he held binoculars. He could make out the traffic light way down there changing to green. He could almost hear the music from the bars that would serve them without asking for IDs so long as Manny was there. 'You thirsty by any chance, man?' he asked.

'You buyin' by any chance, man?' Manny said, grinning.

'*Buenas noches*, Pancho,' they hollered. 'Catch you tomorrow, man.'

'Good-night, guys,' a falsetto voice echoed back from over the wall.

'That ain't Pancho,' Manny said.

'Sounds like the singer on old Platters' records,' Eddie said. 'Ask him if he knows Pancho, man.'

'Hey, you know a guy named Pancho Santora?' Manny called.

'Oh, Pancho?' the voice inquired.

'Yeah, Pancho.'

'Oh, Cisco!' the voice shouted. They could hear him cackling. 'Hey, baby, I don't know no Pancho. Is that rain I smell?'

'It's raining,' Eddie hollered.

'Hey, baby, tell me something. What's it like out there tonight?'

Manny and Eddie looked at each other. 'Beautiful!' they yelled together.

GRIEF

There was never a requiem, but by Lent everyone knew that one way or another Pancho was gone. No wreaths, but plenty of rumours: Pancho had hung himself in his cell; his throat had been slashed in the showers; he'd killed another inmate and was under heavy sedation in a psycho ward at Kankakee. And there was talk he'd made a deal and was in the army, shipped off to a war he had sworn he'd never fight; that he had turned snitch and had been secretly relocated with a new identity; or that he had become a trustee and had simply walked away while mowing the grass in front of the courthouse, escaped maybe to Mexico, or maybe just across town to the North Side around Diversey where, if one made the rounds of the leather bars, they might see someone with Pancho's altar-boy eyes staring out from the make-up of a girl.

Some saw him late at night like a ghost haunting the neighbourhood, collar up in the back of the church lighting a vigil candle; or veiled in a black mantilla, speeding past, face floating by on a greasy El window.

Rumours were becoming legends, but there was never a wake, never an obituary, and no one knew how to mourn a person who had just disappeared.

For a while Manny disappeared too. He wasn't talking, and Kapusta didn't ask. They had quit walking around the prison wall months before, around Christmas when Pancho refused to let anyone, even Manny, visit. But their night walks had been tapering off before that.

Eddie remembered the very last time they had walked beside the wall together. It was in December, and he was frozen from standing around a burning garbage can on Kedzie, selling Christmas trees. About ten, when the lot closed, Manny came by and they stopped to thaw out at the Carta Blanca. A guy named José kept buying them whiskies, and they staggered out after midnight into a blizzard.

'Look at this white bullshit,' Manny said.

Walking down Twenty-sixth they stopped to fling snowballs over the wall. Then they decided to stand there singing Christmas carols. Snow was drifting against the wall, erasing the street that had hardly been there. Eddie could tell Manny was starting to go silent. Manny would get the first few words into a carol, singing at the top of his voice, then stop as if choked by the song. His eyes stayed angry when he laughed. Everything was bullshit to him, and finally Eddie couldn't talk to him anymore. Stomping away from the prison through fresh snow, Eddie had said, 'If this keeps up, man, I'll need boots.'

'It don't *have* to *keep up*, man,' Manny snapped. 'Nobody's making you come, man. It ain't your brother.'

'All I said is I'll need boots, man,' Eddie said.

'You said it hopeless, man; things are always fucking hopeless to you.'

'Hey, you're the big realist, man,' Eddie told him.

'I never said I was no realist,' Manny mumbled.

Kapusta hadn't had a lot of time since then. He had dropped out of school again and was loading trucks at night for UPS. One more semester didn't matter, he figured, and he needed some new clothes, cowboy boots, a green leather jacket. The weather had turned drizzly and mild – a late Easter but an early spring. Eddie had heard Manny was hanging around by himself, still finding bullshit everywhere, only worse. Now he muttered as he walked like some crazy, bitter old man, or one of those black guys reciting the gospel to buildings, telling off posters and billboards, neon signs, stoplights, passing traffic – bullshit, all of it bullshit.

It was Tuesday in Holy Week, the statues inside the church shrouded in violet, when Eddie slipped on his green leather jacket and walked over to Manny's before going to work. He rang the doorbell, then stepped outside in the rain and stood on the sidewalk under Manny's windows, watching cars pass.

After a while Manny came down the stairs and slammed the door.

'How you doin', man?' Eddie said as if they'd just run into each other by accident.

Manny stared at him. 'How far'd you have to chase him for that jacket, man?' he said.

'I knew you'd dig it.' Eddie smiled.

They went out for a few beers later that night, after midnight, when Eddie was through working, but instead of going to a bar they ended up just walking. Manny had rolled a couple of bombers and they walked down the boulevard along California watching the headlights flash by like a procession of candles. Manny still wasn't saying much, but they were passing the reefer like having a conversation. At Thirty-first, by the Communicable Disease Hospital, Eddie figured they would follow the curve of the boulevard towards the bridge on Western, but Manny turned as if out of habit towards the prison.

They were back walking along the wall. There was still old ice from winter at the base of it.

'The only street in Chicago where it's still winter,' Eddie mumbled.

'Remember yelling?' Manny said, almost in a whisper.

'Sure,' Eddie nodded.

'Called, joked, prayed, sang Christmas songs, remember that night, how cold we were, man?'

'Yeah.'

'What a bunch of stupid bullshit, huh?'

Eddie was afraid Manny was going to start the bullshit stuff again. Manny had stopped and stood looking at the wall.

Then he cupped his hands over his mouth and yelled, 'Hey! You dumb fuckers in there! We're back! Can you hear me? Hey, wake up, niggers, hey, spics, hey, honkies, you buncha fuckin' monkeys in cages, hey! We're out here *free*!'

'Hey, Manny, come on, man,' Eddie said.

Manny uncupped his hands, shook his head, and smiled. They took a few steps, then Manny whirled back again. 'We're out here free, man! We're smokin' reefer, drinking cold beer while you're in there, you assholes! We're on our way to fuck your wives, man, your girlfriends are giving us blow jobs while you jack-offs flog it. Hey, man, I'm pumping your old lady out here right now. She likes it in the ass like you!'

'What are you doing, man?' Eddie was pleading. 'Take it easy.'

Manny was screaming his lungs out, almost incoherent, shouting every filthy thing he could think of, and voices, the voices they'd never heard before, had begun shouting back from the other side of the wall.

'Shadup! Shadup! Shadup out there, you crazy fuck!' came the voices.

'She's out here licking my balls while you're punking each other through the bars of your cage!'

'Shadup!' they were yelling, and then a voice howling over the others: 'I'll kill you, motherfucker! When I get out you're dead!'

'Come on out,' Manny was yelling. 'Come and get me, you pieces of shit, you sleazeballs, you scumbag cocksuckers, you creeps are missing it all, your lives are wasted garbage!'

Now there were too many voices to distinguish, whole tiers, whole buildings yelling and cursing and threatening, *shadup, shadup, shadup,* almost a chant, and then the search-light from the guardhouse slowly turned and swept the street.

'We gotta get outa here,' Eddie said, pulling Manny away. He dragged him to the wall, right up against it where the light couldn't follow, and they started to run, stumbling along the banked strip of filthy ice, dodging stunted trees that grew out at odd angles, running towards Twenty-sixth until Eddie heard the sirens.

'This way, man,' he panted, yanking Manny back across the nameless street, jumping puddles and tracks, cutting down a narrow corridor between abandoned truck docks seconds before a squad car, blue dome light revolving, sped past.

They jogged behind the truck docks, not stopping until they came up behind the icehouse. Manny's panting sounded almost like laughing, the way people laugh after they've hurt themselves.

'I hate those motherfuckers,' Manny gasped, 'all of them, the fucking cops and guards and fucking wall and the bastards behind it. All of them. That must be what makes me a realist, huh, Eddie? I fucking hate them all.'

They went back the next night.

Sometimes a thing wasn't a sin – if there was such a thing as sin – Eddie thought, until it's done a second time. There were accidents, mistakes that could be forgiven once; it was repeating them that made them terribly wrong. That was how Eddie felt about going back the next night.

Manny said he was going whether Eddie came or not, so Eddie went, afraid to leave Manny on his own, even though he'd already had trouble trying to get some sleep before going to work. Eddie could still hear the voices yelling from behind the wall and dreamed they were all being electro-cuted, electrocuted slowly, by degrees of their crimes, screaming with each surge of current and flicker of street-lights as if in hell where electricity had replaced fire.

Standing on the dark street Wednesday night, outside the wall again, felt like an extension of his nightmare: Manny raging almost out of control, shouting curses and insults, baiting them over the wall the way a child tortures penned watchdogs, until he had what seemed like the entire west side of the prison howling back, the guards sweeping the street with searchlights, sirens wailing towards them from both Thirty-first and Twenty-sixth.

This time they raced down the tracks that curved towards the river, picking their way in the dark along the junkyard bank, flipping rusted cables of moored barges, running through the fire truck graveyard, following the tracks across the blackened trestles where they'd once shot pigeons and from which they could gaze across the industrial prairie that stretched behind factories all the way to the skyline of downtown. The skyscrapers glowed like luminescent peaks in the misty spring night. Manny and Eddie stopped in the middle of the trestle and leaned over the railing catching their breath.

'Downtown ain't as far away as I used to think when I was a kid.' Manny panted.

'These tracks'll take you right there,' Eddie said quietly, 'to railroad yards under the street, right by the lake.'

'How you know, man?'

'A bunch of us used to hitch rides on the boxcars in seventh grade.' Eddie was talking very quietly, looking away.

'I usually take the bus, you know?' Manny tried joking.

'I ain't goin' back there with you tomorrow,' Eddie said. 'I ain't goin' back with you ever.'

Manny kept staring off towards the lights downtown as if he hadn't heard. 'OK,' he finally said, more to himself, as if surrendering. 'OK, how about tomorrow we do something else, man?'

NOSTALGIA

They didn't go back.

The next night, Thursday, Eddie overslept and called in sick for work. He tried to get back to sleep but kept falling into half-dreams in which he could hear the voices shouting behind the prison wall. Finally he got up and opened a window. It was dark out. A day had passed almost unnoticed, and now the night felt as if it were part of the night before that, all connected by his restless dreams, fragments of the same continuous night.

Eddie had said that at some point: 'It's like one long night,' and later Manny had said the same thing as if it had suddenly occurred to him.

They were strung out almost from the start, drifting stoned under the El tracks before Eddie even realized they weren't still sitting on the stairs in front of Manny's house. That was were Eddie had found him, watching traffic, taking sips out of a bottle of Gallo into which Manny had dropped several hits of speed.

Cars gunned by with their windows rolled down and radios playing loud. It sounded like a summer night.

'Ain't you hot wearin' that jacket, man?' Manny asked him.

'Now that you mention it,' Eddie said. He was sweating.

Eddie took his leather jacket off and they knotted a handkerchief around one of the cuffs, then slipped the Gallo bottle down the sleeve. They walked along under the El tracks passing a joint. A train, only two cars long, rattled overhead.

'So what we doing, Eduardo?' Manny kept repeating.

'Walking,' Eddie said.

'I feel like doing *something*, you know?'

'We are doing something,' Eddie insisted.

Eddie led them over to the Coconut Club on Twenty-second. They couldn't get in, but Eddie wanted to look at the window with its neon-green palm tree and winking blue coconuts.

'That's maybe my favourite window,' he said.

'You drag me all the way here to see your favourite window, man?' Manny said.

'It's those blue coconuts,' Eddie tried explaining. His mouth was dry, but he couldn't stop talking. He started telling Manny how he had collected windows from the time he was a little kid, even though talking about it made it sound as if windows were more important to him than they actually were. Half the time he was only vaguely aware of collecting them. He would see a window from a bus, like the Greek butcher shop on Halsted with its pyramid of lamb skulls, and make a mental photograph of it. He had special windows all over the city. It was how he held the city together in his mind.

'I'd see all these windows from the El,' Eddie said, 'when I'd visit my *busha*, my grandma. Like I remember we'd pass this one building where the curtains were all slips hanging by their straps – black ones, white ones, red ones. At night you could see the light bulbs shining through the lace tops. My *busha* said Gypsies lived there.' Eddie was walking down the middle of the street, jacket flung over his shoulder, staring up at the windows as if looking for the Gypsies as he talked.

'Someday they're gonna get you as a peeper, man.' Manny laughed. 'And when they do, don't try explaining to them about this thing of yours for windows, Eduardo.'

They were walking down Spaulding back towards Twenty-sixth. The streetlights beamed brighter and brighter, and Manny put his sunglasses on. A breeze was blowing that felt warmer than the air, and they took their shirts off. They saw rats darting along the curb into the sewer on the other side of the street and put their shirts back on.

'The rats get crazy where they start wrecking these old buildings,' Manny said.

The cranes and wrecking balls and urban-renewal signs were back with the early spring. They walked around a barricaded site. Water trickled along the gutters from an open hydrant, washing brick dust and debris towards the sewers.

'Can you smell that, man?' Manny asked him, suddenly excited. 'I can smell the lake through the hydrant.'

'Smells like rust to me,' Eddie said.

'I can smell fish! Smelt – the smelt are in! I can smell them right through the hydrant!'

'Smelt?' Eddie said.

'You ain't ever had smelt?' Manny asked. 'Little silver fish!'

They caught the Twenty-sixth Street bus – the Polish Zephyr, people called it – going east toward the lake. The back of the bus was empty. They sat in the swaying, long backseat, taking hits out of the bottle in Eddie's sleeve.

'It's usually too early for them yet, but they're out there, Eduardo,' Manny kept reassuring him, as if they were actually going fishing.

Eddie nodded. He didn't know anything about smelt. The only fish he ate was canned tuna, but it felt good to be riding somewhere with the windows open and Manny acting more like his old self – sure of himself, laughing easily. Eddie still felt like talking, but his molars were grinding on speed.

The bus jolted down the dark block past Kedzie and was flying when it passed the narrow street between the icehouse and the prison, but Eddie and Manny caught a glimpse out the back window of the railroad tracks that curved down the nameless street. The tracks were lined with fuming red flares that threw a red reflection off the concrete walls. Eddie was sure the flares had been set there for them.

Eddie closed his eyes and sank into the rocking of the bus. Even with his eyes closed he could see the reddish glare of the walls. The glare was ineradicable, at the back of his sockets. The wall had looked the same way it had looked in his dreams. They rode in silence.

'It's like one long night,' Eddie said somewhere along the way.

His jaws were really grinding and his legs had forgotten gravity by the time they got to the lakefront. They didn't know the time, but it must have been around 3 or 4 a.m. and the smelt fishers were still out. The lights of their kerosene lanterns reflected along the breakwater over the glossy black lake. Eddie and Manny could hear the water lapping under the pier and the fishermen talking in low voices in different languages.

'My uncle Carlos would talk to the fish,' Manny said. 'No shit. He'd talk to them in Spanish. He didn't have no choice. Whole time here he couldn't speak English. Said it made his brain stuck. We used to come fishing here all the time – smelt, perch, everything. I'd come instead of going to school. It they weren't hitting, he'd start talking to them, singing them songs.'

'Like what?' Eddie said.

'He'd make them up. They were funny, man. It don't come across in English: "Little silver ones fill up my shoes. My heart is lonesome for the fish of the sea." It was like very formal how he'd say it. He'd always call this the sea. I'd tell him it's a lake, but he couldn't be talked out of it. He was very stubborn – too stubborn to learn English. I ain't been fishing since he went back to Mexico.'

They walked to the end of the pier, then back past the fishermen. A lot of them were old men gently tugging lines between their fingers, lifting nets as if flying underwater kites, plucking the wriggling silver fish from the netting, the yellow light of their lamps glinting off the bright scales.

'I told you they were out here,' Manny said.

They sat on a concrete ledge, staring at the dark water, which rocked hypnotically below the soles of their dangling feet.

'Feel like diving in?' Manny asked.

Eddie had just raised the bottle to his lips and paused as if actually considering Manny's question, then shook his head no and took a swallow.

'One time right before my uncle went back to Mexico we came fishing at night for perch,' Manny said. 'It was a real hot night, you know? And all these old guys fishing off the pier. No one getting a bite, man, and I started thinking how cool and peaceful it would be to just dive in the water with the fish, and then, like I just did it without even deciding to, clothes and all. Sometimes, man, I still remember that feeling underwater – like I could just keep swimming out, didn't need air, never had to come up. When I couldn't hold my breath no more and came up I could hear my uncle calling my name, and then all the old guys on the pier start calling my name to come back. What I really felt like doing was to keep swimming out until I couldn't hear them, until I couldn't even see their lanterns, man. I wanted to be way the fuck out alone in the middle of the lake when the sun came up. But then I thought about my uncle standing on the pier calling me, so I turned around.'

They killed the bottle sitting on a concrete ledge and dropped it into the lake. Then they rode the El back. It was getting lighter without a dawn. The El windows were streaked with rain, the Douglass Avenue station smelled wet. It was a dark morning. They should have ended it then. Instead they sat at Manny's kitchen table drinking instant coffee with canned milk. Eddie kept getting lost in the designs the milk would make, swirls and thunderclouds in his mug of coffee. He was numb and shaky. His jaw ached.

'I'm really crashin',' he told Manny.

'Here,' Manny said. 'Bring us down easier, man.'

'I don't like doing downers, man,' Eddie said.

'Ludes,' Manny said, 'from Pancho's stash.'

They sat across the table from each other for a long time – talking, telling their memories and secrets – only Eddie was too numb to remember exactly what they said. Their voices – his own as well as Manny's – seemed *outside*, removed from the centre of his mind.

At one point Manny looked out at the dark morning and said, 'It still seems like last night.'

'That's right,' Eddie agreed. He wanted to say more but couldn't express it. He didn't try. Eddie didn't believe it was what they said that was important. Manny could be talking Spanish; I could be talking Polish, Eddie thought. It didn't matter. What meant something was sitting at the table together, wrecked together, still awake watching the rainy light spatter the window, walking out again, to the Prague bakery for bismarcks, past people under dripping umbrellas on their way to church.

'Looks like Sunday,' Manny said.

'Today's Friday,' Eddie said. 'It's Good Friday.'

'I seen ladies with ashes on their heads waiting for the bus a couple days ago,' Manny told him.

They stood in the doorway of the Prague, out of the rain, eating their bismarcks. Just down from the church, the bakery was a place people crowded into after Mass. Its windows displayed coloured eggs and little frosted Easter lambs.

'One time on Ash Wednesday I was eating a bismarck and Pancho made a cross on my forehead with the powdered sugar like it was ashes. When I went to church the priest wouldn't give me real ashes,' Manny said with a grin.

It was one of the few times Eddie had heard Manny mention Pancho. Now that they were outside, Eddie's head felt clearer than it had in the kitchen.

'I used to try and keep my ashes on until Good Friday,' he told Manny, 'but they'd make me wash.'

The church bells were ringing, echoes bouncing off the

213

sidewalks as if deflected by the ceiling of clouds. The neighbourhood felt narrower, compressed from above.

'I wonder if it still looks the same in there,' Manny said as they passed the church.

They stepped in and stood in the vestibule. The saints of their childhood stood shrouded in purple. The altar was bare, stripped for Good Friday. Old ladies, ignoring the new liturgy, chanted a litany in Polish.

'Same as ever,' Eddie whispered as they backed out.

The rain had almost let up. They could hear its accumulated weight in the wing-flaps of pigeons.

'Good Friday was Pancho's favourite holiday, man,' Manny said. 'Everybody else always picked Christmas or Thanksgiving or Fourth of July. He hadda be different, man. I remember he used to drag me along visiting churches. You ever do that?'

'Hell, yeah,' Eddie said. 'Every Good Friday we'd go on our bikes. You hadda visit seven of them.'

Without agreeing to it they walked from St Roman's to St Michael's, a little wooden Franciscan church in an Italian neighbourhood; and from there to St Kasimir's, a towering, mournful church with twin copper-green towers. Then, as if following an invisible trail, they walked north up Twenty-second towards St Anne's, St Puis's, St Adalbert's. At first they merely entered and left immediately, as if touching base, but their familiarity with small rituals quickly returned: dipping their fingers in the holy water font by the door, making the automatic sign of the cross as they passed the life-size crucified Christs that hung in the vestibules where old women and school kids clustered to kiss the spikes in the bronze or bloody plaster feet. By St Anne's, Manny removed his sunglasses, out of respect, the way one removes a hat. Eddie put them on. His eyes felt hardboiled. The surge of energy he had felt at the bakery had burned out fast. While Manny genuflected to the altar, Eddie slumped in the back pew pretending to pray, drowsing off behind the dark glasses. It never occurred to Eddie to simply go home. His head ached, he could feel his heart racing, and would suddenly jolt awake wondering where Manny was. Manny would be off – jumpy, frazzled, still popping speed on the sly – exploring the church as if searching for something, standing among lines of parishioners waiting to kiss relics the priest wiped repeatedly clean with a rag of silk. Then Manny would be shaking Eddie awake. 'How you holding up, man?'

'I'm cool,' he'd say, and they would be back on the streets heading for another parish under the overcast sky. Clouds, a shade between slate and lilac, smoked over the spires and roofs; lights flashed on in the bars and *taquerías*. On Eighteenth Street a great blue neon fish leapt in the storefront window of a tiny *ostenaria*. Eddie tried to note the exact location to add to his window collection. They headed along a wall of viaducts to St Procopius, where, Manny said, both he and Pancho had been baptized. The viaduct walls had been painted by schoolchildren into a mural that seemed to go for miles.

'I don't think we're gonna make seven churches, man,' Eddie said. He was walking without lifting his feet, his hair plastered by a sweatlike drizzle. It was around 3 p.m. It had been 3 p.m. – Christ's dark hour on the cross – inside the churches all day, but now it was turning 3 p.m. outside too. They could hear the ancient-sounding hymn 'Tantum Ergo', carrying from down the block.

Eddie sank into the last pew, kneeling in the red glow of vigil lights that brought back the red flicker of the flares they had seen from the window of the bus as it sped by the prison. Manny had already faded into the procession making the stations of the cross – a shuffling crowd circling the church, kneeling before each station while altar boys censed incense and the priest recited Christ's agony. Old women answered with prayers like moans.

Old women were walking on their knees up the marble aisle to kiss the relics. A few were crying, and Eddie remembered how back in grade school he had heard old women cry sometimes after confession, crying as if their hearts would break, and even as a child he had wondered how such old women could possibly have committed sins terrible enough to demand such bitter weeping. Most everything from that world had changed or disappeared, but the old women had endured – Polish, Bohemian, Spanish, he knew it didn't matter; they were the same, dressed in black coats and babushkas the way holy statues wore violet, in constant mourning. A common pain of loss seemed to burn at the core of their lives, though Eddie had never understood exactly what it was they mourned. Nor how day after day they had sustained the intensity of their grief. He would have given up long ago. In a way he *had* given up, and the ache left behind couldn't be called grief. He had no name for it. He had felt it before Pancho or anyone was lost, almost from the start of memory. If it was grief, it was grief for the living. The hymns, with their ancient, keening melodies and mysterious words, had brought the feeling back, but when he tried to discover the source, to give the feeling a name, it eluded him as always, leaving in its place nostalgia and triggered nerves.

Oh God, he prayed, I'm really crashing.

He was too shaky to kneel, so he stretched out on the pew, lying on his back, eyes shut behind sunglasses, until the church began to whirl. To control it he tried concentrating on the stained-glass window overhead. None of the windows that had ever been special for him were from a church. This one was an angel, its colours like jewels and coals. Afternoon seemed to be dying behind it, becoming part of the night, part of the private history that he and Manny continued between them like a pact. He could see night shining through the colours of the angel, dividing into bands as if the angel were a prism for darkness; the neon and wet streetlights illuminated its wingspread.

LEGENDS

It started with ice.

That's how Big Antek sometimes began the story.

At dusk a gang of little Mexican kids appeared with a few lumps of dry ice covered in a shoe box, as if they had caught a bird. *Hot ice*, they called it, though the way they said it sounded to Antek like *hot eyes*. Kids always have a way of finding stuff like that. One boy touched his tongue to a piece and screamed '*Aye!*' when it stuck. They watched the ice boil and fume in a rain puddle along the curb, and finally they filled a bottle part way with water, inserted the fragments of ice they had left, capped the bottle, and set it in the mouth of an alley waiting for an explosion. When it popped they scattered.

Manny Santora and Eddie Kapusta came walking up the alley, wanting Antek to buy them a bottle of rum at Buddy's. Rum instead of beer. They were celebrating, Kapusta said, but he didn't say what. Maybe one of them had found a job or had just been fired, or graduated, or joined the army instead of waiting around to get drafted. It could be anything. They were always celebrating. Behind their sunglasses Antek could see they were high as usual, even before Manny offered him a drag off a reefer the size of a cigar.

Probably nobody was hired or fired or had joined anything; probably it was just so hot they had a good excuse to act crazy. They each had a bottle of Coke they were fizzing up, squirting. Eddie had limes stuffed in his pockets and was pretending they were his balls. Manny had a plastic bag of the little ice cubes they sell at gas stations. It was half-melted, and they were scooping handfuls of cubes over each other's heads, stuffing them down their jeans and yowling, rubbing ice on their chests and under their arms as if taking a cold shower. They looked like wild men – shirts hanging from their back pockets, handkerchiefs knotted around their heads, wearing sunglasses, their bodies slick with melted ice water and sweat; two guys in the prime of life going nowhere, both lean, Kapusta almost as tanned as Santora, Santora with the frizzy beard under his lip, and Kapusta trying to juggle limes.

They were drinking rum using a method Antek had never seen before, and he had seen his share of drinking – not just in the neighbourhood – all over the world when he was in the navy, and not the Bohemian navy either like somebody would always say when he would start telling navy stories.

They claimed they were drinking cuba libres, only they didn't have glasses, so they were mixing the drinks in their mouths, starting with some little cubes, then pouring in rum, Coke, a squeeze of lime, and swallowing. Swallowing if one or the other didn't suddenly bust up over some private joke, spraying the whole mouthful out, and both of them choking and coughing and laughing.

'Hey, Antek, lemme build you a drink,' Manny kept saying, but Antek shook his head no thanks, and he wasn't known for passing up too many.

This was all going on in front of Buddy's, everyone catching a blast of music and air-conditioning whenever the door opened. It was hot. The moths sizzled as soon as they hit Buddy's buzzing orange sign. A steady beat of moths dropped like cinders on the blinking orange sidewalk where the kids were pitching pennies. Manny passed around what was left in the plastic bag of ice, and the kids stood sucking and crunching the cubes between their teeth.

It reminded Antek of summers when the ice trucks still delivered to Buddy's – flatbeds covered with canvas, the icemen, mainly DPs, wearing leather aprons. Their Popeye forearms, even in August, looked ruddy with cold. They would slide the huge, clear blocks off the tailgate so the whump reverberated through the hollow under the sidewalks, and deep in the ice the clarity shattered. Then with their ice hooks they'd lug the blocks across the sidewalk, trailing a slick, and boot them skidding down the chute into Buddy's beery-smelling cellar. And after the truck pulled away, kids would pick the splinters from the curb and suck them as if they were ice-flavoured Popsicles.

Nobody seemed too interested when Antek tried to tell them about the ice trucks, or anything else about how the world had been, for that matter. Antek had been sick and had only recently returned from the VA hospital. Of all his wounds, sickness was the worst. He could examine his hacked butcher's hands almost as kids from the neighbourhood did, inspecting the stubs where his fingers had been as if they belonged to someone else, but there were places deep within himself that he couldn't examine, yet where he could feel that something of himself far more essential than fingers was missing. He returned from the VA feeling old and as if the neighbourhood had changed in the weeks he had been gone. People had changed. He couldn't be sure, but they treated him differently, colder, as if he were becoming a stranger in the place he had grown up in, now, just when he most needed to belong.

'Hey, Antek,' Manny said, 'you know what you can tell

me? That girl that saved your life in the meat freezer, did she have good tits?'

'I tell you about a miracle and you ask me about tits?' Antek said. 'I don't talk about that any more because now somebody always asks me did she have good tits. Go see.'

Kids had been trying for years to sneak into the icehouse to see her. It was what the neighbourhood had instead of a haunted house. Each generation had grown up with the story of how her father had ridden with her half-naked body on the streetcar. Even the nuns had heard Antek's story about finding the girl still frozen in the meat freezer. The butcher shop on Kedzie had closed long ago, and the legend was that after the cops had stopped checking, her body had been moved at night back into the icehouse. But the icehouse wasn't easy to break into. It had stood padlocked and heavily boarded for years.

'They're gonna wreck it,' Eddie said. 'I went by on the bus and they got the crane out in front.'

'Uh-oh, last chance, Antek,' Manny said. 'If you're sure she's in there, maybe we oughta go save her.'

'She's in there,' Antek said. He noticed the little kids had stopped pitching pennies and were listening.

'Well, you owe her something after what she done for you – don't he, Eduardo?'

The kids who were listening chuckled, then started to go back to their pennies.

'You wanna go, I'll go!' Antek said loudly.

'All right, let's go.'

Antek got up unsteadily. He stared at Eddie and Manny. 'You guys couldn't loan me enough for a taste of wine just until I get my disability cheque?'

The little kids tagged after them to the end of the block, then turned back bored. Manny and Eddie kept going, picking the pace up a step or two ahead of Antek, exchanging looks and grinning. But Antek knew that no matter how much they joked or what excuses they gave, they were going, like him, for one last look. They were just old enough to have seen the icehouse before it shut down. It was a special building, the kind a child couldn't help but notice and remember – there, on the corner across the street from the prison, a factory that made ice, humming with fans, its louvred roof dripping and clacking, lost in acrid clouds of its own escaping vapour.

The automatic ice machine in front had already been carted away. The doors were still padlocked, but the way the crane was parked it was possible for Manny and Eddie to climb the boom on to the roof.

Antek waited below. He gazed up at the new Plexiglas guard turrets on the prison wall. From his angle all he could see was the bluish fluorescence of their lighting. He watched Manny and Eddie jump from the boom to the roof, high enough to stare across at the turrets like snipers, to draw a level bead on the backs of the guards, high enough to gaze over the wall at the dim, barred windows of the buildings that resembled foundries more than ever in the sweltering heat.

Below, Antek stood swallowing wine, expecting more from the night than a condemned building. He didn't know exactly what else he expected. Perhaps only a scent, like the stab of remembered ammonia he might have detected if he were still young enough to climb the boom. Perhaps the secret isolation he imagined Manny and Eddie feeling now, alone on the roof, as if lost in clouds of vapour. At street level, passing traffic droned out the tick of a single cricket keeping time on the roof – a cricket so loud and insistent that Manny didn't stop to worry about the noise when he kicked in the louvres. And Antek, though he had once awakened in a freezer, couldn't imagine the shock of cold that Manny and Eddie felt as they dropped out of the summer night to the floor below.

Earlier, on their way down Twenty-sixth, Manny had stopped to pick up an unused flare from along the tracks, and Antek pictured them inside now, Manny, his hand wrapped in a handkerchief, holding the flare away from him like a Roman candle, its red glare sputtering off the beams and walls.

There wasn't much to see – empty corners, insulated pipes. Their breaths steamed. They tugged on their shirts. Instinctively, they traced the cold down a metal staircase. Cold was rising from the ground floor through the soles of their gym shoes.

The ground floor was stacked to the ceiling with junked ice machines. A wind as from an enormous air conditioner was blowing down a narrow aisle between the machines. At the end of the aisle a concrete ramp slanted down to the basement.

That was where Antek suspected they would end up, the basement, a cavernous space extending under the nameless street, slowly collapsing as if the thick, melting pillars of ice along its walls had served as its foundation. The floor was spongy with waterlogged sawdust. An echoing rain plipped from the ceiling. The air smelled thawed, and ached clammy in the lungs.

'It's fuckin' freezing,' Eddie whispered.

Manny swung the flare in a slow arc, its reflections glancing as if they stood among cracked mirrors. Blocks of ice, framed in defrosted freezer coils, glowed back faintly, like aquarium windows, from niches along the walls. They were melting unevenly and leaned at precarious angles. Several had already tottered to the sawdust, where they lay like quarry stones from a wrecked cathedral. Manny and Eddie picked their way among them, pausing to wipe the slick of water from their surfaces and peer into the ice, but deep networks of cracks refracted the light. They could see only frozen shadows and had to guess at the forms: fish, birds, shanks of meat, a dog, a cat, a chair, what appeared to be a bicycle.

But Antek knew they would recognize her when they found her. There would be no mistaking the light. In the smoky, phosphorous glare her hair would reflect gold like a candle behind a frosted pane. He was waiting for them to bring her out. He had finished the wine and flung the pint bottle on to the street so that it shattered. The streets were empty. He was waiting patiently, and though he had nowhere else to be it was still a long wait. He would wait as long as it might take, but even so he wondered if there was time enough left to him for another miracle in his life. He could hear the cricket now, composing time instead of music, working its way headfirst from the roof down the brick wall.

Listening to it, Antek became acutely aware of the silence of the prison across the street. He thought of all the men on the other side of the wall and wondered how many were still awake, listening to the cricket, waiting patiently as they sweated in the heavy night.

Manny and Eddie, shivering, their hands burning numb from grappling with ice, unbarred the rear door that opened on to the loading platform behind the icehouse. They pushed out an old handcar and rolled it on to the tracks that came right up to the dock. They had already slid the block of ice on to the handcar and draped it with a canvas tarp. Even gently inching it on they had heard the ice cracking. The block of ice had felt too light for its size, fragile, ready to break apart.

'It feels like we're kidnapping somebody,' Eddie whispered.

'Just think of it as ice.'

'I can't.'

'We can't just leave her here, Eduardo.'

'What'll we do with her?'

'We'll think of something.'

'What about Antek?'

'Forget him.'

They pushed off. Rust slowed them at first, but as the tracks inclined toward the river they gained momentum. It was like learning to row. By the trestle they hit their rhythm. Speed became wind – hair blowing, shirts flapping open, the tarp billowing up off the ice. The skyline gleamed ahead, and though Manny couldn't see the lake, he could feel it stretching beyond the skyscrapers; he could recall the sudden lightness of freedom he'd felt once when he had speared out underwater and glided effortlessly away, one moment expanding into another, while the flow of water cleansed him of memory, and not even the sound of his own breath disrupted the silence. The smelt would have disappeared to wherever they disappeared to, but the fishermen would still be sitting at the edge of the breakwater, their backs to the city, dreaming up fish. And if the fishermen still remembered his name, they might call it again repeatedly in a chorus of voices echoing out over the dark surface of the water, but this time, Manny knew, there would be no turning back. He knew now where they were taking her, where she would finally be released. They were rushing through waist-deep weeds, crossing the vast tracts of prairie behind the factories, clattering over bridges and viaducts. Below, streetlights shimmered watery in the old industrial neighbourhoods. Shiny with sweat, the girl already melting free between them, they forced themselves faster, rowing like a couple of sailors.

Pet Milk

Today I've been drinking instant coffee and Pet milk, and watching it snow. It's not that I enjoy the taste especially, but I like the way Pet milk swirls in the coffee. Actually, my favourite thing about Pet milk is what the can opener does to the top of the can. The can is unmistakable – compact, seamless looking, its very shape suggesting that it could condense milk without any trouble. The can opener bites in neatly, and the thick liquid spills from the triangular gouge with a different look and viscosity than milk. Pet milk isn't *real* milk. The colour's off, to start with. There's almost something of the past about it, like old ivory. My grandmother always drank it in her coffee. When friends dropped over and sat around the kitchen table, my grandma would ask, 'Do you take cream and sugar?' Pet milk was the cream.

There was a yellow plastic radio on her kitchen table, usually tuned to the polka station, though sometimes she'd miss it by half a notch and get the Greek station instead, or the Spanish, or the Ukrainian. In Chicago, where we lived, all the incompatible states of Europe were pressed together down at the staticky right end of the dial. She didn't seem to notice, as long as she wasn't hearing English. The radio, turned low, played constantly. Its top was warped and turning amber on the side where the tubes were. I remember the sound of it on winter afternoons after school, as I sat by her table watching the Pet milk swirl and cloud in the steaming coffee, and noticing, outside her window, the sky doing the same thing above the railroad yard across the street.

And I remember, much later, seeing the same swirling sky in tiny liqueur glasses containing a drink called a King Alphonse: the crème de cacao rising like smoke in repeated explosions, blooming in kaleidoscopic clouds through the layer of heavy cream. This was in the Pilsen, a little Czech restaurant where my girlfriend, Kate, and I would go sometimes in the evening. It was the first year out of college for both of us, and we had astonished ourselves by finding real jobs – no more waitressing or pumping gas, the way we'd done in school. I was investigating credit references at a bank, and she was doing something slightly above the rank of typist for Hornblower & Weeks, the investment firm. My bank showed training films that emphasized the importance of suitable dress, good grooming, and personal neatness, even for employees like me, who worked at the switchboard in the basement. Her firm issued directives on appropriate attire – skirts, for instant, should cover the knees. She had lovely knees.

Kate and I would sometimes meet after work at the Pilsen, dressed in our proper business clothes and still feeling both a little self-conscious and glamorous, as if we were impostors wearing disguises. The place had small, round oak tables, and we'd sit in a corner under a painting called 'The Street Musicians of Prague' and trade future plans as if they were escape routes. She talked of going to grad school in Europe; I wanted to apply to the Peace Corps. Our plans for the future made us laugh and feel close, but those same plans somehow made anything more than temporary between us seem impossible. It was the first time I'd ever had the feeling of missing someone I was still with.

The waiters in the Pilsen wore short black jackets over long white aprons. They were old men from the Old Country. We went there often enough to have our own special waiter, Rudi, a name he pronounced with a rolled *R*. Rudi boned our trout and seasoned our salads, and at the end of the meal he'd bring the bottle of crème de cacao from the bar, along with two little glasses and a small pitcher of heavy cream, and make us each a King Alphonse right at our table. We'd watch as he'd fill the glasses halfway up with the syrupy brown liqueur, then carefully attempt to float a layer of cream on top. If he failed to float the cream, we'd get that one free.

'Who was King Alphonse anyway, Rudi?' I sometimes asked, trying to break his concentration, and if that didn't work I nudged the table with my foot so the glass would jiggle imperceptibly just as he was floating the cream. We'd usually get one on the house. Rudi knew what I was doing.

In fact, serving the King Alphonses had been his idea, and he had also suggested the trick of jarring the table. I think it pleased him, though he seemed concerned about the way I'd stare into the liqueur glass, watching the patterns.

'It's not a microscope,' he'd say. 'Drink.'

He liked us, and we tipped extra. It felt good to be there and to be able to pay for a meal.

Kate and I met at the Pilsen for supper on my twenty-second birthday. It was May, and unseasonably hot. I'd opened my tie. Even before looking at the dinner menu, we ordered a bottle of Mumm's and a dozen oysters apiece. Rudi made a sly remark when he brought the oysters on platters of ice. They were freshly opened and smelled of the sea. I'd heard people joke about oysters being aphrodisiac but never considered it anything but a myth – the kind of idea they still had in the Old Country.

We squeezed on lemon, added dabs of horseradish, slid the oysters into our mouths, and then rinsed the shells with champagne and drank the salty, cold juice. There was a beefy-looking couple eating schnitzel at the next table, and they stared at us with the repugnance that public oyster-eaters in the Midwest often encounter. We laughed and grandly sipped it all down. I was already half tipsy from drinking too fast, and starting to feel filled with a euphoric, aching energy. Kate raised a brimming oyster shell to me in a toast: 'To the Peace Corps!'

'To Europe!' I replied, and we clunked shells.

She touched her wineglass to mine and whispered, 'Happy birthday', and then suddenly leaned across the table and kissed me.

When she sat down again, she was flushed. I caught the reflection of her face in the glass-covered 'The Street Musicians of Prague' above our table. I always loved seeing her in mirrors and windows. The reflections of her beauty startled me. I had told her that once, and she seemed to fend off the compliment saying, 'That's because you've learned what to look for,' as if it were a secret I'd stumbled upon. But this time, seeing her reflection hovering ghostlike upon an imaginary Prague was like seeing a future from which she had vanished. I knew I'd never meet anyone more beautiful to me.

We killed the champagne and sat twining fingers across the table. I was sweating. I could feel the warmth of her through her skirt under the table and I touched her leg. We still hadn't ordered dinner. I left money on the table and we steered each other out a little unsteadily.

'Rudi will understand,' I said.

The street was blindingly bright. A reddish sun angled just above the rims of the tallest buildings. I took my suit coat off and flipped it over my shoulder. We stopped in the doorway of a shoe store to kiss.

'Let's go somewhere,' she said.

My roommate would already be home at my place, which was closer. Kate lived up north, in Evanston. It seemed a long way away.

We cut down a side street, past a fire station, to a small park, but its gate was locked. I pressed close to her against the tall iron fence. We could smell the lilacs from a bush just inside the fence, and when I jumped for an overhanging branch my shirt sleeve hooked on a fence spike and tore, and petals rained down on us as the sprig sprang from my hand.

We walked to the subway. The evening rush was winding down; we must have caught the last express heading towards Evanston. Once the train climbed from the tunnel to the elevated tracks, it wouldn't stop until the end of the line, on Howard. There weren't any seats together, so we stood swaying at the front of the car, beside the empty conductor's compartment. We wedged inside, and I clicked the door shut.

The train rocked and jounced, clattering north. We were kissing, trying to catch the rhythm of the ride with our bodies. The sun bronzed the windows on our side of the train. I lifted her skirt over her knees, hiked it higher so the sun shone off her thighs, and bunched it around her waist. She wouldn't stop kissing. She was moving her hips to pin us to each jolt of the train.

We were speeding past scorched brick walls, grey windows, back porches outlined in sun, roofs, and treetops –

the landscape of the El I'd memorized from subway windows over a lifetime of rides: the chiropodist's foot sign past Fullerton; the bright pennants of Wrigley Field, at Addison; ancient hotels with TRANSIENTS WELCOME signs on their flaking back walls; peeling and graffiti-smudged billboards; the old cemetery just before Wilson Avenue. Even without looking, I knew almost exactly where we were. Within the compartment, the sound of our quick breathing was louder than the clatter of tracks. I was trying to slow down, to make it all last, and when she covered my mouth with her hand I turned my face to the window and looked out.

The train was braking a little from express speed, as it did each time it passed a local station. I could see blurred faces on the long wooden platform watching us pass – businessmen glancing up from folded newspapers, women clutching purses and shopping bags. I could see the expression on each face, momentarily arrested as we flashed by. A high-school kid in shirt sleeves, maybe sixteen, with books tucked under one arm and a cigarette in his mouth, caught sight of us, and in the instant before he disappeared he grinned and started to wave. Then he was gone, and I turned from the window, back to Kate, forgetting everything – the passing stations, the glowing late sky, even the sense of missing her – but that arrested wave stayed with me. It was as if I were standing on the platform, with my schoolbooks and a smoke, on one of those endlessly accumulated afternoons after school when I stood almost outside of time simply waiting for a train, and I thought how much I'd have loved seeing someone like us streaming by.